Praise for SCOTT CIENCIN

"ONE OF TODAY'S FINEST
FANTASY WRITERS."
Science Fiction Review

"There are too few writers today who can
weave a tale the reader simply can't put down.
Scott Ciencin is such a storyteller."
Stuart M. Kaminsky, Edgar Award-winning author of
Lieberman's Day

"EXCELLENT."
The Scream Factory

"SCOTT CIENCIN IS SOMEONE TO
WATCH OUT FOR."
Cemetery Dance

and for THE ELVEN WAYS, Book One: The Ways of Magic

"An entertaining story that combines accessible
characters and familiar landscape with some clever
new reworking of the established apparatus of
both theology and myth."
Tom Deitz

Other AvoNova Books in
THE ELVEN WAYS *Trilogy by*
Scott Ciencin

THE ELVEN WAYS, BOOK 1:
THE WAYS OF MAGIC

Coming Soon

THE ELVEN WAYS, BOOK 3:
NIGHT OF GLORY

Avon Books are available at special quantity discounts for bulk purchases for sales promotions, premiums, fund raising or educational use. Special books, or book excerpts, can also be created to fit specific needs.

For details write or telephone the office of the Director of Special Markets, Avon Books, Dept. FP, 1350 Avenue of the Americas, New York, New York 10019, 1-800-238-0658.

THE ELVEN WAYS

Book 2

ANCIENT GAMES

SCOTT CIENCIN

AVON BOOKS • NEW YORK

This is a work of fiction. Names, characters, places, and incidents either are the product of the author's imagination or are used fictitiously. Any resemblance to actual events, locales, organizations, or persons, living or dead, is entirely coincidental and beyond the intent of either the author or the publisher.

AVON BOOKS
A division of
The Hearst Corporation
1350 Avenue of the Americas
New York, New York 10019

Copyright © 1997 by Scott Ciencin
Cover art by Darrell K. Sweet
Published by arrangement with the author
Visit our website at **http://AvonBooks.com**
Library of Congress Catalog Card Number: 96-97098
ISBN: 0-380-77981-1

All rights reserved, which includes the right to reproduce this book or portions thereof in any form whatsoever except as provided by the U.S. Copyright Law. For information address Siegel & Siegel, P.O. Box 20340, Dag Hammarskjold Center, New York, New York 10017.

First AvoNova Printing: April 1997

AVONOVA TRADEMARK REG. U.S. PAT. OFF. AND IN OTHER COUNTRIES, MARCA REGISTRADA, HECHO EN U.S.A.

Printed in the U.S.A.

RA 10 9 8 7 6 5 4 3 2 1

If you purchased this book without a cover, you should be aware that this book is stolen property. It was reported as ''unsold and destroyed'' to the publisher, and neither the author nor the publisher has received any payment for this ''stripped book.''

To my loving wife, Denise

Prologue

The 323rd year of the Millennium
Ten years ago

MATTHEW DUBROVNIK STOLE A GLANCE TOWARD the window. It was a beautiful day outside. Like any ten-year-old, he longed to run and play. Instead, he was trapped inside a classroom.

"Young Matthew," said a gruff voice.

He turned to see his teacher staring at him. The man was lean, dark-haired, and hawk-faced, with deep blue eyes and a heavily lined brow. The rest of the class also looked at Matthew. He stared back at twenty young acolytes like himself, all dressed in white silk robes, with partially shaven heads to denote their status in the school and their proficiency in the Teachings.

"Would you care to explain what is so interesting outside, what wonders lie out there that cannot also be experienced in my company?" asked the teacher.

Matthew was not afraid. "I was simply noting the greater glories of God, Lord Wagner. They are manifest outside that window, inside this classroom, and most importantly, within all of us. That is His miracle."

Lord Wagner nodded and went back to his lecture.

For the rest of that hour, Matthew made a point of keeping his gaze trained directly upon Lord Wagner. He took note of every word his teacher said and was prepared at any time with an appropriate response.

Finally, he was called upon again. "Matthew, give us an example of the primitive state of medicine before the arrival of the Heavenly Host."

"Yes, lord. A healer in the times of darkness may have come upon someone with a broken leg and said that to effect a cure, they should cut off the leg of a live rabbit, shave a few hairs from its belly, and let it go. Turn the hairs into a thread and use it to tie the rabbit's foot to the troublesome limb. That was all that was needed!"

The class exploded into laughter.

"There's more," said Matthew. "The cure was supposedly even more effective if one could find a rabbit's anklebone in wolf's dung and add that to the charm. Provided, of course, that it had not been touched by a woman. And best of all, the person taking the rabbit's paw and wool was supposed to hurl the rabbit away and yell at it, 'Flee, flee, little rabbit, and take the malady with you!' "

All around Matthew, students laughed even harder. It wasn't until Lord Wagner raised his hands that the sound abruptly stopped. His expression was grave.

"Very good, Matthew," said Lord Wagner. "Today, of course, a limb is bound and medicinal herbs, blessed by the angels if at all possible, are applied. Nails and other couplings are used to take the place of bones that cannot heal, and limbs are kept exercised so that muscles cannot atrophy. Ours is a civilized culture. But what's most alarming is that it was so-called men of God who handed out such superstitious drivel. We must always be on our guard against agents of the Enemy, who would gladly undo all the progress we have made."

Matthew understood and agreed entirely with what his

The Elven Ways: Ancient Games

teacher said. In the back of his mind, however, he was running free in the lush rolling hills outside, playing games with his friends.

It was an idle fantasy, of course. Matthew had no friends at the First School of Light. He was liked well enough. An amiable, handsome young man, with a flare for quoting scripture, both popular and obscure, and an even temperament. But it was well-known that his father was a Curacas, and that he was being trained to assume those esteemed duties one day. He intimidated his peers. They bowed before him, averted their eyes, and spoke to him with only the greatest reverence.

He hated it.

After class, Matthew was in the gardens, contemplating the scriptures and wishing that he had been among the small group that ran off to go skinny-dipping in the lake a mile north of the school, when Lord Wagner approached with a red-haired boy about his age.

"Matthew Dubrovnik, I would like you to meet Garth Shae. He is new to us, and I was hoping that you could help to make him feel more at home."

Bowing to his teacher, Matthew said, "God is merciful, God is good."

"Never forget that," said Lord Wagner as he walked away.

Anxiously, Garth echoed Matthew's sentiment, but the departing figure of the teacher gave no reply. Then he was gone.

"Have you seen the school?" Matthew asked. "I mean, has anyone given you the tour yet?"

"Yes, yes, they have. Impressive. So vast. Nothing like what I was expecting."

"What were you expecting?"

Garth shrugged. "Where I come from, we often live three to a room. My quarters here are large enough to house two or three families!"

"It is no less than we deserve," said Matthew. "We are the chosen few. The gifts of knowledge are not to be squandered on those who are undeserving. Just think what heathen barbarians would do with the sacred gifts of reading and writing. Not that they could be any worse than those smelly Prostinks."

"The Protestants, you mean?"

"Who else? The Protestant Liberation Front is a terrible threat that must be eliminated."

Garth shrugged. "I suppose. Tell me, what do you do for fun around here?"

"Fun?"

"Yes, you know . . . What games do you play? How do you keep yourself occupied? You can't just sit around and contemplate the mysteries of God all day, now can you? I mean, it's been more than three centuries since the angels arrived to put mankind on the One True Path. When was it? Um—"

"The year 1500," said Matthew. "By the old calendar."

"Right. Then there was the Thirty Years War. So that would make the date 1853 now if they hadn't shown up, right?"

"Such things are best not contemplated," said Matthew, looking around, worried. "We had lost our way. By the mercy of God in His Nine Vessels, that which was lost is found again."

"Indeed it is," said Garth. "But you didn't answer my question."

Matthew frowned. "Fun and games, what do we do for fun and games?" He wished that the question wasn't so difficult. Then it came to him. "We could . . . sneak away to the lake. It's about a mile distant."

"Now that would be *bad*, wouldn't it?" Garth asked in a teasing voice.

"Well, I suppose. If we were caught. But others do it all

the time. It's hot, and a little dip would be just the thing, don't you think?"

Garth nodded. "The medicinal waters in the baths here do have a smell to them, don't they?"

"I thought it was just me that felt that way!"

"Oh, no. True, they make a body feel more relaxed, but there's something to be said for being close to nature. It is, after all, as God intended, is it not?"

"I'd say so," said Matthew, feeling strangely daring.

The two boys glanced back at the School of Light. It was an imposing building: four stories high and composed entirely of white marble. Bold columns marked the entrance, and steeples that looked like guard stations waited at each of its four high corners. Certain that no one was watching, they fled the gardens and stole into the woods.

Within minutes they reached the lakes. The sun was high, the clouds far distant. The perfect blue of the sky was reflected in the lake's surface. A half dozen boys were playing in the waters, racing from one end to the other.

They froze when they saw Matthew. Not one of the boys tried explaining their actions. They simply waited to see what Matthew would say.

Would he condemn them for leaving the grounds of the holy school? Threaten to expose this brazen act to the Lord of Discipline?

Instead, Matthew disrobed. The young man beside him did the same. With a whoop and a holler they took a running leap and jumped into the lake!

Water splashed up all around them. Matthew laughed as he paddled swiftly to keep from sinking. He wasn't much of a swimmer, but he also wasn't about to drown.

"Race ya!" said John Leopold, a stringy lad with a wild grin. John was always getting in some kind of trouble.

Matthew hesitated. Beside him, Garth seemed to sense the reason behind his reticence. It was obvious that Matthew wasn't the best of swimmers. This boy, John, simply wanted to be the first to show Matthew up. And that wasn't what this little break from the monotony of school was supposed to be about.

"Race *me,* if you dare!" Garth growled, arcing into the water without waiting for a reply to his challenge. John took off after him, swimming as fast as he could. But he was no match for Garth, who beat him soundly in three of three matches.

It took time, but as the minutes stretched into hours, Matthew found himself becoming accepted by the small group of truants.

"Did you know," Matthew said as they rested together on the shore of the lake, "that baths were popular with the Greeks and Romans, then after Rome fell, they were no longer used? The angels made baths popular again because they couldn't stand the smell of unclean mortals!"

It was the closest thing to heresy that he had spoken in quite some time.

"Dubrovnik, you talk too much," John said with a smile.

"It's true. We stank! We were unclean! The angels have more highly developed senses than we do. That's why we have to bathe with Dead Sea Salts, eucalyptus, and spearmint oils. So that our scent will be more pleasing should a warrior of the Almighty happen to visit the school."

"No, it isn't," said Garth. "The simple truth is, those things cost money, and there's plenty of it wrapped up in that school. They want us to smell of our station."

Matthew didn't like *that* very much. He was taken aback by the vehemence with which his friend—his friend?—had spoken.

Garth looked over and grinned. His eyes were sparkling. "Or maybe I'm just having one over on ya!"

Everyone laughed at this, even Matthew, though he felt there was more than a small amount of conviction in Garth's tone.

That night, after final classes, dinner, and prayer, Matthew visited Garth in his chamber.

"Do you believe all this?" Garth said, gesturing at the four-poster bed and the white silk curtains. His furniture was elegantly designed and neatly arranged. It consisted of a hope chest, a wardrobe, three dressers, and two bookcases. In his lap was the second book of Callibreyas, first Emissary to the Ninth Vessel of God, the keeper of the Almighty's innocence.

"All of our rooms are the same," said Matthew. He was beginning to wonder why he'd come to Garth's room. All he knew was that despite how happy he'd been this afternoon, he couldn't rid himself of the unhappy feeling that Garth had meant the minor heresy he'd said at the lake today. It was as if a knife had been jammed between his ribs, and he desperately needed his friend—yes, there, he knew this time that it was so—to remove it.

Garth rose and crossed to the window. Then he pointed up at the stars. "Have you ever wondered what it must be like to be God? To have all creation as your playground?"

Matthew flinched. "God does not take his responsibilities so lightly."

"Oh come on," said Garth. "God placed the ability to love and laugh in our hearts, and has told us that we were made in His image. That means He must have a sense of humor, don't you think?"

Matthew didn't know how to respond to that.

"There are such mysteries in the world," said Garth. "The Naturals, who held these lands for so very long before the angels came along, had a song of prayer. 'Behold, a sacred voice is calling you; all over the sky, a sacred voice is calling.' Lovely, don't you think?"

"The Heavenly Host thinks highly of the Naturals. They agreed to share these lands."

Garth nodded. "All right, then. Here's another one: 'The man form is higher than the angel form; of all forms it is the highest. Man is the highest being in creation, because he aspires to freedom.' "

Matthew was moved to anger. "That's blasphemy! Why are you saying such a thing?"

"Because it's all a matter of perspective, isn't it? Every culture has its own point of view, and the Host didn't like that. There is to be only one point of view—"

Matthew put his hands to his ears and squeezed his eyes shut as he chanted, "God is good, God is just—"

"Why should knowledge be in the hands of only a few?" Garth went on. "Knowledge is strength. And power. Look at my face!"

Trembling, Matthew opened his eyes and allowed his hands to fall from his ears.

"See my freckles? My great-grandmother said that in some cultures, freckles are considered angel kisses."

"You mean to say that your kind are blessed?"

Garth shook his head. "You should hear yourself. 'Your kind.' We're all the same, aren't we? That's what the Teachings tell us."

"Why are you doing this to me?" Matthew cried. Tears fell from his eyes. "If this is really how you think and feel, why couldn't you just keep it to yourself? Why tell me?"

"Because of what I sense is in you. A questioning nature, like my own."

"You couldn't be more wrong."

"Time will tell, I suppose."

Nodding, Matthew left Garth's chamber. Although His own room was on the same floor, he didn't go there. Instead, he went downstairs, to Lord Wagner's room.

"Yes?" Lord Wagner said.

Matthew told him everything. It pained him to do so, but he felt that he had no other choice.

"I wanted Garth to be my friend," Matthew sobbed. "I needed a friend. But his views are wrong. They're dangerous. I couldn't risk what he might say to some of the younger, more impressionable students..."

"Of course," said Lord Wagner. "Wait here."

Matthew waited in his teacher's chamber for close to half an hour. He was on his knees, lost in prayer, when Lord Wagner returned. He wasn't alone.

Garth was with him.

Matthew rose to his feet. He had prayed for strength, and now he could feel it coursing through him. At the very least, Garth would be sent home in disgrace. For his part in the minor transgression of leaving the school grounds, Matthew would also be punished, but not so severely.

"What did I tell you about this one?" asked Lord Wagner.

"He is far from a disappointment, I agree," said Garth.

Matthew stared at them, unsure of what to make of their exchange. "My lord?"

Lord Wagner smiled. "Have no fears, most honored student. You just underwent a test."

"A test?" asked Matthew.

"Yes. Garth is no heretic. But it was important for us to know how you would react should one espousing such threatening views ever come into your circle, even under the auspices of friendship. And I'm happy to say that you acquitted yourself admirably. You placed the needs of all those around you above your own. Would that there were more like you."

Garth smiled and took Matthew's hand. "I wish I was staying. I believe you, and I could be friends. Our faith could sustain most anything, don't you think?"

Shocked by all of this, but doing his best to hide his reaction, Matthew simply nodded.

Later, in his own chamber, Matthew lay on his bed, staring at the volume Garth had been looking at earlier—Teachings by the first Emissary to the Ninth Vessel of God.

One passage had caught his attention and would not let go. It read:

"For whatever you ask in my name, I will do it . . . if you ask anything in my name, I will do it."

Matthew closed the book and began to pray. *Lord, it is a sin to beseech Thee for selfish reasons. I know this. Yet I am troubled. Did I rail so against Garth when he spoke so openly against the Teachings because I am pure of heart, as Lord Wagner says, or because a part of me felt that Garth's word had merit, and I was so frightened that I had to persecute him to make up for my own failings? Show me the way, oh Lord, for I am lost . . .*

Matthew waited. He didn't know what, if anything, he expected to happen next.

An hour passed. Suddenly, horns sounded. Matthew wondered what could be happening so late. Was the school receiving a visitor? An angel, perhaps?

He ran to his window and looked outside.

A half dozen boys were being led across the vast green lawn. Each carried a lantern to enhance the pale moonlight. The Lord of Discipline, a burly man with a great auburn beard, stood before them.

Matthew could make out John's face. He realized suddenly that these were the students he had played with at the lake. They were receiving punishment for their transgression. And, notably, Matthew was not.

John looked up to Matthew's window. There was no hatred in his eyes, simply resignation, and a sense that he should have known better than to trust a Curacas-in-training.

"Do not sag, do not slouch," the Lord of Discipline recited. "You will stand here, at attention, until such time as I dismiss you. Should you fall, for whatever reason, you will be made to rise again, and your punishment will outlast that of your fellows. Have I made myself clear?"

The acolytes nodded.

Matthew turned away from the window. There would be nothing for him to see. Not for a while, anyway.

The punishment John and the others were being forced to endure was very simple. They had only to stand at attention, holding their lanterns out before them. The lanterns in their hands were meant to represent the light of truth. That light was said to be unwavering. For that reason, the boys could not move. Whatever their needs—for food or sleep, to relieve themselves, an end to the pain and the burden of remaining like statues for hours on end—they could not move.

It was said that the punishment could go on for days. Matthew knew that when it was over, none of these lads would ever trust him again. Not one would look upon him with even a trace of friendship.

He would be alone, again, and that was all.

Matthew turned back to his bed. He picked up the book, then hurled it from him. It slammed against the wall above his desk, then dropped behind it.

He considered leaving it there, but soon decided to crawl under his desk to retrieve it.

It was then he noticed a stain on the wall that seemed to shimmer. Some trick of the light, surely nothing more.

Reaching for the book, Matthew found that his hand was moving past the book, toward the spot on the wall.

It was cold and filled with motion, like a freezing whirlpool.

Matthew pulled back his hand in fright.

What was that? he wondered. Then a proverb entered his mind, practically unbidden: "Do not fear, only believe."

He didn't know if the shimmering light had been there before he began his prayers. It was possible that he simply hadn't noticed it. What he wanted to believe was that his prayers had been answered, that this was some private doorway to truth. But that seemed unlikely.

Several other holy passages came to Matthew's mind.

"Put me to the test, says the Lord of hosts, if I will not open the windows of heaven for you and pour down for you an overflowing blessing." "Fear not, little flock, for it is your Father's good pleasure to give you the kingdom."

Encouraged, Matthew reached out his hand once more. He touched the shimmering pool of light and felt the same odd pull upon his fingers, as if something lay on the other side of that light, something that was attempting to lure him toward it.

Could this be a sign of the Enemy?

It was possible. These were times of great miracles, of Heavenly Cities coming to earth and warrior angels teaching man the error of his ways.

A final bit of scripture worked itself into his mind. "For a good angel will go with him, his journey will be successful, and he will come home safe and sound."

Matthew thrust his hand into the whirlpool. The sensation of being pulled forward strengthened, but it was not so great that he couldn't fight it if he so desired. Matthew did not feel that desire. A part of him knew that he should go to Lord Wagner or one of the other teachers, but he ignored such thoughts.

First one hand went into the light and the cold. Then another. Steeling himself, he thrust his head forward. A dazzling array of shimmering silver lights burst into his sight. He saw odd runes taking shape before him, like those the angels burned into the sky as they created the spells of Convergence. He had seen a Heavenly City arrive on earth once; it had been a magnificent sight. But this was somehow even more impressive.

Wind howled in his ears. He heard the whispers of spirits, mournful and forlorn, then the cries of the blessed as they reached the ecstasy that could only be found in the house of the Lord. Fanciful thoughts, perhaps, but his mind and body felt as if they were being transformed into something other than flesh and blood. Something magical and transcending earthly boundaries.

A flurry of strange images was imprinted directly upon the fabric of his imagination: warrior angels fighting great Crusades; dark women with many, many eyes; crystal caves through which the breath of creation itself could be felt.

He felt his entire body being tugged toward some unknowable destination, then suddenly, there was a cessation of all sight and sound. Matthew found himself in a void.

Was he dead? Where had he been taken?

He drew a deep, shuddering breath, then let it out again. He could feel something cold beneath him. A floor. And from somewhere close, a gentle breeze was blowing.

If he was dead, would he feel such sensations as he had when he was alive? There was no way for him to know for sure, but he thought it unlikely.

So he was alive. Where was he?

A door opened, and a blinding sliver of light fell upon him. Matthew scrambled back and felt his buttocks press against something hard. Was the gateway closed?

"I thought I heard a noise," said a low, rumbling voice.

"You're always hearing noises." This voice was richer, more pleasing.

Footsteps followed, then silence.

Matthew shuddered. He looked around and saw what appeared to be a darkened study. Only—the walls, what little he could see of them, seemed to be changing, describing one odd abstract image after another. He felt something rippling against his back, like fingers caressing him.

With a tiny cry he shoved himself away from the wall he'd been leaning against and turned to see a tide of movement. Rising unsteadily, he crossed to the door and peered out. He saw a marble floor, dark grey, almost black, and walls of mist. There was light in this corridor, but no sound that might betray the presence of those who had entered this room before. He stepped into the corridor, then looked back to the doorway. All he could see was a sliver of darkness carved out of the flowing mist.

What was this place?

Matthew prayed for strength. He could feel the cold sting of his tears upon his flesh. Words leapt into his mind:

"And God shall wipe away all tears from their eyes; and there shall be no more death, neither sorrow, nor crying, neither shall there be any more pain: for the former things are passed away."

That passage . . . It described Heaven.

Was he in Heaven?

Matthew saw a vaulted window at the end of the corridor. He approached it slowly. There was a crimson light filtering through the open window, and a chill that made him shiver. Soon, he was close enough to peer out the window, but he could not bring himself to look up from the floor. Something told him that such sights as those that lay outside this window were not for him.

He forced his gaze upward and was greeted by a rapture unlike any he had experienced before. Clouds surrounded this strange edifice, and rising from those clouds were the spires and domes of great buildings. A crimson sun lay low upon the horizon, causing many of these aerial dwelling places to be cast in shadow. As if to combat the coming darkness, a sparkling inner radiance was flowing from the towers and the reaches of the tall buildings outside. Bridges appeared, linking some buildings to others. They rose and fell, twisted and turned. Spiral staircases made of crystal held the crimson light of the sun, and tiny figures climbed the stairs, while others flew about them.

Matthew was suddenly seized by the knowledge that he had either just gone mad, or he had somehow been taken to one of the countless dwelling places of angels.

Yet . . . The sun in the distance was fading. How could there be a dying of the light in such a place? The very notion of twilight in Heaven was aberrant to Matthew's thinking.

Then you must amend your way of thinking, said a voice within Matthew's mind. The voice of Lord Wagner, his teacher.

There were other questions. Why hadn't he been noticed? God was all-knowing, all-seeing. Why had his warriors not been alerted to Matthew's presence?

Perhaps because he was dreaming this. He might have contracted some terrible fever and was being visited by these delusions as part of his illness.

No, Matthew told himself. This was real. His every sense told him that.

An idea formed in Matthew's mind. It was pure hubris, he knew that, but he could think of no better explanation: God *wanted* him to see these sights. The time had finally come for man to walk boldly within the dwelling place of the Almighty, and Matthew was the herald chosen to take back his knowledge and share it with mankind.

Matthew turned away from the window. Now he was giving way to self-aggrandizement. The *angels* were the heralds of God, not mortals like himself.

The corridor before him had changed. He could see doorways now. There were twelve all told. The first door was made of jasper; the second, sapphire; the third, a chalcedony; the fourth, an emerald; the fifth, sardonyx; the sixth, sardius; the seventh, chrysolite; the eighth, beryl; the ninth, a topaz; the tenth, a chrysoprase; the eleventh, a jacinth; the twelfth, an amethyst.

It was the fourth door, the emerald, through which he had come.

A part of him said, *return, go now, while you still can. Flee before you are discovered.*

But he had a sense that his purpose here was only just begun. Falling to his knees, Matthew prayed for guidance. He looked upward—

And froze.

There was no ceiling. Swirling grey-black clouds loomed overhead. Lightning surged as the clouds rolled and trembled, parting to make way for a sight that Matthew's mind nearly crumbled beneath. For in the center of the clouds was an eye the size of palaces, the size of infinity. The eye was no single color. Rather, it was at once all colors and none.

It was the color of despair and of hope, the color of madness and reason.

Matthew looked full upon the Eye of Silence and thought surely that he must die . . .

"Didn't anyone ever tell you that it's not polite to stare?" asked a voice behind him.

Matthew spun. No one stood there. When he looked up again, the eye was gone.

The boy wanted only to flee. But he could no longer tell the difference between the twelve doors. They had blurred and faded back into the walls of mist.

He chose one at random and passed through it.

Suddenly, Matthew found himself in a vast courtyard. The limbs of a gigantic tree snaked all through this place. They looked as if they'd been turned to stone. A strange music seemed to radiate from within them.

Two angels stood before him. Matthew hid behind one of the twisting roots. He didn't wish to incur the angels' wrath for trespassing upon this most holy place.

As they spoke, he listened carefully to their voices. Neither was the being who had teased him in the corridor of mists.

Matthew had seen angels before. These two were dressed much as he expected, in charred black armor, with silver Sigils imprinted upon breastplates and helm. Their pale, almost white skin shimmered with a pale light. Their eyes were crimson, their hair long, dark, and flowing. Each was armed with a short sword and a broadsword. Gauntlets bearing many jeweled rings adorned their hands.

One angel was on his knees before the other. The one who bowed was thin, with strange runes imprinted upon his cheek. The other wore a beard that looked like the primordial greyish black clouds Matthew had seen above the corridor. Tiny strands of lightning moved in his beard, his eyebrows, and in his eyes themselves. Matthew was, as always, awed to be in the presence of divinities.

The angel on his knees said, *"In the house of Dusk, live lord and priest, live the wizard and the prophet, live those whom the Vessels have anointed in the abyss, Dusk is their nourishment, and the food is crimson bands of Twilight."*

"On your feet, Sraosha," said the bearded angel. "I have told you a thousand times, there is no need for such formalities between us. We played together as children. And our little dramas continue to amuse the Thrones and the Vessels. But this is a time of Rest, and all formalities and affectations need not be considered."

The angel lowered his gaze. "I would feel unclean were I to honor you in a manner any less fitting. Especially as I have come seeking a favor."

"Very well, very well. Tell me, Angel of the Hidden Word, how may Aesthma, Angel of Violence and Anger, not to be confused with that clod in Abaddon, the Angel of Rage, be of service?"

"My son is dying."

Aesthma's face lit up with alarm. "Why in the name of all the Vessels didn't you say that earlier?"

"I—I—"

The Angel of Violence hauled his companion to his feet. "Where is he?"

"Outside the Gates of Dusk. There was no time to reach one of the cities and immerse him in the healing waters of Lethe. I prayed that your power would be equal to the task."

Aesthma drew his sword and sliced at the air before

them, causing a tear to occur in the fabric of reality. A shimmering, crimson light poured through the gateway.

"Come with me, and let us both pray that your dawdling hasn't cost fair Mithra his life. Have you sent word to Rashnu? And the Yazatas?"

"There was no time," said Sraosha as he crossed through the boundary with his friend, "and no one to bear the messages..."

Matthew heard their voices dwindle, then fade.

Suddenly, the voice he had heard before was at his left ear. "What are you waiting for? Follow them!"

Matthew spun, and this time he caught the barest hint of movement. A shadow darting for cover. But there was no one behind him.

Shaking with fear, Matthew approached the crimson rift in the air. He passed through and found himself at the top of a staircase, looking down over a railing at a room that was bare except for a long wood table, a fireplace, and a collection of beautiful rugs. The fires burning here were emerald and gold, casting an odd light upon the marble walls.

He heard grunts of exertion, then saw the pair of angels enter the room, carrying a third who'd been wounded and was bleeding upon the ornate rugs. Matthew saw the patterns of the weave altering with each drop of angel's blood that fell upon them. The wounded angel had the most beautiful face Matthew had ever seen, though it was now twisted in pain.

"How in the name of all that's holy did this happen?" cried Aesthma.

Sraosha hesitated.

"Well?"

"It was a terrible clash with an agent of the Enemy!" cried Sraosha.

Aesthma frowned as he examined the younger angel's wound. "Isn't it always?"

The fallen angel tried to speak.

"Save your strength," said Sraosha.

"He's an Angel of Truth," said Aesthma. "And your attempts to salvage his honor with lies shame him all the more. Keep him still while I find what I have of healing waters."

The Angel of Violence left them alone for a few moments.

Mithra said, "Father, he is right. Truth is God's greatest gift, the embodiment of His love..."

"I know," said Sraosha. "Forgive me, gentle one, I know..."

Above, Matthew watched as Aesthma returned with four small vials filled with glowing silver-white liquid. He handed two to his companion and kept two for himself.

"A blessing, please," said Sraosha, as he took the stopper from the first of his two vials.

"By all that's holy," muttered the Angel of Violence. "Fine." He straightened his back. "I call to you, spirits of the Wastings, embodiments of our brethren's pain. Listen well, for the power of Shamash is at hand. *'The net, the spell of Shamash would fall upon thee and seize thee. He who trespasses on what is Shamash's, Shamash will punish him with his own hand.'*"

Sraosha shuddered and murmured, "Yes, oh Lord, yes..."

"And I proclaim Mithra's life and goodness to be mine," the Angel of Violence growled, "so dare not take them from me!"

With that fiery proclamation, the two angels poured the healing liquids into the wounds of the fallen angel. Mithra screamed as agony tore through him.

But even as the angel writhed, his wounds began to heal.

"When this is over, you're going to owe me," said the Angel of Violence.

"Anything."

Aesthma nodded. "Your son is an Angel of Truth. Not everyone wants to hear the truth. And sometimes the truth needs to be defended. Let me train young Mithra here to be a warrior. That way, should he ever encounter those who would seek to harm him because his very nature keeps him from telling even the most gentle and pleasing of lies, he'll not end up with his guts about his ankles for his troubles. That is what happened, is it not?"

Sraosha nodded grimly.

"Thought as much. I assume the perpetrator has been bound and is being delivered to the twins for judgment? And from there swift passage to the Ring of Punishment?"

"Yes."

"Then justice is done, at the very least. Ah, did I tell you that I have a visitor? A young man. A scholar. Despite that, he's handy with a sword, and cool enough of temperament to know when to use it. I'm surprised all the noise hasn't roused him. I'll summon him when Mithra here is well..."

Matthew turned away from the tribulations of the angels. What he'd just seen was fantastic. He knew, of course, that the angels were mortal. They had sacrificed Paradise to walk among men and attempt to lead them onto the One True Path.

So... Did that mean that he was on earth, but in a Heavenly City?

From the exchanges Matthew had overheard, it seemed that man's baseness had corrupted the pure hearts of some angels. The sacrifices they'd made for mankind could not be underestimated. Others might see them as weak and petty, after learning that angels attempted to slay one another over matters as venal as pride and an unwillingness to face certain truths. Matthew saw them as even more noble than ever. They were suffering for man's sins, experiencing them firsthand so that they could better understand the evil that must be expunged from humanity.

Matthew felt ashamed of his race. He couldn't watch anymore. He turned and found himself once again in the corridor of mists. Glancing over his shoulder, he saw that the room below had vanished. He looked up. The Eye of Silence was not above him.

For a brief moment, the twelve doors flared in brilliance. Then their light failed and only the emerald door, which was still partly ajar, seemed to beckon with its light.

Matthew went to the door and slipped into the darkened room. He searched around, praying that he would find a shimmering patch of light like the one he had discovered in his room.

The light did not appear.

Fear seized him. Was he trapped in this place? He'd often read that mortals who were taken to the Heavenly Cities to look upon God's glories never returned.

What would he do here? He couldn't avoid the angels for long, that much was certain. In fact, he'd already been seen by the Eye and by the playful angel who'd spoken to him twice but had not yet appeared to him.

In desperation, Matthew got on his hands and knees and began feeling along the wall. It undulated beneath his touch, which was unnerving, but he refused to allow himself to be dissuaded from his task.

Suddenly, his hand came upon a fiery, thick substance that pulled at him as it scalded his flesh. The gateway.

His eyes were now adjusting to the darkness, and he saw that from this side there was no light, only a greater area of shadow. He drew his hand away, then took a deep breath and thrust himself against the portal.

Matthew screamed as fires licked at his soul. He felt as if he was being reborn to a world of deep agony and sorrow. Quickly, he'd passed through, and found himself crawling on the hard floor of his room. Soft dim light washed over him, though he was hesitant to raise his head and acknowledge the brilliance.

Groping blindly, his eyes squeezed shut, Matthew's hands closed on something cool and made of leather.

Opening his eyes quickly, he saw that he had grabbed someone's boot. He looked up and gasped.

An angel sat next to his bed.

A very *young* angel.

The dark-haired youth sitting before him did not wear the leathers and armor of a warrior. His tunic was made of green velvet, his leggings were thin black hose. His boots were worn. He looked exhausted.

"You must be surprised," the angel said.

Matthew's entire body quivered. "Lord, I beseech you, make my punishment swift, for I meant no harm."

The angel slid a knife out of his belt. "You don't say."

Matthew froze. He closed his eyes and waited to feel the slight breeze and the biting pain of a blade cutting across his neck.

Nothing happened.

"Wouldn't you be more comfortable sitting on the bed?" asked the angel. He was picking at the spaces between his teeth with the knife.

Trembling, Matthew said, "If that is where you wish to administer my deliverance, lord, I shall not deny you."

The angel frowned, then looked at the blade he held. "Do you think I mean you harm?"

Matthew wasn't quite sure how to answer that. But he'd been taught that there was no sense in telling lies to an angel, or holding back the truth. They could always sense duplicity.

"Are you not the Angel of Death, come to punish me for bearing witness to sights meant for no mortal eyes?" Matthew asked.

"As a matter of fact, I'm not." The angel put the blade away.

"I—I'd assumed you were that being and that you'd

taken a form that would seem familiar to me, that of a lad my age, I—"

"I'm not one of death's angels, I've already told you that. Don't take on so."

"Then why do you look like me?" Matthew asked, quickly adding, "if I might humbly request an answer, though I am undeserving . . ."

Shaking his head, the angel said, "Do you have a name?"

"Matthew."

"Fine. Mine's Komm Kayriel. If you're trying to ask why I seem the same age as you, that's simple. We're both children, though you wouldn't know it by listening to you. What is this place?"

"You don't know?"

"I wouldn't be asking otherwise."

Terrified of trying the angel's patience, Matthew told Komm Kayriel everything he could about the school.

"Fair enough," said the angel. He gestured at the pulsing mass of light beneath Matthew's desk. "What do you know about *that*?"

"Only that it took me to a place of unimaginable sights, of miracles and dreams."

Kayriel chortled. "You left out tedium and backbreaking labor."

"Pardon?"

"Aesthma doesn't believe in the bindings, and has no spirits to perform the day-to-day tasks. It's one of the reasons I was sent to him. So that I could be toughened up. And it seems to have taken."

Matthew stared blankly at the angel.

"Never mind." Komm Kayriel got up and gestured toward the shimmering portal. "I've heard of phenomena like this, though to be honest, such things have never interested me much. Not until tonight."

Matthew fell to his knees before the angel once more.

"Lord, let me serve you. Let me pledge my life, my soul, all that I am and all that I ever will be to you."

"*No,*" said Komm Kayriel. "That's stupid. If you're going to be like this, I'm going home and that's the end of it. I'll tell Aesthma about the rift and have someone come to tend to it."

"How have I offended you? Tell me, that I might make amends."

"You're mewling, for one thing. I hate that. I've never been able to stand all this formality. When I saw you, I was hoping—never mind. It's pointless."

"Please," Matthew said, "Tell me."

"I was hoping for a friend. Someone to share some adventures with. Not someone trailing behind, desperate for a chance to kiss my feet. Where's the fun in that?"

Matthew was astounded by this. Was it possible that this child angel was lonely, too? "But you're a part of God, one with his Holy Essence."

"So are we all. That doesn't make either of us any less bored."

"Why do you say I'm bored? The Teachings are my life!"

Kayriel shrugged. "Maybe because looking at you, I feel as if I'm holding up a mirror to myself. I believe in the Ways. Have no doubt of that. But worship and ritual . . . It can't mean everything in a person's life!"

"It does if you live here."

"My life's much the same! What I want—what I *need*—is something more. What about you?"

"Lord, are you testing me?" Matthew asked hesitantly.

"Fah!" Kayriel said, hauling Matthew's desk out of the way so that he could reach the portal with greater ease.

"Wait!" Matthew cried. "Yes. I'm devout, but I'm not happy. My father says that I will one day be a great man, and that I must take all my responsibilities seriously. But I can't stand the way the other students look at me. Have you seen what's going on outside? The way those boys are being punished? Tortured?"

Kayriel nodded.

"That's my fault." Matthew told the angel what had happened.

Kayriel went over and placed his hand on the boy's shoulder. "Matthew, I can't help but think that it's a part of God's plan that we meet like this. Do you agree?"

"All that happens is part of God's plan."

"Then let's do something about what's happening outside."

Matthew looked at the angel strangely. "What can we do?"

The angel grinned. "Tell me once again about this punishment the Lord of Discipline is so fond of."

Dutifully, Matthew recounted the particulars.

"And are there any caves nearby? I can smell the fresh breezes that come only from the sea. All I need is a bit of moss, and I think we'll be set."

"There is a shore about five miles from here. I've been told there are caves—"

"Oh, and a cape of some kind!"

"I have a cloak for the winter months."

"Bring it!"

"Where?"

"To the caves. There's something we need."

"But it was leaving the school that started all of this."

"And it will be leaving the school that finishes it. Are you with me?"

Matthew nodded. "But there's something you have to know."

"Enough talk. Come on!"

Komm Kayriel opened the door and stepped into the hallway. Matthew waited for the sound of voices.

None came.

He followed the angel. The man he'd expected to find standing fast in his duties to keep the students in their rooms at night was slumped over his desk.

"Sleeping," said Kayriel. "I've worked a bit of Influence to make sure we can slip away unnoticed. After all, neither of us wants to have to explain to our guardians what mischief we've made this night, yes?"

Matthew nodded, his shoulders sagging in bold relief.

Before long, they were far from the school. As Kayriel had promised, no one saw them leave.

"This may seem funny to you," said Kayriel, "but there is an angel for every task. An Angel of Laughter, an Angel of Itches, and an Angel of Body Hair."

"No," Matthew said with a smile.

"All right, I made up the last one. But we all have Power in our lineage. Mine is to make my way unseen. To skulk, putting it bluntly. Most of my family is gone, and the Power was bequeathed to me. Now I have to learn to control it, whether I like it or not."

"It sounds difficult," Matthew said.

"Yes, but I'm happy to say that tonight, at least, my Power is truly a blessing."

Matthew nodded. As they neared the shore, the rushing of waves filling their ears. Matthew asked Kayriel if he had been the one guiding him on the other side.

"Of course."

"I couldn't tell by your voice, it sounded different."

"When you're cloaked in shadows, that is the way of it." To demonstrate, Komm Kayriel took Matthew's cloak and threw it around himself. He reached out with his Power and seemed to pull a cloak of pure darkness around himself with the cloth. His appearance darkened and he nearly faded from sight.

"Lord Kayriel?" asked Matthew.

"Don't call me that!" said a lower, echoing voice that

seemed to come from everywhere and nowhere at once.

"I'm sorry," said Matthew.

Kayriel uncloaked himself. "No harm done. Look, we're here!"

They spent an hour in the caves gathering what they needed, then hurried back toward the school. Despite the hour, and the many miles he'd traveled, Matthew didn't feel the least bit tired.

Stopping nearly a mile from the school, Matthew and Kayriel set to work. They smeared glowing moss all over the cloak. The angel worked a spell upon it, making it glow so brightly that it was nearly blinding. Then he dimmed its light with his mastery over shadows.

"When we get there, let me do the talking," said Kayriel.

"Yes," said Matthew. His enthusiasm was giving way to fear. What if their plan didn't work? What if he was discovered?

No, he told himself, *be calm in all things, be at peace with the stillness of God.*

The fear remained, but he could control it, and use the nervous energy it gave him to his advantage.

That, or he would faint the moment they broke from the woods.

Matthew and Kayriel walked side by side. They reached the edge of the woods and could see the small group of young men standing at attention, several of their lanterns wavering.

The Lord of Discipline was a statue.

"Remember to enjoy yourself, Matthew," said Kayriel. "Remember that above all things."

"I'll try."

"Do better than that."

Nodding, Matthew walked forward. Beside him, Komm Kayriel vanished into the shadows. Matthew was startled to realize that when he looked down, he could barely see himself.

Soon he was close to the Lord of Discipline, standing between him and his charges. The burly man blinked several times, as if he wasn't quite convinced that his senses were being honest with him. Earlier, Matthew had stared at Kayriel wearing this cloak, and so he knew exactly what the teacher was seeing: an ebony, amorphous shape that hung before his vision, separating him from at least one or two of the lantern bearers.

"Ohhh, ahhh—" the burly man stammered. He was rubbing at his eyes and shaking his head.

Matthew smiled, enjoying the response he was eliciting. He had never seen the Lord of Discipline at a loss, not until this very moment.

Enjoying himself? Yes, that seemed entirely possible.

Suddenly, Komm Kayriel removed the shadows. A startling brilliance radiated from Matthew. He saw the Lord of Discipline's expression turn from confusion into fear and awe. The man began to tremble.

"MORTAL MAN!" boomed a voice that seemed loud enough to crack open the heavens.

Matthew wanted to put his hands to his ears, but he didn't dare. Kayriel had instructed him thoroughly, and he knew better than to deviate from a plan laid down by an angel. As the forces of magic coursed through him, Matthew wondered if this was what if felt like to be an angel. A thousand fingers kneaded his flesh, and a sizzling energy made his hair ripple and flow.

"WHAT HAVE YOU DONE? WHY DO YOU MAKE THESE CHILDREN SUFFER?"

"I—I—" the Lord of Discipline stammered.

"WHAT IS THIS? WILL YOU NOT *BOW* BEFORE ME?"

Matthew grinned. The rules of this particular punishment

were simple. If the Lord of Discipline broke form, for whatever reason, then the punishment was at an end.

"DO YOU WISH TO INCUR MY WRATH?!"

"No, dear lord, no!" cried the burly man, tears suddenly streaming from his eyes. He sank to his knees.

Matthew heard the grass behind him whisper softly as a dozen knees fell upon it. The plan had worked! John and the others were free!

"These children were willful!" the Lord of Discipline mewled. "They left the grounds, broke our rules!"

"HAVE YOU NO MERCY? NO TOLERANCE?"

"They were swimming in the lake, they—"

"AND THUS I WILL COMMAND YOU! FOR ONE WEEK, YOU WILL RESIDE IN THAT LAKE! TAKE FISH FROM IT TO LIVE, AND DO WHAT YOU *MUST* IN ITS DEPTHS!"

"Merciful angel, I beg of you—"

"DO NOT TRY MY PATIENCE, OR YOU WILL FIND YOURSELF IN A LAKE OF FIRE!"

The Lord of Discipline sprang from his knees and bolted toward the woods. He ran so quickly that he nearly fell twice. Bits of his clothing flew up in the air and he cried out as if the Enemy himself were in pursuit.

Matthew spun to face his schoolmates. He gestured for them to follow him into the woods. They seemed frightened, evidently believing him to be an angel, just as the Lord of Discipline had believed. They went where he commanded.

As they walked upon a well-trodden path through the heavy trees, Matthew saw his light fading and heard a whisper.

"I'll see you again, Matthew. Soon..."

Komm Kayriel. He was leaving.

"Thank you, my friend," Matthew whispered in return. "Thank you—and let God's love and mine be with you always."

Matthew peeled off the cloak as he confronted John and the others. "What'd you think of my performance?"

John stared at him, gape-mouthed. "But—the angel—"

"Call him the Angel of Reason and Good Sense," said Matthew, wondering if there was such an angel. "It wasn't right, what they did to all of you. I had to make it right."

"But the light," John said, pointing at the cloak.

"Moss," Matthew said. "The kind found in caves near the shore. The last of it, I'm afraid."

Matthew waited, hoping that his story wouldn't be questioned, and that no one would accuse him of blasphemy for impersonating an angel.

John started to laugh. His friends joined in.

"Can you picture it?" asked John. "The Lord of Discipline paddling around naked, turning into a prune in the lake for the next week? Bugger, it's brilliant!"

"We have to bury the cloak. Quickly," said Matthew. It was still soaked through with magic, and any visiting angels would detect it unless it was buried among the offensive smells of the earth. Fortunately, the ground was soft and the cloak was easily hidden.

"That's the last time I accuse you of thinking you're better than us," said John.

"I'd just like to be as good as you fellows," said Matthew. He held out his hand. "Friends?"

John clasped it with both hands. "Never doubt!"

Laughing, the small group headed back to the school.

In the shadows, Komm Kayriel smiled. There was no malice in his smile, only satisfaction that he had done a kind turn to a lonely boy like himself.

Perhaps one day, someone would do the same for him. In the meantime, he swore inwardly that he would content himself with Matthew's friendship, and never want more in this world than to make it a better place for the mortals who worshiped his kind.

Standing alone that night, he was perfectly confident that no power in heaven or earth could make him stray from the path he was now on.

One

The 333rd year of the Millennium
The present

KOMM KAYRIEL LEAPED AT AITAN. TOM SAW THE LIVing shadow descend upon his friend. The angel never stopped his recitation, but he managed a flicker of a smile.

The monstrous, twisting form of Komm Kayriel engulfed Aitan, but only for an instant. Suddenly, he was brought down to the size and shape of a man. Tom saw Aitan grappling with the nightmare made flesh. Kayriel's eyes glowed red, and Aitan's form seemed to shimmer and lose its shape, then regain it again.

Aitan looked to Grin, and nodded once.

The former Emissary called upon his magics and suddenly a fiery red pit formed beneath Aitan and the Enemy. Tom recognized the Ring of Punishment and heard the screams of the angels cast into it. It was a burning, reddish gold rose made entirely of angels and their suffering.

Aitan's gaze moved to Tom. He nodded once again, very slowly, then turned and dragged his struggling nemesis deep into the pit with him.

Then he was gone. The screams, the flames—all of it—gone.

"AITAN!" Tom cried, rushing forward. But it was too late.

Tom bolted awake. He shuddered. For the longest time tonight he'd been unable to fall asleep. He'd told himself it was because he'd been spoiled by having a bed to sleep in for the past week during his recuperation in the city of Paridian. The hard ground of his campsite, with snaking roots beneath him, was far less luxurious than the room his lover had rented for them.

But he'd been kept awake by more than that. The former Emissary Grin had told Tom that he now had the gift of prophecy, though it was nowhere near as powerful as his other blessing. A part of him had *known* that if he went to sleep tonight, he would dream of Abaddon's fall. He would see his friend be taken from him again. Even now, after the dream had passed, the image remained, burning upon his mind.

He rolled onto his side and looked at the woman next to him. Her emerald eyes were closed, and her raven's hair was tangled in her face. Her breathtaking, voluptuous body was covered by a blanket. She was seventeen, three years older than he, though not for long. Tomorrow was his birthday.

His life had changed so much in the past month, since Aitan Anzelm first came to the small town of Hope. Tom had begun as the squire to an angel, though he had no training in the vocation, and ended up blessed with magical gifts and the love of a woman he adored more than life itself.

Tom ran his hand through the young woman's hair, gently moving it out of her face. She stirred. "Tom?"

He kissed her cheek. "Go back to sleep, Kayrlis. Everything's fine."

She grunted and rolled onto her side.

They had camped in the woods ten miles outside of Paridian, and were traveling parallel to the coastline. There was a barge sailing north that they hoped to catch in Port Henry. Kayrlis's brother, Cameron, kept watch.

Tom shifted his gaze to the ten-year-old leaning against a tree on the other side of their fire. His head was nodding forward; he was having a hard time staying awake.

Rising, Tom went to Cameron and said, "It's time. I'll take the next watch."

Cameron didn't argue. Grunting and wobbling, he went to his bedroll, slipped inside, and settled into a deep sleep almost instantly. Tom took his place. Sitting on the ground was a small book that Cameron had been reading. Books were rare and expensive. Few could read. Tom had been taught by a friend who remained at a school for the chosen long after he was expelled. It surprised him that Cameron had the knowledge.

Then again, he really didn't know much about Cameron and his sister, other than that he loved Kayrlis and that her brother had saved him from the Scourge, a disease that was beginning to sweep through their world. Most people believed that there was no cure for the Scourge. But they didn't know about the waters from the River Lethe that ran through the Heavenly Cities—or the touch of this boy's hand.

If Tom hadn't known better, he never would have believed that Cameron held the Blessed Gift of purifying the bodies of those racked by the dread disease. Cameron was a fine-looking lad, but there was nothing unusual or striking about his appearance. Of course, Tom knew that was true about himself, as well.

Tom looked down at the book. The title was *Bright Angel*. He flipped through it and saw that it was a text devoted to the beings who ruled their world. He read a passage at random.

"When you see a band of fifty, you are lost in amazement. They seem clothed with golden plates, constantly moving, like so many suns."

Tom had seen more than his share of the angels. And he knew more about their true beginnings than they did.

Those who called themselves angels were really the Elven, beings from a dying world who had come to Earth to plunder its natural and magical resources. The nine Vessels—in fact, now there were only eight, one had been killed by Komm Kayriel—were not reflections of the Almighty's varied aspects. They were a group of Elven who had gained unspeakable power and transformed themselves into gods, then made it nearly impossible for any to follow in their footsteps.

The Vessels had chosen to deceive not only the humans but also their own people. The masquerade had been played for so long that those who called themselves angels truly believed that they were the avatars of God. Only a handful of people knew the truth. Komm Kayriel had been the first. He'd learned the secrets in a strange book of magic called the Mysts Arcana. Aitan Anzelm and the former Emissary Grin also possessed this knowledge, but they, along with Kayriel and the Angel of Blood, had vanished from the mortal and heavenly planes. Tom had sworn to find his friends and bring them back. And he had to find a way to do so without also freeing Komm Kayriel, who wished to become a power greater than the eight remaining Vessels and shape two worlds in his own image.

Tom had an idea of where to start in his search. Aitan had a Patron in the mystical arts, an angel more powerful than himself who would surely help. He knew where the Patron made his home, in a city far to the north. That was where they were bound.

So far, Tom had honored Kayrlis's wishes and had told her brother only the vaguest details of his experiences in the dying Heavenly City of Abaddon. Cameron knew that they were on a quest to free from the darkness a pair of angels who'd sacrificed themselves to see Komm Kayriel there himself. What he couldn't understand was why they didn't simply seek out the help of other angels in their quest.

Cameron was devout in his faith. He was certain that the flame guardian who visited both him and Tom in their dreams was an avatar of the angel's will, an Emissary to one of the Vessels.

Tom suspected that this was not the case.

Still, Cameron was very young, and he looked at Tom with the same kind of adulation that Tom had showered upon Aitan when they'd first met. It was Tom who'd saved Cameron from the Scourge by giving him water from the River Lethe. Cameron would do whatever Tom said, whether he understood or agreed with Tom's approach.

Suddenly, a clanking sound came from the road.

Although the road was a quarter mile away, Tom didn't think it odd that he'd heard the noise at this distance. The night was still, so sounds traveled easily through the woods.

Putting the book down, Tom decided to see what was making the noise. He stole through the darkness until he came to the forest edge. Hiding himself behind an oak, Tom heard the sound again. He could hear it more clearly now and identified it as chains rattling.

Torches appeared. Tom watched as a somber progression of Arrow Riders on horseback passed by. The peacekeepers' armor resembled those of Roman Centurions. Three sets of riders passed silently. Then another horse followed, this one carrying a man bound in chains that rattled and *chinked* with every slight movement. Three more sets of riders brought up the rear.

Tom's attention was fixed on the prisoner they escorted. He was swarthy, with long dark hair that fell in waves. A scruffy beard had formed on his hard face. His bare chest was rippling with muscle, hair, and scars. The chains kept his strong arms pinned to his sides. Torn trousers were his only clothing. His feet were filthy. They had made him walk a distance, Tom guessed.

The man looked Tom's way, just for an instant. Tom was startled. Had he been discovered?

The prisoner shifted his gaze away and said, "I didn't kill the woman."

Remaining hidden, Tom felt his Power rise up in him. The fire of truth burned in his heart and he knew the man *wasn't* lying!

"Say nothing," snarled one of the Arrow Riders.

"That is the crime I'm to die for, isn't it? Well, I didn't kill her. Nor her husband."

A sharp crack sounded in the night. One of the Arrow Riders used a whip to apply yet another wound to the prisoner's back. The dark man buckled and made a rough sound of pain, but he kept his balance on his mount.

Tom felt his blessed Power again. The chained man was telling the truth. He was *innocent*.

The procession moved on.

Tom went back to his campsite. Cameron and Kayrlis were sound asleep.

He knew that just up ahead, the road leading away from Paridian branched off. One path continued on along the coastline and went directly to Port Henry, about two days' ride from here. The other veered off and led to New Florence.

Tom was willing to wager—though he knew it was a sin—that the prisoner was being taken to New Florence. Many Pilgrims from Italy had settled there, and this man looked like one of them.

He woke Kayrlis first.

"I didn't do it," she muttered as he shook her arm.

"Sweetheart, it's Tom. You've gotta get up."

Her eyes opened slowly. Looking around, she said, "I don't see any sunlight."

"Kayrlis—"

"Good night, Tom. We can sneak off and have some fun tomorrow night, okay? I'm tired."

"No, it's not that," Tom said, though if the circumstances had been different, that might not have been a bad idea. He was still astounded by the pleasures—the ecstasies—of the flesh to which she had introduced him.

"What is it, then?" she growled.

He told her what he'd seen.

She sat up. Her throat was dry. She found a water bag and took a sip. Then she sighed, and said, "You know if we do this, if we try to help this man, we might not make Port Henry in time."

He lowered his head and thought of his lost friends. If they were at his side, what counsel would they give?

"I think it's what Aitan and Grin would want me to do," Tom said.

"And both of us are gonna have to say we're older than we are. I know you don't like lyin', but—"

"No. Agreed." While in Paridian, they'd had false papers made up for them in case they had to present themselves to a Curacas. According to the scroll they carried, they were married and Cameron was Tom's stepson. They couldn't risk being detained because of their ages. And if they were made to explain what roles they played in the Heavenly Service, they needed a ready answer. Now they had one.

Tom bit his lip. "I know this isn't what we talked about, I know everything we have to do, but—"

Placing her finger gently on Tom's mouth, Kayrlis said, "Sweetheart, you saved my brother's life. You helped him become something like a miracle on two legs. I'll go anywhere and do anything for you."

The fourteen-year-old in Tom rose up. "Anything?"

"Within reason."

He laughed. "We've done some things I didn't even know were possible, let alone within reason."

"Behave."

"Not what you were saying last night."

"Tom—"

"Sorry." He kissed her. "Just with the fire playing in your eyes like that ... I mean, can you honestly tell me you're not in the mood?"

She knew better. "Wouldn't do me any good if I did, I guess. You being able to tell when people are lying and such. What about Cameron?"

"He's sound asleep. And I found this nice spot when I was on my way back here, far enough away that we could make some noise."

"I thought you said it was the sound of the chains drifting all this way that got you started—"

"All right, all right. So we'll be quiet."

She lunged at him, kissing him hungrily, openmouthed. His hands settled on the thin shift she wore. As his kisses traced the long, elegant line of her neck, Kayrlis cleared her throat. It was a brutally loud sound, and it caused Cameron to wake.

"What? Huh?" Cameron murmured. "Is everything okay?"

"Fine," Kayrlis said. "But we need to get ready. We're leaving here soon."

"We are?" Cameron asked, only a slight whine in his voice.

"Yes," she said in a tone that would brook no arguments. "We are."

As Cameron gathered his things, Tom turned his gaze to his beloved. "I thought you said—I mean, I *know* you were in the mood!"

"Can't make everything so blasted easy on you!" she

said, turning her back as she searched for her dress.

Cameron started laughing.

"You *hush*," said Tom.

Cameron's laughter turned into giggles. He couldn't stop. Tom launched himself at the boy, tickling him and making it even worse.

Kayrlis shook her head, smiling, and took advantage of the opportunity to get dressed. By the time she was done, she saw Tom and Cameron lying on their backs, chests heaving, wide grins on their faces.

"So is the barge leaving early?" Cameron asked.

Tom rose and explained to Cameron what he'd seen and where they were going.

"But what about the angels?" cried Cameron in distress. "Aitan Anzelm and Lord Skalligrin! They're trapped in the netherworld with the Enemy."

"And we *are* going to do everything we can to find them and bring them out. But right now, there's a terrible miscarriage of justice about to occur, and we have to do something about that."

"God'll provide for the man you saw. He won't let him be put to the Extraordinary Question."

Tom felt a shiver pass through him at the very thought of that horrible way to die. He sighed. Though he knew that Cameron would do as he asked, he preferred not to command him.

"Cameron, consider this: Does it really sound likely, or at all *natural*, the way I heard those chains from such a distance? It didn't seem strange to me at the time, but the more I've thought about it—"

"Yeah?" Cameron asked, his attention absolutely captured.

"Well, the sounds, and the way the prisoner turned his head and looked right to the spot where I was hiding, then said just what I needed to hear to realize what was happening... Like I said, think about it.''

''You mean—''

''I think God *was* providing for that innocent man. He was providing *us*...''

Two

EVEN FROM A DISTANCE, NEW FLORENCE AT DAYbreak was a lovely sight. Tom, Kayrlis, and Cameron stood on a rise overlooking the valley cradling the settlement. Tom could see narrow cobbled streets, dozens of art galleries, several museums, and at least two parks. Most impressive of all were the seven Schools of Art and Devotion.

"When I was a kid, I used to dream of coming here," said Tom. "All I wanted was to be an artist."

"What happened?" asked Cameron.

"I don't know," Tom said, returning to his mount. "Grew out of it, I guess."

"But you still draw," said Cameron, scurrying to his own horse.

Kayrlis was the fastest of them, leaping bareback onto her mount. "Best not to mention that to anyone while we're here."

"If you have gifts, you should be proud of them," Cameron said. "You should use them for the greater glory of God."

"That *is* what I'm doing," Tom said brightly. Though

he had learned the truth about the angels, he still had faith in God.

They rode down the crest, into the valley. It was getting cooler. Summer was passing into fall.

There *had* been a time when Tom thought of becoming a student here. His dream had been to enter one of these schools and emerge a great artist, but then he'd learned that the angels ran these schools, carefully controlling the students' every brushstroke, dictating what they could or could not render, and what particular style they might use. Tom had visions of his own that he wanted to pursue, and in schools like these, those visions would never be allowed.

Maybe someday . . .

Aitan Anzelm, the angel Tom desperately hoped to save, had charged Tom with the task of using his talent as an artist to make a record of what he'd seen in the Heavenly City: its many wonders and its terrible fall.

So far, Tom hadn't quite gotten around to the task. All the days he'd spent in Paridian had been devoted to his recuperation from his own bout with the Scourge—cured by Cameron's touch—and figuring out the best way to reach Aitan's Patron.

Besides, Tom had decided that if at all possible, it would be best to let the angels tell their own stories. Writing down what had happened and illustrating the tale would be like creating a memorial, and he *knew* that they were still alive.

"By the way," Kayrlis said as they rode toward the settlement, "happy birthday."

Her brother enthusiastically echoed the sentiment.

"When are your birthdays?" Tom asked.

There was a long silence.

Tom laughed. "What, did I ask something bad?"

"The past is the past," said Kayrlis. "It doesn't matter much."

"Of course it does," said Tom. "I was born and raised in Hope. Until Aitan Anzelm came along—"

"I know the story, Tom. I've heard it enough times," Kayrlis said.

"Oh," Tom said. "Sorry."

He looked away and let the subject trail out before him as he hoped Kayrlis or her brother would leap upon it.

They didn't.

All he really knew about their past was that Kayrlis and her brother had been trained in China as acrobats, and that when he'd met them, they'd been traveling with the Carnival of Wonders, a very small troupe of entertainers.

He also knew, of course, how they felt about him. Kayrlis loved him and Cameron was amused by him. He wanted to know more, but he'd come to realize the hard way that badgering them was pointless. They'd tell him what he wanted to know when they were ready, and not before.

Soon they had reached the settlement's outskirts. They came to a group of young men who sat looking up at the dawn.

"God's in His glory!" one of them called.

"Yes—and in all of us," responded Cameron.

"So what are you fellas doing?" asked Kayrlis. "I thought classes were in session before the dawn!"

One of the students rose and came over to her. He was tall and lanky, with long straw-colored hair. "Haven't you heard?"

"We've been traveling," said Tom. "Plying our trade."

"I'm Oberon," said the young student. "What trade is that?"

"Well, I was a knife sharpener, but there was an accident. Some falling rocks down by Winding Way. Our mule was killed, my rig crushed. But I'm good with my hands, I can work stables, I can cook—"

"Please," said Kayrlis, "our young friend here wasn't looking to hire, I'm sure."

"Just curious," Oberon said, a little embarrassed.

Tom nodded. Kayrlis had warned him about his tendency

to tell more than was really needed, and how it made him sound nervous and suspicious.

"Now," said Kayrlis, "what were you talking about before? You mentioned something we hadn't heard anything about."

"The angels," Oberon said. "They're gone. All but one."

"Which one?" asked Tom.

"Lord Thegri. His is the dominion over—"

"Beasts," said Cameron, quickly.

Oberon nodded, impressed. "We have to learn how to portray all things in our works. Lord Thegri stayed behind to keep the lions, tigers, and bears in line."

"My, my," said Kayrlis.

"Why did they leave?" asked Tom.

"The Fall of Abaddon, of course. You've heard that much, I hope."

Tom nodded.

"The Heavenly City was swept away in a terrible battle with the Enemy and his minions. The angels from our school have gone to honor their fallen comrades."

Tom was surprised. There'd been no mass exodus of angels in Paridian, at least, not while he was there. It must have happened suddenly, just after they left.

Even so, news of Abaddon's destruction had caused some panic in the city. A small number of people had fled Paridian, afraid of the Enemy sweeping their way. Others took comfort in their faith and believed that they would have fair warning if they were in any danger.

The official story sanctioned by the angels was that the Enemy had been chained, and would remain in the fiery torment he so richly deserved until the end of the Millennium.

The story was, in ways, not far from the truth.

"I thought perhaps you were here for the trial and the sentencing," said Oberon.

Tom tried to act casually. "What trial is that?"

"Juno Meazzi. He lay with his neighbor's wife, and when his mistress tired of his attentions, he slew her and her husband."

"You sound like you were there," said Tom quickly and with an unmistakable edge of annoyance in his voice.

Oberon flinched as if he'd been struck. "I think it's time that I return to my meditations and silent prayers, Grinder."

Kayrlis looked at Tom and mouthed the word, "Smart." Then all three rode ahead, toward the first few buildings of the settlement.

"We have to ask questions," said Tom, in his own defense.

Kayrlis shook her head. "What we have to be is subtle, blast it. We're strangers here. I'd figure that the opinion of most in New Florence is that Juno is guilty of this crime. When we talk to people, we gotta take whatever they say as a given. Let them lead us to the truth."

"Subtle," repeated Tom.

"Yes."

"My mistake."

"I'd say." Kayrlis angrily rode on. Tom and Cameron fell in together two dozen paces behind her.

"What'd I do?" asked Tom.

"You didn't do nothin'," Cameron said. "She's scared, that's all."

"Her?"

Cameron nodded. "She always gets like this when something's giving her the frights."

"Gets like what?"

"Blunt. You just gotta get used to it."

"I guess." Tom yawned. He was grateful that the nightmare had woken him last night or else he might have never become aware of Juno's plight. On the other hand, he was exhausted.

As the trio entered the main cobblestone street of New

Florence, a small delegation came out to meet them. Three men and two women. Each had raven's hair and piercing eyes. They were dressed in dark, elegant clothing. Long violet overcoats, with occasional touches of white silk for contrast, dark leggings, pointy-toed boots. An accordion pattern had been embroidered upon the breasts of each coat like family crests. Collars were high, reaching to the chin, serrated at the center. The women were dressed no differently from the men.

"God be with you, travelers," said a green-eyed gentleman who stepped out from the others. "How may the people of New Florence help you this day?"

"God be with you," said Tom. "Is there somewhere we could get a meal and a bath? Perhaps a place to sleep?"

"Of course," said the man. "Though I must warn you, the galleries are closed and construction on the Arcadia proceeds apace. The noise may not be helpful—if sleep *is* your true goal . . ."

"Why wouldn't it be?" asked Kayrlis. "Some young men on the road made mention of a trial, but I have no taste for such things."

"Suit yourselves, then." The welcoming committee quickly departed.

Finding an inn with vacancies was easy enough. The innkeeper was a pleasant man in his fifties, his hair an unnaturally solid shade of black. He called for two young women to take the travelers to their rooms while a man in his thirties with short auburn hair saw to their horses.

"This is something we didn't expect," said the first of the young women. She was barely out of her teens, with short, blond, curly hair, and a hard edge to her otherwise pleasing features.

"What do you mean?" asked Tom.

"So many people are leaving," said the second, an olive-skinned young woman with hazel eyes.

"Why's that?" Kayrlis ventured.

"The Fall of Abaddon," said the first. "It's been chaos ever since word arrived and the angels left. I heard that Vittorio saw a group of anarchists prowling the streets last night, talking about hunting down the Angel of Beasts. Foolish thought, that. Beyond the heresy involved, I mean."

"Anarchists," Tom said, stunned. "Walking around in public? Were they wearing their masks?"

"Oh, yes. Or so Vittorio tells the story."

They reached the landing and were shown to a pair of rooms off to the left. The olive-skinned lass brushed past Tom as she went to open the curtains letting the noises of the city float in. He smiled at her, and she gave a small laugh in return.

"I think we can take care of the rest ourselves," said Kayrlis as she ushered the young women from the room.

"Shouldn't we show the young sir to his room?" the pretty darker-skinned woman asked. She held out her hand to Cameron, who shifted his gaze uneasily between the woman and his sister.

"No need," said Kayrlis, barely restraining an urge to slam the door in the young women's faces. A moment after the door closed, giggling resounded in the hall along with a pair of voices.

"—thought he was very cute—"

"—so shy, I could do something about that—"

Cameron smiled crookedly at his sister as he reached for the door. "I'm sure you two want some time alone..."

"Don't even think about it," Kayrlis said.

Cameron laughed. "Just playin' with you. The Vessels didn't make us to act like wanton beasts, I know that."

"Fine," said Kayrlis, turning down the sheets of the bed she would share with Tom. True, it was a sin for them to lie together, but in their hearts and minds they were joined. There was love between them, and that had to make a difference. "We need to find out what's going on here. And fast."

"How do you want to go about it?" asked Tom.

Kayrlis frowned. "As I was saying before, we can't be too obvious about—"

Suddenly, a voice erupted from the street over the sounds of crowds and construction.

"Juno Meazzi returned to custody! Some say spirits of the dark have taken his soul. Today we'll find out as he stands trial for his life. Arguments begin at three. How long will it take for evil to be found out and punished? Not long, many feel. Not long at all!"

"The town crier," Tom said.

Nodding, Kayrlis went to the window and listened to the rest of the day's news.

Tom tried to concentrate on the words of the crier, but his attention was stolen by Kayrlis's beauty. The sun struck her elegant profile and became white-hot fire against her soft flesh. Her hands were finely crafted, beautiful and delicate, angular and strong. He watched the way the light traced the length of her long, sensuous neck, a waterfall of brilliance leading to the hollow where she loved to be kissed.

There was so much about her he didn't know, yet—was it really important? So long as her heart was his, so long as the mysteries of her exquisite body were open for his explorations—

Stop that, Tom chided himself. *There's a child present. Her brother, for heaven's sake.*

Tom looked away from his beloved.

For Heaven's sake . . .

"Tom?"

He looked up sharply. "I'm sorry?"

"I said that we should go out," said Kayrlis. "If anyone

asks us why such weary travelers as us are not asleep, as we pledged, well—''

The sounds of construction in the distance rose up.

''I'd call that an explanation, wouldn't you?''

Tom nodded. ''Let's go.''

Three

THE STREETS OF NEW FLORENCE WERE FILLING WITH people by the time Tom, Kayrlis, and Cameron left the inn. The brick and stone buildings stood in clusters; their windows seemed to be made of black glass, the rooftops triangular, domed, or steepled. The cobblestone streets were filled with people dressed in brilliant clothing, rushing, heads down, expecting everyone else to get out of their way.

There were many businesses. Moneylenders, clothiers, toy shops, and bakeries. Public baths had recently been installed, and hawkers stood on the street, attempting to lure clients by comical means—either making cracks about their odor or going right up to them, taking a whiff, and fainting on the spot. The advertising was effective. Tom was feeling pretty ripe himself after witnessing the display. A rat catcher bumped Cameron, the corpses of vermin tied to his belt, swaying and slapping against his hip. Town criers spoke again of the trial, which would take place in the Eisenkranz Plaza.

Tom passed a shoemaker and wondered what it would be like to have enough money to own several pair of shoes, to discard boots when they were giving out instead of repairing them again and again for years. They passed the shops of saddlers, wheelwrights, goldsmiths, knife grinders, and many other craftsmen. Chimney sweeps hacking away passed with downturned eyes. Street cleaners did their job while ducking carriages and horsemen.

"Are you hungry?" Tom asked his companions.

"I am!" cried Cameron.

"He can always eat," said Kayrlis.

They visited a shop that made sweets and served desserts that looked so rich, Tom worried that he would feel queasy for an hour after his meal. The server, a thin, swarthy-skinned youth, nervously eyed a trio of women seated off to the rear. Near the door stood a pair of Arrow Riders.

After the server left, Tom said, "I wonder what's bothering him."

"Those three," said Kayrlis, nodding to the women.

The noise from the street ebbed, and the women's voices drifted toward Tom and his companions. Only two spoke. The third watched with growing concern and evident anger, to which her companions were oblivious.

"I tell you, Juno Meazzi is a beast. If anyone in this settlement deserves what's coming to them, it's him."

"Not a very charitable attitude."

"I had to fend off his advances more than once. Perhaps that left me feeling less than charitable. Besides, I heard that even those louts he drank with believe him to be guilty. What more proof does one need? Beatrice may have been a bit open with her favors, especially for a married woman, but that wasn't a sin great enough to die for."

"Well, you won't get any argument from me, he was hated in this settlement, I'll give you that."

"And he had motive. With the head of the Builder's Guild in his grave, who stood to take his place? That animal, Meazzi, that's who!"

Suddenly, the third woman rose up and dashed for the door, tears streaming down her face.

"Luchia!" one of her companions cried. "What is it?"

Kayrlis touched Tom's hand. "We should catch up with her."

He looked to Cameron. "Stay here, and you can have all our treats."

"Great!" cried the boy.

Kayrlis left money on the table, then walked unhurriedly to the door, Tom right behind her. "I'm telling you," Kayrlis said loudly, "if you can't keep me in the style to which I am accustomed in this ridiculous profession of yours, then you'll just have to take that position with your father, whether you like it or not! You *don't* want me to be unhappy, now do you?"

The Arrow Riders acted as if they were paying no attention to the display, but Tom had a sense that they were.

"Of course not, sweetheart," he groused, playing along.

"Weakling," one of the guards said. The other laughed.

Once they were on the street, Tom said, "Was that really necessary? And if so, would you mind telling me *why*?"

"Was it necessary? In my opinion—yes. I didn't want the Arrow Riders to think we were leaving to follow this Luchia. They might have stopped us and asked questions we didn't want to answer. I got an idea that they're *very* protective of the people in this settlement. Maybe that guilds pay them and grant them favors that the angels won't. 'Sides—it was fun."

They saw Luchia entering an outdoor market. She'd placed a veil before her face to hide her tears.

Tom and Kayrlis followed her. Luchia had a basket and was collecting fruit. At one point, Kayrlis drifted close beside her. Then she eased away, pulling Tom along with her.

"She's married," Kayrlis said. "I wanted to get close enough to see if she was wearing a ring."

"Do you think it's true that Juno made a habit of romancing married women?"

"It'd explain why Luchia got so upset. But I'm afraid it

doesn't paint a very flattering portrait of this man we're trying to save.'' Kayrlis hesitated. "Tom, are you *sure* that the Power didn't mislead you?"

"Positive," said Tom.

"I just don't know what we can do for him. It's not like we can come right out and say that you've been Blessed and that's how you know he's innocent. Even if we could prove that you have the Power, they'd call you a Transformed Being. An agent of the Enemy. Or worse, they'd take you to the angels. If that happened—"

He squeezed her hand. "I know. So we have to find another way, that's all."

By the time they returned to the inn, the place was packed. It was lunchtime, and many of the builders had come here to feast—and to drink.

Cameron wasn't feeling well after his rich meal of sweets. He went upstairs directly. Tom and Kayrlis were about to join him when they heard a man cry, "To Juno Meazzi!"

Everyone in the taproom froze at that.

The man who'd spoken was swarthy-skinned, with a single bushy eyebrow that lashed itself over his hooded eyes. He smoked a cigar and wore many rings on his thick fingers. He was fatter than Juno, thickly built and mean-looking. But otherwise, he was close enough in appearance to the condemned man to pass for his brother.

"Don't mind Reni!" cried a thin man missing several of his front teeth. "A joke! A joke!"

The man who'd spoken rose up. "By the blood and spit of the Enemy it was *not*!"

The innkeeper whispered something to one of his boys. The young man raced off. Tom decided it was probably to summon a few of the Arrow Riders.

"No need for talk like that here," said the innkeeper.

The loutish man sat back down. "My apologies. But Juno Meazzi was our friend. He may have sinned—and sinned mortally. But we knew he was a man of passion. He used those passions in our behalf many times. Remember how he fought to keep us from losing any chance of seeing our families when the guild masters would make us do a job again and again for no reason other than to torture us?"

Several people in the taproom murmured and nodded their heads.

"Do I believe he killed Antonio and his wife?" Reni continued. "Yes, probably. And I don't condone his actions if he did. The Vessels will judge him more wisely—and with more finality—than we ever could. All I say is that we should raise a glass to him for all the good he once did, and out of a prayer that his soul finds peace, should he be found guilty and strung up. That's all."

Reni raised his glass once again. "To Juno Meazzi."

No one else raised a glass.

Enraged, the brute smashed his glass down on the table, shattering it. He cut himself, his blood leaking into the brew he'd spilled.

The thin man beside him laid down enough gold to pay for the damage and raced to the innkeeper, talking quickly, and begging the man's understanding.

Reni stormed toward the exit. Kayrlis stopped him.

"Here, let me see that," she said, snatching up a towel from a nearby table and wrapping it around his bleeding hand.

"You're—most kind," said Reni. He looked to Tom. "Your woman?"

"Her own, actually. But I'm lucky enough to be married to her."

Kayrlis smiled at this, despite herself.

Reni laughed. "Good answer, lad. Keep that frame of mind and you'll be married a long time. Just don't say such things in front of the boys, if you can help it."

Frowning, Kayrlis tightened the towel a bit more than

she had to. Reni winced. Then he laughed and said, "No offense, tender one."

"None taken," said Kayrlis. "Sorry about your friend."

"Did you know Juno?" he asked, suddenly very interested.

"Never met him. But it seems that he's been judged harshly."

"True enough." He looked down at his wounded hand. "Foolish thing to do, I suppose. You have my thanks. Is there a way I can pay you back?"

Tom shrugged. "None that I can think of right now."

"Let me know," said Reni. Crossing his arms over his chest to hide his wounded hand, he slipped out the door as the Arrow Riders entered.

"You really think he'll confess before the trial's over?" asked the first Arrow Rider, a hawk-nosed man with thin lips.

"Don't they all? We have the might of the angels on our side. And if he goes to the other side with a lie on his lips, he'll be judged all the more harshly when he arrives."

"True, true. Still . . . Have you seen the way he looks at us? So smug and superior?" The first man's hand grazed the whip hanging from his belt. "It's all I can to do contain my urge to see him punished here and now, for his lack of respect."

"In time, in time," said his companion as they went to the innkeeper.

Tom turned to Kayrlis. "And you told me to be subtle. *I think he's been judged harshly . . .* "

"Yeah, well . . ."

"I don't know what else we can do," Tom said. "The trial's only a few hours away."

"I can think of one thing," said Kayrlis.

Tom raised an eyebrow. "Really?"

"Uh-huh. Sleep. We're both going to need a few hours at least."

They went upstairs, hand in hand, oblivious to the looks they were receiving from two men at a table near the door. Each was handsome, with raven's hair and sky blue eyes. One wore a thin beard shaved to a point, the other a mustache. In every other regard, they were identical.

Angelico and Benevenuto Canova didn't like what they'd just seen.

"Why do you think she spoke with Reni?" asked Angelico, the bearded one. "The way she looked at him when she bound his wound—"

"She's probably a very Godly woman. Let it go."

"I'm worried. If the truth comes out—"

"You're always worried. Juno will say nothing. He'll go to his grave saying nothing. That was the pact he made. And as much as you or I might think him a fool for placing his personal honor above everything, even his life, that is who and what he is. There's nothing to worry about. I guarantee you this."

Angelico nodded. "I'll just feel better when it's over, that's all."

"We both will," said his brother. "We both will . . ."

Four

Tom, Kayrlis, and Cameron arrived early enough to get seats near the tribunal and the witness box. The four elegantly dressed people who had greeted them when they first arrived in New Florence sat close by.

"I thought you had no interest in the trial?" the woman asked.

Kayrlis shrugged. "It's all anyone in this settlement talks about. Bound to get a person's curiosity up."

"True, true..."

Tom was impressed with Kayrlis's display of nonchalance. He found it very difficult indeed to contain his excitement. A part of him felt a tremendous guilt at having taken this detour from the path of finding his friend and mentor Aitan Anzelm. Still, he knew this was what Aitan would have told him to do. Besides, Tom had more than a little doubt as to how effective his search for the missing angels could possibly be. This, at least, was something that perhaps was not beyond his power to affect or control.

The prisoner was brought into the plaza, his chains announcing him. Everyone stood and turned to see Juno being led into the makeshift court. He looked as if he'd been beaten many times, but his eyes were not downcast. He grinned at several of the women.

"Vitola, have you put out that fire of yours yet?" he cried to one of them.

The Arrow Rider leading Juno yanked hard with the chains. Juno grunted, but never lost his smile. The woman to whom he'd spoken shook her head and cried, "Still the same, eh? A headsman's ax could be inches from your neck and you'd still be looking down the front of a woman's blouse!"

"With her approval!" Juno cried out in a rough voice.

The court was set up like a stage. Juno was led up several steps onto a platform, where he was made to stand at the easternmost flank. Three podia were set up, one for the judge, another for the defense, and another for the prosecution. The man assigned to protect Juno's life entered next. Short, overweight, and balding, he was a penguin of a man who seemed uncomfortable with his role this day.

The prosecutor was tall, silver-haired, and surprisingly youthful. He stood with his back bolt straight, confidence radiating from him. Finally the judge entered.

"All rise. The Honorable Enrico Marsalles presides!"

The judge was from the southwestern settlements. He had hard eyes, sleek black hair, a mustache and goatee, and appeared close to Tom's father's age. Intense and seemingly filled with wrath, the judge wore black robes trimmed with turquoise and crimson. The particular style had been transplanted from the Lahu people of the eastern Yunnan province in China.

He was New Florence's Curacas.

"Sit," he said simply. Everyone followed his command.

Tom glanced around. The plaza was filled. No wonder they couldn't hold this trial in a usual place of judgment. It seemed that every resident of New Florence had turned out.

There was no jury; the judge would render his decision alone.

Tom took Kayrlis's hand as Juno's representative addressed the judge and the vast audience.

"This man, Juno Meazzi, is innocent," the pear-shaped man stammered. "He knew the victim, of course he did. He worked for him, after all. And they argued, no denying that. Many times. Before countless witnesses. He secretly met with the slain Beatrice, that he has admitted, though not for the purpose of a romantic liaison. He was at the scene of the murder that night, that he does not deny. But he did not kill this unfortunate couple. This he maintains on his word as a man, and in the solemn office of facing the Almighty's wrath. He gives his word, what more do we need? Thank you."

The round little man went back to his podium, shaking.

For a few seconds, there was a stunned silence. Then laughter broke out among the crowd, quickly rising to a deafening roar. The Arrow Riders restored order before long.

"Why don't they just take his head now?" Tom whispered angrily.

Kayrlis squeezed his hand so hard it hurt.

The judge said, "I have allowed the public to be a part of these proceedings because the victims of this foul murder were beloved in this community and everyone here has a right to see justice done. But I will not brook any more disturbances of this kind. Should they occur, I will move this trial back to my private court."

His proclamation sobered the crowd. They didn't want to miss a minute.

The prosecutor stood up. "I almost don't know what to say. It seems my work has already been done for me. However, however . . . I am here today on a most serious matter. Murder has been done. A valued member of our community and his wife have been savagely cut down. Someone must pay for that. The person who has shattered God's law—Juno Meazzi!"

The crowd rose to its feet in applause. This time, the Curacas did nothing to stop them.

Tom, Kayrlis, and Cameron rose to their feet but didn't applaud.

Order was finally restored. Witnesses were called.

Three women of low character testified to Juno's wanton nature. The last, a blue-eyed woman named Miranda, laughed and said, "He would brag about all the married women he had taken to his bed. Even when we were—well, you know—he would tease me with them, telling me they were so desperate for fire and passion that they made the best lovers, and that I'd have to break a real sweat to even come close."

Murmurs of disgust drifted through the plaza. Tom looked over to see Juno smiling wistfully.

Did the man *want* to die? Tom wondered.

Soon, Juno's friends from the inn were called. They testified uniformly that Juno was a man of passion and dark lusts. But they also maintained that he lived by a strict code of honor and that he never lied. The last to testify was the man who had hurt his hand at the inn.

"Juno never named names," Reni said. "And he never spoke of the fair and fallen Beatrice. I know only that there was one woman he truly loved but could never have. He spoke of her often."

"But she was never named," said the prosecutor.

"Never."

"Was she married?"

Reni hung his head. "She was."

Another burst of outrage filled the court. People turned to one another, their anger growing. Tom glanced around. He saw the young married woman from the marketplace. She seemed withdrawn, her eyes unfocused. A much older man sat beside her, shaking his fist in the air, calling for

Juno's blood now, right now, protocol be damned!

Kayrlis whispered in Tom's ear, "Any lies yet?"

"None," Tom said gravely.

The prosecutor continued, "Juno was your friend?"

"He *is* my friend," Reni growled. "Your butchers haven't gotten to him yet."

"I stand corrected. Do you believe that he's capable of this crime?"

"No," said Reni.

Tom looked to Kayrlis and shook his head. Reni was lying.

"What about the words you spoke at the Florentine Inn today? You seemed to be willing to acknowledge the possibility then."

"I've given it more thought. Juno is a hard man, but he is not a killer. I have to believe that he would not take a man's life except in service to the angels."

"Yes, yes," said the prosecutor. "You served in several holy crusades with Juno, did you not?"

"I did."

"The blood of heretics ran freely, yes?"

"It did."

"I believe that Juno had a prescribed method of execution for those the angels proclaimed unclean, is that not so?"

Reni shrugged. "Perhaps."

"You know this to be a fact; you adopted the method yourself."

With a deep growl Reni cried, "If you know so much, why don't you just spit it out and stop asking me stupid questions!"

Some people laughed at this. Juno was one of them.

The prosecutor looked to the judge.

"Yes, go on," said the Curacas.

"Juno took the hands, then the hearts, of those he slew," said the prosecutor. "Correct?"

"They'd sinned against God!" Juno roared suddenly.

An Arrow Rider spun and smashed her armored elbow into Juno's face. He staggered back, then put his hand to his face, where blood flowed freely. Holding up his crimson hand he said, "Now that's what you've all come to see, isn't it?"

The Arrow Rider struck Juno with the hilt of her sword. It doubled him over, but his smile soon returned.

"This man is one with the Enemy!" the Arrow Rider proclaimed. "Let me take him now!"

She drew her sword.

"Do nothing!" cried the Curacas.

Shaking, the Arrow Rider sheathed her sword and bowed.

"Should have done it," said Juno. "Spared us all this farce."

Reni was excused.

Juno said, "You're a good man, Reni. A good friend. I'll raise a drink to you on the other side."

Tom noticed the way the judge and the prosecutor smiled at that. He wondered why.

"My point to all this," said the prosecutor, "is to draw attention to the gruesome manner in which the victim and his wife were slain. They were bound, then their hands were severed, followed by their hearts."

A buzzing began among the crowd.

"And where were these dark and terrible prizes found? In the home of the accused, along with the weapon that most assuredly was used for this dark deed."

Someone rose up and threw a stone at Juno. It struck him on the side of the head, and he teetered but did not fall.

Men that Juno had worked with testified that Juno often started fights, that he swore, drank, and bragged endlessly about his conquests. A wiry man with dark eyes was the last to be called upon.

"Who would gain from the death of the master builder and head of the Builder's Guild?" the prosecutor asked.

"Juno, of course. No matter what else you could say about him, he knew his job. He had a talent and a passion for creating works that will outlive us all."

"Yet he and the deceased argued frequently?"

"Oh, yes."

"Why is that?"

"It's wrong to speak ill of the dead, sir."

The prosecutor shook his head. "This is a place of truth. We all have our flaws. Tell the court."

"The master builder was a good man, a kind man, but he wanted everything to be perfect. He would work us long into the night, which would have been fine, except—well, he never really knew what he wanted. We'd have to do a job a half dozen times, then he'd tell us to take it all down and do it the way we had in the first place. He said that he was seeking his bliss, acting on inner visions . . ."

"Hmmmm," said the prosecutor, "if he was so incompetent—"

"He was not! I never said that!"

"Forgive me. But all that we are and all that we do is in service to the greater glory of the Heavenly Host and the Almighty. Master Antonio's quest for perfection could hardly be faulted in that light, wouldn't you say?"

"When you put it like that . . ."

"And this was why he and Juno argued? Over the work and no other reason?"

"I wouldn't know," said the man. "They often went to more private places to have their discussions."

"Discussions which you could hear a mile off, I understand."

"They were loud and heated, yes."

"Can you think of no one but Juno who stood to gain from Antonio's death?"

The man hesitated. Then he said, "I cannot."

Near the front of the crowd, Tom felt the Power rise up in him. "Liar," he whispered.

Kayrlis glared at him, then said, "Really?"

He nodded.

More witnesses were paraded through the trial, women who testified to the rumors always spreading about the slain Beatrice and her poor deluded husband.

"He thought she loved him," said one woman. "And he loved her, that much was for sure. But though he was handsome, and by appearances, quite capable—"

Laughter came from the audience.

"Yes?" asked the prosecutor.

"It was common knowledge that she had appetites that couldn't be satisfied by one man. She was beautiful. She could have whoever she wanted. And she did."

"Those were the rumors."

"Indeed."

Next, Lorenzo Cellini was brought forward. He was a thickly built man, his muscles soft, his arms and chest hairy like a bear. His eyes were wide and filled with grief.

The prosecutor established that Cellini had been made the new master builder and head of the Guild in place of Juno.

"Tell me," said the prosecutor, "did you have any reason to feel enmity toward Juno Meazzi?"

"No," said Cellini.

Tom felt it. A lie.

"Do you feel that you profited by Antonio Chuiddo's death?" asked the prosecutor.

"In that I gained his title and responsibilities?" asked Cellini. "No. I never wanted this position."

The fire of truth rose in Tom again. He began to sweat. A shudder passed through him. More lies.

"And would you categorize the defendant, Juno Meazzi, as an ambitious man?"

"Yes."

Tom began to feel faint. Did this man *ever* tell the truth?

"Last question," said the prosecutor. "Can you think of anyone other than Juno who would have profited from Antonio's death? Anyone who would have motive to kill this man and his wife—the lover who had lured him into her embrace then spurned him when he no longer proved entertaining?"

"None."

Tom felt the fire of truth slice through him like a molten blade. "Well," he whispered, "we know where to start."

"You are excused," said the prosecutor.

Juno leaned in close to his overweight defender. "You're doing a *great* job. Thank you so much."

The man frowned and looked away.

Next a young man named Giovanni Perugino was called. He had short blond hair, dark blue eyes, and an innocent-looking face.

"Please tell this court your relationship to the deceased," said the prosecutor.

Perugino nodded anxiously. "I was hired by Antonio Chuiddo to protect his home and his belongings. There had been several burglaries in the area, along with several beatings of those who were home at the time. Antonio feared for his wife's safety on those nights when he was working late."

"When were you hired?"

"Two nights before the . . . Before—"

"Yes. Before Juno Meazzi brutally slew Antonio and Beatrice."

No one said a word.

The young man said, "I had wanted to be an Arrow Rider, but my feet weren't the right type. But I am good at what I do. I've caught five thieves and several other criminals over the last few years."

"Your reputation precedes you," said the prosecutor.

"And as you can see, no one is calling your credentials into question."

"No," said Juno, nodding toward his defender, "not even the lump over here."

Several people laughed at that.

Tom listened carefully. So far, the young guardsman had told the absolute truth.

"Did you see Juno Meazzi meet with Beatrice secretly?" asked the prosecutor.

"Twice. They thought it was secretly. But I saw them."

"Yes, at her house," said Juno, "with a snooping little pup right at the doorstep. Exactly what we'd have done if we were carrying on a mad *passionate* affair."

The Arrow Rider beside him turned and struck Juno. Something crackled in his jaw. He spit out a tooth.

"Silence," said the Curacas. "Prosecutor?"

"Did you see Juno Meazzi the night of the killings?"

"I did," said Perugino. "I was in the house at the time. I saw Antonio Chuiddo and his wife enter their study, where the murder took place. Then Meazzi arrived and went in after them."

"How did he seem?"

"Agitated. Alarmed over something."

"Then?"

"I went in after him, to make sure everything was all right. Antonio told me to wait outside. So I did."

"There were no windows in the study, no doors except that one?"

"Yes."

"What happened next?"

Perugino paused. "I heard raised voices. A scream."

Tom felt something flare within him. This was not a lie, but there was something wrong . . .

"Go on," said the prosecutor.

"I burst into the room. Beatrice and Antonio had been murdered. Butchered."

"Did you see the defendant?"

"No. Someone clubbed me from behind. I heard a man running off behind me. And that was all."

Tom felt it. The fires telling him that a lie had been spoken. *And that was all.*

No, Tom thought. It most certainly was not.

The young guardsman was excused.

"I have one final witness to call," said the prosecutor. He nodded, and two of his young assistants raced from the plaza. Moments later, the rear doors opened and a shining figure entered.

The Angel of Beasts had arrived.

Five

THE ANGEL WAS NOT AT ALL WHAT TOM EXPECTED. Most of the angels he had seen were perfect. This one was hardly that. The Angel of Beasts was enormous, covered in so many layers of shining silver-and-gold robes that he looked like a huge bell floating across the floor. His feet were entirely hidden by his clothing.

His plain features were thick, and he seemed a bit groggy. His hair was fashioned in tight little ringlets, and his chubby fingers were unadorned. A series of gold links looped around his wrists jingled as he walked.

Approaching the platform, he glanced at the stairs, shook his head, and spread his arms. His body rose up from the floor and was gently deposited on the platform.

The crowd made cries of blessing and reverence.

Tom said nothing. He tried to force away the anger in his heart. *You're Elven. A pretender. But I suppose you don't even know that. You think you really are a messenger of God, just as you were raised to believe. Fooled by the lies, just like all of us.*

The prosecutor bowed before the angel. "Lord Thegri, we are honored by your presence."

"Of course," said the angel in a voice that was soft and not at all commanding.

"I understand that you have had dealings with the accused."

"I have," said the angel. "When Juno was a child, he studied at the St. Michael School of Art, where I am also an instructor."

"Was he a student of yours?"

"Ghastly though it is to admit—yes."

The audience laughed. The angel looked up sharply, as if he was being mocked. The crowd fell silent. Many wept with sudden terror, fearful that they would be damned on the spot for their impertinence. Then the angel looked up at a spot on the ceiling and seemed to forget about the incident.

"Lord?" asked the prosecutor.

"Yes?" said the daydreaming angel. He looked down and turned his gaze fully on the prosecutor. "Yes. Juno Meazzi. I am the Angel of Beasts, but they at least are one with God. Juno Meazzi is unclean."

The audience gasped at the pronouncement.

"Benevolent and kind lord," said the prosecutor, "would you share with us your reasons for describing the defendant so?"

At the edge of the platform, Juno made a loud meowing.

The angel whirled. "Evil! You are wedded to the Enemy, you are a servant to darkness and filth! You cannot die soon enough!"

Juno grinned.

The prosecutor fell to his knees. "Lord, I beseech you!"

"Do not," said the angel as he drew a pattern in the air. A fiery Sigil appeared. It grew until it became large enough to encompass a man.

"Divine judgment is at hand!" someone screamed.

"No," said the angel. "Illumination."

Suddenly, a large black panther dived from the vortex.

It padded onto the stage and growled. The second it saw Juno, it advanced on him.

"Desist!" the angel cried.

The panther stopped.

Tom noticed immediately that the animal had no tail.

"When Juno was a child, though to describe a creature such as he with a term that denotes innocence seems foul to me," said the angel, "he decided upon a little experiment. He tied together the tails of this poor creature and several others. They went mad attempting to get away from one another. Poor Stumpy here was never the same again."

The angel actually wept.

At first, it seemed that Juno might laugh. Then he saw the genuine grief in the angel's eyes, and he lowered his gaze. "I am sorry, lord. It was a foolish, wretched, and childish thing I did."

The angel looked up sharply. "Do you think I would accept your apology now, after so much time has passed?"

"Apparently not," said Juno.

The angel waved his hand again. Two wraithlike figures appeared. They corralled the tailless beast back into the fissure the angel had created in reality, then departed with the beast.

"Who were *they*?" Tom cried, despite himself.

"Anastasia and Theodorus," said the elegantly dressed man beside him. "Spirits who have dedicated themselves to our lord's service for all eternity."

Tom nodded. Spirits who had been bound, more likely. Tom had learned much about the magics of the angels from Malkiyyah, the Angel of Blood. He knew that a severed soul had to be captured quickly, and the ceremony of binding was a painful one.

Tom felt repulsed by what everyone else here accepted as right and good.

The angel bellowed at the Curacas, "I tell you, Juno Meazzi is a foul creature from lower depths. If anyone in this settlement deserves what's coming to him, it's Juno.''

The prosecutor smiled. "Lord, do you feel that Juno Meazzi is capable of committing the heinous acts of which he stands accused?"

The angel shook his head slowly and with conviction. In his lofty voice he said, "I believe he is capable of *anything*."

"I have nothing further," said the prosecutor.

The angel left the plaza.

Juno's representative finally spoke. "Have you anything to say for yourself?"

"Only that you're all fools," said Juno. "I welcome death if it means an end to suffering your presence."

"Is that all?" counsel asked. "Did you kill Beatrice and Antonio Chuiddo?"

"No, I did not. As God is well aware."

This created an uproar in the court. After several minutes of shouting to make himself heard, the Curacas restored order.

"Do you know who did kill them? Did you have an accomplice who performed the actual deed while you watched?"

"Kill me and have done with it," Juno said. "I have nothing more to say to you. I have nothing more to say to any of you."

"You may not feel that way tomorrow," said the Curacas. "I have heard all I need to hear. My judgment is made. I find Juno Meazzi guilty of the murders of Antonio and Beatrice Chuiddo. He will die at dawn tomorrow. God shall have no mercy on his soul."

The crowd rose up a final time, cheering and spitting at the condemned man. Tom looked around and saw that the young married woman and her husband had gone. But near the edge of the crowd, he saw an old woman who wept and several other people who gathered around her. Juno's family, Tom guessed, wondering if there was anything they could tell him.

Kayrlis and Cameron followed Tom as he made his way toward them, but the crowd quickly obscured them from view, and the quest soon became an impossible one.

Tom and his companions left the plaza and found a quiet side street.

"The guardsman wasn't telling everything he knew," Tom said. "And the new master builder lied the entire time. Somehow, we have to find out what they know, and we have to be able to prove it."

It was early evening. The sky was darkening.

Kayrlis looked to her brother. "You know what to do, don't you, Cameron?"

He grinned.

"Take the guardsman. I'll deal with the builder."

Cameron ran off toward the crowd. Kayrlis moved to follow him, then stopped as she realized that Tom meant to come with her.

"Go back to the room, Tom. There's nothin' else you can do."

"What do you mean?"

"Do you trust me?"

"Yes."

"Then go. Wait for me. And use the time to think about what you've heard and seen. Just keep in mind—with your Power, you might *know* that this man's innocent. But there's a big difference between knowing something and being able to prove it."

"Don't do anything—"

"Careless?" she asked. "Wouldn't dream of it."

With that, she was gone.

FIRST INTERLUDE

Genesis, the New York Colonies

LILITH FOUND HER PREY EASILY. SHE SHADOWED HIM FOR days, learning his responsibilities, his habits, his joys and private fears. Though the image that had been placed in her mind had been that of a child, Lilith knew the adult Matthew Dubrovnik the moment she saw him. It seemed that all those who had trafficked with her lord, the renegade Komm Kayriel, bore a certain mark upon their souls that she could spot instantly.

Matthew had not married. It seemed that he had little interest in companionship of any kind, though he was greatly admired by most of his charges. Many women wanted him, but none seemed capable of attracting his eye.

This would be no challenge at all.

Matthew was the Curacas of a village that was steadily growing in stature among the colonies. The Hierarchy knew that Matthew was from a long line of Curacas and he had proven himself to be a wise and fair man, incapable of being corrupted by the power that had been placed in his hands.

Lilith had tired of merely watching Matthew. The time had come to act.

She positioned herself along the route he usually took to reach his modest home. A man approached. Not Matthew. This one was doughy in the face and around the middle, a poor specimen in all regards.

He would do nicely.

Lilith stepped out before him. She had raven's hair and soft, seductive features. She pulled an ebon cloak around her, obscuring her breathtaking body.

The man stopped before her, startled. He stared at her openly for a moment, unable to stop himself. She knew that it had probably been a long time since he'd been this close to a woman like herself. Their faces were close enough that if she wished, she could kiss him simply by leaning forward.

But a kiss was not what she wanted.

"Kill me," she whispered.

"Ma'am?" he said, eyes wide, his face instantly growing pale.

Lilith reached forward. Her hand slid through his chest, as if she were a wraith—though she was not.

He shuddered with silent agony as her semi-intangible hand worked itself upon his tender organs.

"Kill me—or I will kill you instead," she whispered.

"What, what are you—"

She gave a little squeeze, and soon he was fighting for his life, clawing at her, beating her, kicking and screaming and calling her every foul name he could possibly imagine. The man didn't notice when she stopped fighting back. When she fell to the ground he kicked at her face and chest.

The moment it looked as if he might withdraw from the attack, Lilith allowed her mistlike hand to penetrate his ankle, bringing a cold raw fire to his nerve endings. He lost his balance, toppled down upon her, and with a scream of animal rage, wrapped his hands around her throat.

At that very moment, as Lilith had planned, Matthew Dubrovnik came upon the scene.

"Are you insane?" he roared. "Let her go!"

Lilith's victim didn't hear the words of his Curacas. All he knew was that an agent of the Enemy, an unclean beast in a pleasing form, had set its sights upon him. He had to destroy it! He had to!

Matthew dragged the man from Lilith.

"You want some of what she was getting?" the man roared. "Do you?"

Matthew leveled the man with a single blow, employing an Eastern style of fighting the angels had taught during his years of service to God's army. He felt nothing when he brought the man down. No elation, none of the dark joys that sometimes come from beating another human being, dominating them, proving one's superiority. He was cold and detached, doing what had to be done.

Then he saw the woman's face.

"You're like an angel," he whispered, aghast.

Her face was bloody and bruised, but to Matthew, it was the most pure and radiant sight he had ever beheld.

A crowd was starting to form. Matthew commanded two of the men who appeared to keep an eye on Lilith's attacker. Then he demanded that another find their doctor.

"You'll be all right," he said, stroking the warm forehead of the woman.

He barely even noticed that for an instant, her blood was on his hands. An instant later, it had vanished into his flesh, leaping into him like water hungry for a sponge.

"Why?" she whispered, sobbing. "Why did he—"

"I don't know," said Matthew. "But I'll make sure he never hurts you again. I'll make sure that no one ever hurts you again."

Lilith reached up. Matthew's hand closed on hers. Their fingers entwined.

A single tear left her eyes.

Without thinking, Matthew bent down and kissed it

away. There was a collective gasp from the crowd, but Matthew didn't notice.

Lilith restrained a smile. The act of corruption that she had traveled so far to commit had begun. When it was over, she would possess the means to bridge the gap between the worlds of light and darkness, and call back her lord, Komm Kyriel.

Six

TOM SAT IN THE ROOM, LOOKING OUT THE WINDOW. The moon was full and he felt an old urge to sketch it. Then the desire fell away and he found himself drifting down into darkness...

The crystal chamber burned with a reddish fire. A man made of flames stood before Tom.

"There is much you have yet to learn. Much you have yet to seek. What has happened to your bold and questing heart?" the flame guardian asked.

"I'm afraid," Tom said.

"Of life? Of finding that you cannot possibly succeed in your quest to free your friends from the place they went of their own accord?"

"Yes."

"Don't be a coward and a fool. You know there is a way. But you must believe in it. You must believe in yourself. If you lose that, you have nothing."

"These Powers you gave me—"

"I gave you nothing. You took what you wanted. What you were ready to receive."

"Are the Powers a blessing or a curse? When I was

walking through the marketplace, I could feel one of them inside me, so many people, so many lies..."

"It's the way of things, Tom. Your life isn't going to get any easier. You've chosen a path. Even if you turn your back on it, the longing to know what might have been will remain, and it will be a far worse form of suffering than the uncertainty plaguing you now."

"What are the other two Powers?"

"You will know soon enough, but only if you persevere."

"This man, Juno... I know he's innocent, but how can I prove it?"

"You feel trapped, don't you?"

"Yes."

"As if the key to your freedom is at hand, but for some reason, you can't touch it."

"You know everything about me, don't you?" Tom asked. "And I know nothing about you."

"Not true. You know that I'm trying to help you. The whys and wherefores aren't really important. Not yet. Think about what I said. Consider whether or not there are any others in New Florence who are bound as you feel bound. Perhaps you can help each other..."

Tom woke suddenly as he felt a hand on his shoulder. Kayrlis was beside him. Cameron was perched on the edge of the bed like a cat about to leap. Brother and sister shared a wild look in their eyes, and a flush of excitement.

"We're halfway there," Kayrlis said. "Cameron and I pieced the whole thing together. The tough part—"

"The impossible part," said Cameron, "but who cares?"

"—is proving it."

"Where've you been?" Tom asked.

"The Spider and the Fly have been out building a web, that's all," said Kayrlis excitedly. "I love this settlement.

The buildings are close together. The roofs are easy to scale. And people don't think to close their windows before having important—and if you don't mind me saying it—*damning* conversations!"

"Penelope!" Cameron cried in horror. He never used his sister's real name.

"Come on, now," she said. "Just having a little fun."

Tom nodded. He was beginning to wonder if the extent of their training in China was even more far-reaching than simple acrobatics...

"What I'm worried about right now is you," Kayrlis said, running her hand through Tom's hair. "You looked like you were having a nightmare."

"The flame guardian," Tom said, running his hands over his face and suppressing a yawn.

Cameron leaped down. "The Avatar of the Almighty! You've seen him again?"

"Um... Yes," said Tom. One day, he and Cameron were going to have to talk about what Tom had learned in the Heavenly City. "He said there's a way to free Juno. But we need allies. Allies who are just as stuck as I am."

"Pardon?" Kayrlis asked.

"Nothing." Tom kissed her quickly.

"Do you want to know what I found out?"

"Yes," said Tom. "I want to know."

Cameron and Kayrlis spoke for about an hour, taking turns. Tom interjected comments now and then, drawing conclusions based on their discoveries, until soon, the entire mystery had been unraveled.

Tom rose from his chair. His back was stiff. "All right. So now we know everything. But what do we do about it?"

"I want to go to the angel," said Cameron. "He'll help. He'll guide us."

"To his foodstock, perhaps," Tom mumbled.

Suddenly, Cameron was before him. "Take that back!"

"What?"

"You blasphemed against an Avatar of the Almighty. We might all be damned this very minute—"

"Oh, come on," said Tom. "They're different, but they're not—"

"Tom," Kayrlis said quickly.

A ragged gasp escaped him. "All right. I apologize for any slight to the Angel of Beasts."

"That's better," said Cameron.

Tom sometimes forgot that Cameron was still just a child. Even worse, he was just as deluded as Tom had been when he had first met Aitan Anzelm, because Cameron was devout in his faith.

Then it struck him.

"You're right," Tom said. "We should go see the angel."

Kayrlis looked at him strangely. "Are you sure?"

"Finally!" Cameron cried, squealing with delight.

"Under certain conditions," said Tom.

Cameron's wailing ceased. "Like what?"

"Well," said Tom, "we both know that the Vessels choose their Emissaries very carefully."

"Oh, yes."

"And as the flame guardian has appealed to us directly, not through the auspices of other angels, there has to be a reason, right?"

Cameron thought it over. "I guess that makes sense."

"I know for a fact that there are angels who know about our Power and what we're meant to do with it."

"You do?"

Tom nodded. "But there is the Enemy to consider. He can assume a pleasing form, even that of a kindly angel. We *must* wait until an angel recognizes us for who and what we are before we may say anything to them, before we can appear to be anything more than a couple of devout believers. Do you see?"

"You think the Angel of Beasts is in league with the Enemy? That's why he didn't leave New Florence when all the other angels were called home to mourn the dead in Abaddon?"

Actually, Tom simply thought that the angel was too old and lazy and fat to make the journey. "It's possible."

"Imagine what the flame guardian would say if we caught a *renegade!*"

"That's not what I have in mind, either. We're on a mission. We can't lose sight of that. And most importantly, we can't draw a lot of attention to ourselves. It just wouldn't do. In fact, it'd be like breaking a holy covenant."

Cameron's eyes grew wide. "I never thought about it that way."

"We have a responsibility to uphold. Now go to your room and get your book of angels. We're going to need it."

Seven

Lord Thegri's manor was found at the northernmost border of New Florence. The view from his windows was spectacular. They all faced the wide expanse of nature stretched out beyond the town. No schools were visible, nothing that resembled a city in the making. The unspoiled lands were breathtaking.

Two separate buildings lay to the west of the manor. One held the animals over which Thegri held direct dominion, the other housed his human servants.

Tom knocked on the front door of the manor. Kayrlis and her brother waited several hundred yards away. One of the wraiths answered, a man in a long coat with an upturned collar. Mist clung to the figure. Tom could see through him.

"How may I assist you?" the spirit asked in a gentle, kindly voice.

"Exactly what I've come here to ask you," Tom said softly. He knew that he was taking a risk, but he could see no other way. "I know the Spell of Binding, and I know how to break it."

The spirit was expressionless.

Tom waited. If the spirit was indeed a devout soul who willed his immortal self into service and had not been bound and trapped, like the revenants in the holy City of Abaddon, or if he had not since come to loathe his captivity, then the plan could backfire quickly.

"Tell me more," said the spirit.

Tom sighed with relief. He revealed only enough of his plan to entice the spirit, and to convince him that he was not an agent of his master sent to test his loyalty. Tom genuinely knew how to free him from his unearthly chains and had the Power to do so. And the motivation.

"I'll have to consult with my companion," said the spirit. "Wait here."

The spirit returned in moments. "Hide in that grove of trees over there. What you seek is in my lord's private chamber. When you see my companion in the window, come back. She will lead you to the cabinets and see that you are not discovered while my lord entertains your wife and her brother."

Tom went to Kayrlis and Cameron. He told them what they had to do, then took his position in the woods.

They went to the door and knocked much louder than he had. The wraith opened the door and let them in. Several minutes passed. Tom saw lanterns burst into life in several rooms. Finally, the silver-white form of a young woman appeared in the window and beckoned.

Tom retrieved the two prizes, and had only one near encounter with the angel and his new friends.

"No one has ever asked me to perform such a service!" the angel said as he led Kayrlis and Cameron to a study. "I will not only sign this wonderful book, I will place a blessing upon it!"

Once they were out of view, Tom's companion led him downstairs. He stole down the road and waited for Kayrlis and Cameron.

They appeared nearly an hour later.

"Sorry," Kayrlis said. "He insisted on introducing us to some of the animals."

"I couldn't believe it!" Cameron cried. "Those fellows we met on the road weren't kidding. Lions, tigers, bears . . . I actually got to touch Stumpy!"

Tom hugged Kayrlis, then said, "I'll have to stay here. The boxes can't travel too far from the manor. If they do—"

"I understand," said Kayrlis.

"Can I see them?" Cameron asked. "Can I?"

"Cameron," Kayrlis said in a chiding tone, "how would you like for someone to hold the key to your heart and what's most precious to you, and have them go peeking at it when you've trusted them to respect your privacy?"

"I just wanted a look," he said, but he made no more out of it than that.

During the night, several men came to the angel's manor. Tom wasn't able to get a decent look at any of them. He spent several hours with the spirit boxes, performing magical rites that he'd been shown by the Angel of Blood. By the time he was finished, he was one step away from completing his end of the bargain.

The rest would wait until the spirits had completed theirs.

As dawn approached, a procession left the angel's manor. The angel and several of his attendants walked down the road and passed Tom's hiding place in the nearby grove.

Suddenly, the female wraith appeared before Tom. He cried out, but Kayrlis had moved with lightning speed, clamping her hand over his mouth in time to muffle the sound.

"The men who came in the night," the wraith said. "It was the Curacas and the prosecutor. They asked our lord to perform a binding."

"Juno," Tom said.

"They mean to take his soul and force it into unmentionable service. We'll have to be swift. I was a child in these parts. I can get you to the place of execution long before the angel arrives there. And they won't start without him."

"We'd better move fast," Tom said.

The small party drifted through the woods as if they were carried on the winds. In a bag strapped to her back, Kayrlis carried the spirit boxes Tom had stolen. Within these boxes were the physical anchors that prevented the spirits from moving on to the true afterlife. After Tom completed the Spell of Separation, the contents of the boxes would have to be destroyed.

Soon, they reached the outskirts of a great crowd. The execution was set to take place upon the lawns of New Florence's largest school of art.

"We won't be able to get close enough," Tom said.

Kayrlis nodded toward a rooftop. Tom climbed awkwardly behind his beloved and her brother, nearly losing his footing twice. They moved with remarkable grace and speed.

Atop the roof, Tom joined Kayrlis and Cameron. He was relieved to find no other observers. Both spirits were with them now.

"You know what you have to do," Tom said.

"Remember your promise," said the first of the spirits.

Tom nodded.

Below, he saw what lay at the center of the gathering. Juno was there, chained and stripped to the waist. A large stump had been chosen for his execution. A man dressed as a noble performed tricks with his sword to amuse the crowd. Another man, who might have been his brother, stood nearby.

"Angelico and Benevenuto Canova," one of the wraiths said. "They are to be the executioners. One for the hands. Another for the heart."

Tom felt a chill pass through him. Juno was to be killed in the exact manner as the victims.

An uproar exploded below. The Angel of Beasts and his entourage had arrived.

"Go, it's time," Tom said to the wraiths. They vanished.

He turned to Kayrlis. "We've done all we can do. Now we wait."

"And pray," she added.

Below, the Angel of Beasts was brought close to Juno. He touched the man's forehead and Juno flinched. Then the angel withdrew and the Curacas stepped forward.

"Juno Meazzi, you have been tried and found guilty of the crime of murder. This morning, justice will be served. Do you have anything to say for yourself?"

Juno laughed. "What are you going to do with my head and hands? Mount them on your wall as trophies?"

"You are foul," said the Curacas.

"At least I'm not a deluded fool who mistakes a morning's entertainment for justice. The real murderers are at large. In this crowd, I would wager. They will one day be brought to justice. If not man's justice, then God's."

"Are you finished?"

"One more thing. For those of you in the crowd who would weep for me, and I know you are few—save your tears. Laugh if you can and weep only with happiness. My body may die this morning, but my soul will be free."

The Curacas and the angel exchanged knowing glances.

"*Now* are you finished?"

"In more ways than one, it seems," Juno roared, and the crowd tittered in response.

Suddenly, two fiery wraiths rose up from the crowd. The crowd gasped. The Curacas and the swordsman brothers stumbled back. The figures were so bright they were blinding to look upon.

"*There will be no killings this day!*" said the first wraith. "*Not in our names!*"

"Antonio and Beatrice!" someone gasped.

"Impossible," cried the angel, but he hardly sounded convinced.

"*Juno Meazzi did not take our lives,*" said the second wraith.

"A spirit may not lie," said a woman in the crowd. "That's what we've always been told!"

"It must be the truth!"

"This is a hoax!" roared the Curacas. "Lord Thegri, dispel these illusions created by the Enemy!"

The angel stiffened. "Curacas, did you just *attempt* to give me an order?"

The Curacas fell to his knees. "No, oh lord, of course not, forgive me—"

"Rise before you become tiresome. Speak, good spirits. For it is true, you are bound to tell nothing but the truth, as are all spirits."

Suddenly, the young guardsman stepped forward. "But I told the truth! I saw Juno go in after Antonio and Beatrice. Then I heard screams—"

"You told the truth," said the wraith who appeared to be Antonio said. *"But not the whole truth. After Juno went into Antonio's chambers, you fell asleep. It was the sound of screams much later that woke you."*

Everyone stared at the young guardsman. He shuddered, then nodded. "Yes."

"You never saw Juno leave and the true murderers arrive because you were asleep."

The guardsman wept in shame. "I was . . . I never meant to see anyone harmed, I believed in Juno's guilt, I—"

"Enough!" bellowed the Curacas. He saw that several people were backing away from the gathering. "Arrow Riders! Make sure that no one leaves here!"

The Arrow Riders closed on the ring of spectators.

The female spirit spoke next. *"Master Builder Lorenzo Cellini. You swore in the presence of God that you did not covet all that belonged to Antonio Chuiddo. With the exception of his wife, that was a lie."*

"Shadows!" Cellini cried. "Shadows sent to mislead us. Creatures of filth and degradation. How can you listen to what they say?"

"Silence," cried the Curacas. "The truth, or your tongue will be cut from your head by my hands!"

Cellini hesitated. "Yes. I wanted his power, his position. But I didn't kill him for them."

"You know who did," said the male wraith.

"The heads of the other Guilds. They wished to do the very minimum of what was required during the building. Antonio's insistence on perfection in the name of the angels' greater glory was standing between them and their profits. He could not be reasoned with, he could not be bribed. And so they hired rogues to murder Antonio and his wife, laying the blame firmly on Juno. The guard's ale was drugged that night. One of Antonio's trusted servants was a part of the conspiracy."

The wraiths looked away from Cellini, who fell to his knees. "God forgive us all."

"God perhaps," said the Curacas. "Not me."

Three men broke from the crowd: the heads of the guilds. The Arrow Riders stopped them easily.

The female wraith drifted forward to Juno. *"Tell them why you met secretly with Beatrice."*

"I cannot," Juno stammered. "I gave my word."

"I release you from your vow."

Nodding and looking away, Juno said, "Beatrice had lain with men other than her husband. Two brothers. They stand nearby, swords in their hands."

Angelico and Benevenuto Canova raised their weapons. Angelico, the bearded one, cried, "I won't listen to this!"

Suddenly, an Arrow Rider appeared and leveled a crossbow at him. It was the woman who had taken such delight in beating Juno the day before. "Ah, but you *will.*"

Angelico lowered his sword.

Juno continued with his story. "She had an affair first with Benevenuto, then with his brother. It was an amusement to her, nothing more. She thought a rift would be caused when the brothers learned that they had both carried on liaisons with the same woman. But instead, their bond overcame any such jealousies and both turned on Beatrice. They each threatened her. They said that they would destroy her comfortable life and make her fool of a husband see her as a harlot." Juno looked up at the wraith. "Their words, milady. Not mine."

The wraith nodded. *"Go on."*

"Beatrice became fearful that they might harm her husband. She met with me secretly to ask if I would watch over him."

The second wraith drifted forward. The one everyone believed to be Antonio said, *"You? But you and Antonio were enemies!"*

"No," said Juno. "I envied him. His passion. His dedication. I had wished to be an artist once, but I didn't have the discipline. He had the calling. In a way, I hated him for it. But in a way, I loved him, as well. When we argued, it was because I didn't want to admit that he was right. That nothing mattered more than serving the greater glories. Beatrice sensed this about me. And she knew that I was a hard man, that few would dare move against her husband if I was around. But I failed. I was summoned to the house that night. It surprised me, but I went. Neither of them seemed to know why I was there. I didn't know what to make of it, so I left."

"Why did you say nothing of this when your life was in peril?"

"I'd given my word to Beatrice. Made a vow. I may be many things, but I am not without honor. And I failed her. I failed them both. It just seemed that they were in no real danger. The brothers had as much to lose from the affair becoming public knowledge as she did. They only meant to frighten her. Like petulant children."

"I'll have your heart and your hands for that," Angelico swore.

Juno shook his head. "I have no quarrel with you or

your brother. But when the dead command, what can any of us do, except speak? The truth brings suffering, yes, but it brings freedom, too. Look!''

Everyone turned to stare at the wraiths. The shining figures were becoming dimmer, less distinct. Their hands touched one last time, then they appeared to melt into one another, becoming a final burst of light before they vanished.

On the rooftop, Tom smashed a brooch he had found in one of the spirit boxes while Kayrlis dropped a crinkled letter down a chimney chute, into a fire below.

The spirits were free. It was over.

During all the confusion in the wake of the aborted execution, no one noticed the trio climbing down from the rooftop. They were on the narrow streets, midway back to the inn, when an old woman stepped out of the shadows.

"You saved my son's life," she said. "By day's end, he and I and several others will quit this settlement. If you ride with us, we will pay you back."

Tom was stunned. He looked to Kayrlis, then back to the old woman. "I don't know—"

"True, there is much you don't know. Such as, you are not the only ones to have been visited in dreams by the man of flames. You do not know who he is or what he wants."

"And you know?" Tom asked, incredulous.

"You have mysteries, I have answers. Consider my offer. I wish to make good on this debt. To help you, as you have helped me. Such is the way of the Strega."

"The Strega?" Kayrlis asked.

"It is not a word you would wish to speak aloud again in this place," said the old woman.

"Is it heresy?" asked Cameron.

"Not to us," said the old woman. She darted back into the shadows and seemed to meld with them.

Tom raced after her, anxious to ask her more questions.

The alley was empty.

"So how are we supposed to find them if we want to go with them?" Tom asked.

"I think," said Kayrlis, "that they'll find us...."

SECOND INTERLUDE

IN ONLY A FEW SHORT DAYS, LILITH HAD BECOME EVERYthing to Matthew. She sated desires that he never knew he had, and awakened longings within him that had been buried since he was a child. What she did with his flesh was little more than a precursor to what she would do with his soul.

Or so she had been commanded.

Lilith sat with Matthew by his fire. The amber flames played upon his healthy, naked form, tracing patterns and casting delicate shadows that provided endless intrigue for her. She followed each of these with fingers and tongue, declaring the grooves and niches of his body a playground in which she could lose herself for hours on end.

But it wasn't the carnal aspect of what she'd found with him that made her feel troubled. She'd been with other men, countless men, both before and after she'd been transformed by Komm Kayriel. In terms of pure physical prowess, she'd known better lovers than Matthew. One in particular had been able to keep pace with her for days on end. He'd been a fine distraction until the day she'd been forced to take his life.

And with many others, she'd been able to reveal her

unnatural powers and use her wild and wicked talents to heighten her pleasure—and that of her lover. Matthew believed her a far more fragile creature than she really was. In fact, he believed her to be human. His inability to perceive her as something far more—and far less—should have earned little more from Lilith than her contempt.

Yet, that wasn't what she felt for him. Instead, she held a tenderness in her heart for this man. A feeling that had been lost to her for so very long.

Why was she feeling this at all? And why with him?

It wasn't so much the physical act that had caused Lilith to cry out with true ecstasy and caused tears to flow from her eyes when their bodies were joined. It was that they had made love.

Created love.

Felt love.

And that was something that should have been beyond one like her. Beyond one who was damned.

She knew all that she had awakened in him. But what had he awakened in *her*?

"Matthew," she whispered.

His head lay against her thighs. He looked up at her and murmured, "Ummm?"

"What's on your agenda for tomorrow?"

"You mean . . . What's going to keep me from being at your side every minute of the day?"

Laughing, she said, "Yes."

Matthew sat up. "Beyond my normal duties? Well, there is the matter of Jumping Dan Hatch. Have you heard of him?"

Lilith shook her head.

"He says that he's the second coming of Jumping Sam Patch, who died leaping drunk into the Genesee Falls. This man has repeated all of Jumping Sam's great leaps, diving off every bridge and high building into any body of water he can find. He's creating quite a stir. So to speak."

"I have heard of this man," Lilith said. " 'Some things can be done as well as others.' "

"That's his catchphrase, all right. His predecessor, who was found frozen in a block of ice more than thirty years ago, created it. Now this man's brought it back."

"Why's he come here? There are no great falls in Genesis."

"No, but there is the tower at the outskirts of town."

"The Spire of Truth."

Matthew nodded. "And there's a small pond at the base of it. He means to climb the spire and leap into the pond. He's a madman and a fool. I'll have to be on constant guard to make sure he doesn't end up killing himself. Never mind the fact that climbing the spire for any reason other than worship is heresy. Even if he survived his jump, he would find himself facing a quick trial and a final judgment."

She leaned over, kissing the underside of his chin, and ran her nails along the sides of his neck. "There is *no one* but you who can see to this man?"

Matthew sighed in pleasure and defeat. "All right. I'll place Isiah in charge of that little problem."

"Good."

"But I will have to attend to at least one bit of official business."

"And what's that? Inspecting the widow Bramley's home to see if she's kept up with her dusting?"

"Lilith," he said in mock warning.

"Or putting your blessing to yet another arranged marriage that is sure to end in heartbreak and misery?"

He frowned. "Now you do me an injustice. I know many Curacas who will do such things, but I have never—"

She grabbed his right nipple and twisted. He cried out in pain.

"Why'd you do that?" he demanded.

"To get your attention."

"Well, you certainly have it now!"

She kissed him. "I was only playing with you when I spoke of forcing young woman into arranged marriages. I know you are a good and honorable man. It's one of the reasons I love you."

"Ah," he said.

"So tell me, what's this other bit of pressing business?"

Sadness came into Matthew's eyes. "John Leopold, an old friend of mine from school, is stopping by for a visit."

"Really?" Lilith asked. Suddenly, her every nerve was on fire. Her instincts warned her that this was what she'd been waiting for.

"Can't he visit another time?"

Matthew shrugged. "Well . . . It's a bit too late to stop him. Besides, I'm afraid my friend has a disappointment to face, and I must be the one to confront him with it. Believe me, it's not a chore I'm looking forward to."

"Tell me more," Lilith said, intrigued despite herself.

Matthew sighed. "John has wanted to be a Curacas for a very long time. And he's deserving. No one would argue. But his family is not highly placed. And no one from his line has ever served in such a position."

"What's this news you have to tell him?"

"John had been told that there was a position waiting for him in Conviction, a settlement not far from here. I put him forward as a candidate and have supported him in every way I know how. But the Curacas's son, who is— ah, I wouldn't want to speak ill of the fellow . . ."

"No, tell me. We have no secrets between us." Lilith nearly choked on those words.

"He's not worthy of the position. Not like John."

"I see."

Matthew looked to the flames. "I don't say that lightly. This young man is lazy and mean of temperament. The few times he's acted as Curacas in his father's absence have been hard days indeed for the people beneath him."

"Could he grow into the role?" Lilith asked. "There

must be a terrible pressure placed on him to live up to the high standards set by his father."

Matthew shook his head. "My father was a Curacas. I know those pressures well. If he had within him what it took to force away such concerns and become a good leader on his own, I of all people would be sensitive to his potential. But he doesn't. I wish . . ."

"Yes?"

"Nothing," Matthew said. He pulled Lilith close to him. "Such thoughts are unworthy of me. And certainly they could be of little comfort to you, were I to share them."

She stroked his hair. "Then sleep. I will be here when you wake. I will be here all your days, if you will have me."

"I will," he said, nuzzling against her neck. "I will, my love . . ."

Lilith sat quietly with Matthew. She stared into the flames, listening as her lover's breathing changed, growing slower and deeper. Soon, he was sound asleep.

It was a perfect moment. A time to be cherished.

Anger welled within her. Until tonight, she had viewed her existence with perfect clarity. The world of man had hurt her, and she in turn wished to see it destroyed. This flawless vision had been a gift of Komm Kayriel. He had taken her mad, chaotic existence and given it order and purpose.

What was it about Matthew that had brought about so profound an effect on her? He was nothing special. And if he knew the truth about her, he would no longer love her.

Lilith allowed her hand to become discorporeal. It would be a simple matter to ease it within his chest and crush his heart. Then the order that had suddenly fled from her life would be restored.

Of course, if she murdered Matthew, Komm Kayriel would not be freed, and the world would not be plunged into darkness—but what of it?

In fact, was Kayriel himself even needed? All he had learned had come from a book he had found. The Mysts Arcana. She could find the book, learn its secrets, and become the Enemy herself. That would be far more satisfying a destiny than simply serving as a handmaid to darkness and disaster.

Wouldn't it?

Matthew shuddered in her arms. Willing her hand into flesh once more, she grabbed a shawl from a nearby chair and wrapped it around her lover.

The gesture, she knew, was far more damning than any fate she could wish upon either of them.

"If you are cold, I will warm you," she whispered, stroking the side of Matthew's face. "If you are hungry, I will feed you. If you are lonely, I will stand by your side until the end of time."

She had said those words to only one other living being, someone who had been taken from her and delivered into God's "merciful hands" many years earlier.

Such would not be the case with Matthew.

The course of action that Komm Kayriel would wish for her to follow was now clear to her: seduce Matthew into the murder of the incompetent young Curacas so that his more deserving friend could take the position. Already, a few drops of her blood were within him, working their dark magics, causing him actually to consider dark deeds when before he would have fallen to his knees, praying for guidance and deliverance from the Almighty. His inhibitions had been lowered, and, rather than invoking one scripture after another, he was putting his tongue to more pleasurable uses.

Getting him to commit murder would not be difficult, but her heart was not in the task.

There had to be another way to free Kayriel.

Closing her eyes, Lilith did something she once swore she would never do again: She prayed.

Lilith prayed to the God she was no longer sure existed, and to any being who would listen. She prayed for a means of completing her task that would not involve the destruction of Matthew's soul. It was important to her that on the day the world was plunged into darkness, and she was revealed as one of the damned, that he would still have the power to look at her with love.

Suddenly, the knowledge she required came to her. There was no great thundering to greet its arrival. Windows did not explode inward as they might in a storm. The earth did not tremble. The knowledge came quiet, peacefully, as if on invisible wings.

What she would have to do would be unthinkable. An act that Matthew could never forgive, were he to know the truth.

Well then, she would simply have to keep him otherwise occupied. And his ignorance, along with another's pain, would provide her bliss....

Eight

TOM KEEPER AND HIS COMPANIONS STOOD OUTSIDE the stables, waiting.

Cameron was getting impatient. "Why can't we just go? We're never gonna get safe passage north at this rate!"

Kayrlis nodded. It was almost night. They had lost an entire day that could have been spent traveling waiting around for the old woman Tom had spied in the shadows. And there was another concern.

"Lord Thegri may not be the most formidable angel I've ever seen," Kayrlis said, "but he's got to know by now that someone stole his spirit boxes and freed his servants. We've transgressed against an angel. That's not good. And we're waiting around here for someone to notice. That's even worse."

"He's a renegade angel," Cameron said. "What we did was just."

Kayrlis and Tom exchanged worried glances.

Tom said, "Lord Thegri has no reason to connect us with what happened."

"He could use his magics to divine the truth."

"If anything was going to happen, I think it would have

by now. Besides, this gave us a chance to restock our supplies, have one last decent meal before getting on the road, and to visit a few of the schools."

Kayrlis's expression softened. "Are you thinking about what you missed by not attending a school of art?"

"What I escaped is more like it: Every artist slaving away to paint in the same style. Approved colors. The seemly and unseemly choices in light and shadow. Mediums—"

"I understand. So . . . Why don't you draw my picture?"

"Sometime."

"Now's as good as any."

"Not here. Someone might see. You know what would happen then."

"Well . . . Only if they think you're any good."

Tom smiled, and whispered, "You know? I really don't care what they or anyone else thinks. When I start up again with my art, it's going to be because I want to. Not because someone tells me to, or thinks I should."

Kayrlis shrugged. "I guess you told me."

"That wasn't how I meant it. I just—I'm not ready, that's all. Besides, I've been using my talents in other ways. And I haven't heard you complaining."

"Would it have done any good?"

"Oh? Oh, fine. I'll remember that the next time you're after something that's going to leave me with a sore neck and an aching back for days."

"Don't be a whiner, Tom. Doesn't suit you. You signed on for the job, you'll just have to put up with what comes with it."

He kissed her, and she melted into his arms. Finally, Tom said, "The old woman will be here."

"Then what?" Cameron muttered. "We wait around until morning? Or are we supposed to do all our traveling by night?"

"Why not?" asked a voice behind them. "It's cooler, and you can make better time."

Everyone turned to see Juno and a small entourage emerging from the stables with horses. The old woman was with him. So was the gruff man from the bar whose hand Kayrlis had bandaged—and the young married woman who had wept for Juno.

"You've met my benefactor," Juno said, gesturing at the old woman.

"I am Mother Jael," she said. "I thank you for your patience."

"You already know Reni," Juno said, nodding toward the burly man with the bandaged hand. Juno touched the arm of the young woman. "This is Luchia."

"Tom Keeper. My wife, Kayrlis, and her brother."

Juno grinned. "You seem a little young to have a wife."

"You seem a little old to be without one," Tom said.

With a hearty laugh, Juno slapped Luchia's backside. "Maybe we should do something about that, eh?"

"Maybe," said Luchia. "But not right away. You kept me waiting long enough. Time for you to feel what it's like."

Juno grinned. "We were betrothed until the Curacas convinced her family that dried-up old Vecillio was a better match for her than me. Even made me believe it, for a while. I was a damn fool."

"Please," said Cameron.

"Sorry," said Juno.

"He's not much in social skills," said Reni. "But he's a good man to have watching your back."

Juno went on, "In light of the Curacas's blunder, nearly taking my hands and heart for no good reason, he granted her freedom as payment."

"That's why I asked you to wait," Mother Jael said.

Luchia nodded. "My thanks."

"Speaking of gratitude," said Mother Jael as she looked

at Juno. "Don't you have something to say?"

"Yes," Juno said. "We've wasted enough time on introductions. Let's be away from this wretched settlement."

"No," the old woman said firmly, her dark eyes suddenly filled with a frightening energy. "You know the debt you owe these people. Acknowledge it."

"Really," said Tom. "I don't know what you're talking about. We were just—"

"Thank you for my life," Juno said in a low, throaty rush.

Tom took a step back. They knew. They were aware of *everything* he'd done.

"The spirits?" Tom asked, wondering if the wraiths had told them. "Did they tell you?"

"In a way," Mother Jael said.

"Don't let her scare you," Juno said as he climbed upon his mount. "She really doesn't know all the secrets of the universe. Just most of them."

Tom felt his Power tremble within him. Juno was telling the truth.

The small party left New Florence without looking back. No one waved to them. Their passing barely seemed noticed at all.

"I'll miss the project," Juno said. "I wanted to see the Arcadia finished."

"We can always come back someday," said Luchia.

"No," Juno said. "Never."

They traveled several miles in silence. The sun set, and stars appeared.

Cameron clearly felt uncomfortable traveling with these strangers. It wasn't until Luchia rode up beside him that his tension seemed to ease.

"You're a devout young man, aren't you?" she asked.

"Faith is everything to me!"

"Really? So—you don't enjoy playing games or listening to stories or anything of that sort."

Cameron looked at her strangely. "Sure, I do!"

"I know a story."

"Is it about the angels?"

"Oh, yes. One that helped me when I was almost lost to despair."

Cameron nodded gravely. "I felt that way when our parents died. It was on a ship heading for China. Kayrlis and I were the only survivors."

Tom looked over in shock. His beloved and her brother wouldn't tell *him* about their early life, but Cameron was talking about it with a total stranger, and Kayrlis wasn't stopping him.

He listened closely, hoping to learn more about their past.

Instead, Luchia spoke. "You know that angels don't always appear to us in the flesh. Sometimes they are unseen hands guiding our journey."

"The invisible world," Cameron murmured.

She nodded. "Dreams. Visions. Or sometimes just a whisper beside you. A gentle push that steers you away from disaster."

"I know all about dreams," said the ten-year-old. "You wouldn't believe the ones I get."

"If you ever need to talk, I'm here."

Cameron nodded, smiling. "Tell me the story."

"It happened when I was about your age. I was playing with a friend. Clarisima. We loved to climb."

"That can be fun," said Cameron. "But you've got to know what you're doing."

"We thought we did. There wasn't a building in New Florence we didn't climb. Even the ones they were still putting up." She laughed. "Some of those were the most fun!"

Suddenly, Luchia brought her legs up under her and knelt

on her horse. "Takes a lot of balance, see?"

"Luchia!" Juno roared. "You'll get yourself killed!"

She slid down into a normal position on her mount.

"Hey, wanna see something?" Cameron asked.

"Getting a little dark, hard to see much."

"Watch." Cameron flipped onto his hands and spun around as his horse continued to trot along.

"Stop showing off," Kayrlis warned.

Cameron lowered himself so that the top of his head nearly touched the soft hair of his mount. Then he pushed up and somersaulted, landing in a sitting position. His horse let out a whinny of disapproval.

"Wanna see what else I can do?" Cameron asked enthusiastically.

"No more," said Luchia. "Please. I don't want your sister getting upset."

"You should see the things *she* can do!" he said.

"Cameron!" cried Kayrlis.

"It's true," said Cameron. "We were headliners. The Emperor had us perform for him at least once a month."

Tom watched it all and shook his head. The Emperor? The ruler of China?

"Pride is a sin," Kayrlis warned.

"So are some other things I could think of," Cameron muttered.

"What was that?" Kayrlis called.

"Nothing!" Cameron turned to Luchia. "Tell me the rest of your story. You and your friend were climbing."

"We were three stories high. It had been raining on and off that day. We should have known better. But we were almost to the roof. So we kept going. My hand was on a rail that I thought was secure. It wasn't."

"What happened?" Cameron asked breathlessly.

"I fell."

He stared at her. "Three stories? You must have been—I mean, how'd you—"

"I felt an angel's hands upon me."

"Were you scared?"

"I was terrified. But I believed in the greater glories."

"What happened?"

"The angel slowed my fall. I struck the ground. Nothing was broken. I was bruised, but that's all."

"It *is* true," said Juno. "Impossible as it may sound."

From that moment on, Cameron and Luchia became inseparable.

"I wonder why the flame guardian hasn't told him the truth," Tom said to Kayrlis. "I mean, about what the angels really are."

"He didn't tell you," Kayrlis replied. "If he had, you'd have thought it heresy, wouldn't you?"

Tom reluctantly admitted it was true. The flame guardian had allowed Tom to find out the truth for himself. Perhaps that would also be the case with Cameron.

"But *you* believe me," he said. "I know you do."

"It's different with me," Kayrlis said. "I've never been all that devout. I've always seen—I dunno—inconsistencies in the way the angels run things. And I've had plenty of cause to have a suspicious mind."

"Something to do with your parents?" Tom asked.

Kayrlis looked away quickly. "It's not important."

"I miss my dad," Tom said. "And Catherine and Gus. The angels probably told them I'm dead. That's what they've got to believe. That everyone died in Abaddon. I wish there was a way I could get word to him that I'm all right."

"We can't," Kayrlis said firmly. "The second the angels know you're alive—"

"I know," said Tom. "Can't blame me for wishing, though."

"I don't," she said, looking off into the distance. "Believe me, I don't."

The Elven Ways: Ancient Games   107

The group entered a gauntlet of trees. A canopy had been formed by heavy overhanging branches.

Suddenly, a branch snapped and a voice from above cried out, "Hold where you are!"

Tom looked up to see the trees crawling with activity. A half dozen men, maybe more, looked down at them. Each was armed.

"Brigands," Luchia whispered. "We're trapped..."

Nine

"SHOW US YOUR VALUABLES, THEN THROW THEM down. Cooperate and you'll ride out of here unhurt. Resist and you won't live to see daylight," the robber said from the shadows above.

"Don't you fear the wrath of God and His angels?" asked Cameron.

Laughter sounded from above. "The angels have fled. The Scourge and the Fall of Abaddon have them running scared. This world is ours again!"

Not likely, Tom thought. The True Lands were dying. Leaving this world to the humans was *not* an option for them.

"Let's start with me," Juno said, turning and opening a saddlepack.

The distinctive sound of bowstrings being pulled taut came from above.

Juno drew out a heavy sword. "Now this was used in nine campaigns. With it, I took the hands and hearts of a hundred godless men."

"Throw it down!" came a gruff voice from above.

Juno turned slowly and balanced the sword on his horse's back. "I once threw it thirty feet and caught a poor fool in the throat. Perhaps its days of service to me are over. Perhaps not.''

Reni was next. He pulled out a handful of daggers. ''Here, girl!''

Kayrlis whirled, somehow certain that Reni meant her. The burly man tossed a pair of knives her way.

''No!'' Tom shouted.

The blades spun end over end. Kayrlis plucked them from the air by their hilts in a lightning motion.

Reni laughed. ''I had a feeling about you.''

Tom stared at his beloved, stunned.

She shrugged. ''Good reflexes.'' She couldn't meet his gaze.

''You people seem to think we're playing here,'' called one of the archers above.

''No one thinks you're playing,'' Tom said evenly. He turned to his companions. ''Just give them what they want.''

''They're heretics,'' said Cameron.

''They're heretics with arrows trained at our hearts,'' Tom hissed. ''Do it!''

Mother Jael rode up alongside Tom. ''No.'' She pulled back her hood and craned her face upward, so that a stray shaft of moonlight revealed her features.

''Mother Jael,'' one of the brigands whispered.

''These people are under my protection,'' she said. ''You may be cursed with hunger or desperation or simply foolishness. Anything's possible. But do you want to be cursed by the Strega? Do you wish the *Malocchio* branded upon you?''

''Move along!'' one of the brigands called, his voice high and shaky. ''Pass before we change our minds!''

''They won't,'' Mother Jael told Tom.

''A pity,'' Juno said, gripping his sword as he urged his mount onward. ''I was hoping to see if I could still launch this sword like a spear, as I did when I was young.''

Mother Jael rode up beside Juno and slapped him. "Think of your betrothed and not just yourself."

His hooded eyes were suddenly downturned. "Forgive me. The old fires—"

"Find something else to do with them."

"Now there's an idea," Juno growled. "Luchia, have you any itches I can scratch for you?"

Luchia glared at Juno, then looked away.

He laughed. "She loves me. She really does."

"Not sure why sometimes," Luchia growled.

"Maybe it's because I always tell the truth. Ask the boy here. He can tell you."

The group edged onward.

Kayrlis gripped each of her blades as she guided her horse forward through the canopy. Scurrying sounds from above followed Tom and his companions.

Soon, they were on the open road once more.

"We should do something about the robbers," Cameron said once they were clear. "Double back. Make sure they don't hurt any other travelers."

"No," said Kayrlis. She slipped Reni's blades into her own bags.

"It'd be easy," Cameron said. "The Spider and the Fly—"

"*No*," said again.

"But they're heretics. You heard them."

"There are some things that just can't be fixed," Kayrlis said. "Fools are everywhere. If we set ourselves the task of giving them all some learnin', we'd have no time for our true purpose, now would we?"

Cameron shook his head. "I guess not."

"Besides," said Kayrlis, "you're too precious to me—to everyone—to risk your life for any reason."

"I agree," said Mother Jael. "From what I can tell, both your husband and your brother are *very* special indeed."

The Elven Ways: Ancient Games

Kayrlis rode ahead so that she wouldn't have to look at the old woman.

"The Lare have been kind to us," said Luchia softly. She glanced abruptly to Cameron, and seemed relieved to note that he hadn't seemed to hear a word she said.

But Tom had heard . . .

A few hours later, the group found an isolated spot near a clear mountain stream and made camp. Cameron built a small fire to keep them warm.

Mother Jael tapped Tom on the arm. "I think it's time we talk. Don't you?"

He nodded and followed her as she walked toward the edge of the clearing. Long flat stones led downward to the water in uneven tiers. When he saw her approaching the rocks he said, "Be careful."

She ignored him, gazing up at the moon and stars as her feet found exactly the right patterns of stones to take her downward to the water's edge. Tom carefully followed her. But he hesitated when he saw her step into the waters themselves—and seem to walk upon them!

"Stones just beneath the surface," she said, turning back. "Place your feet where I place mine and you will follow."

Tom turned to see if Cameron was looking their way. If he saw this—

No. Luchia was keeping him busy, along with Kayrlis. Reni and Juno glanced their way, but said nothing. They didn't seem at all disturbed by the spectacle.

Tom followed Mother Jael. He trod carefully, tapping the waters with each foot, making sure that he wasn't about to drop into the stream instead of walking upon the stones. He never faltered.

They reached the other side of the stream, where the steady rush of waters would obscure their voices from their companions.

"I never saw any stones," Tom said.

"But you believed you wouldn't fall into the waters," Mother Jael replied. "Belief is very important, Tom. You've been set upon a path. You are trying to learn The Ways. What we call, La Vecchia."

"You know about my dreams."

"I've seen the fiery man. The portal he protects. You've entered that portal. You've become more than you were in some aspects, less in others."

"What do you mean?" asked Tom.

"You don't need me to tell you. Look at the waters."

Tom did as she asked.

"Can you see your reflection?"

"Not very well. The waters are moving too fast."

Mother Jael reached into her pockets. She drew out a pinch of something that smelled like spices, gestured, and blew upon her hand. A black mist struck the waters like a stone. Circles radiated outward then vanished.

Tom was startled to see a patch of the waters grow still, ignoring the current that rushed around and encircled them. In those waters, he saw his own reflection as clearly as he might in a looking glass.

"Magic," he said.

"More a form of communion, really. All things are connected. Your friend Aitan tried to teach you that."

"How do you know so much about me?" Tom asked.

"Look at the waters, Tom. When the chaos is stilled, you can see into them more clearly, yes?"

He nodded. "You didn't answer my question."

"The answers are inside you. The only answers you really need."

Tom felt his Power surge within him. Everything she said was true. And yet—he couldn't make sense of it.

"But there's a difference between what you really need and what you think you need," said Mother Jael. "And it seems that you won't be able to focus in the manner required until some of the mysteries plaguing you are put to rest. So ask your questions, Tom. I'll answer them as best I can."

Tom nodded. "When those people tried to rob us. You threatened them with the *Malocchio*. What did you mean by that?"

"The *Malocchio*. The Evil Eye. Some call it the overlook. If it is cast upon you, you can become very ill without warning. Terrible headaches will keep you from going about your chores, or make you lie awake all night in agony. Or it can make you listless, take away your drive to do anything at all. Make you a failure at anything you try. A Strega like me can cast such a spell or cure one. Those men knew that. So they let us go."

"What do you mean by a 'Strega'?"

"It's an ancient word. It refers to women like me. Weavers of natural magic. You are on your way to become a Streghe. The same, only a male. You see?"

Tom found himself struggling with all that Mother Jael was telling him. "What you're telling me is forbidden. It's—well, I mean, it's—"

"It's heresy, and I could be put to death for revealing these simple basic truths to you. I know that. But I'm placing my trust in you, Tom. As you are placing yours in me simply by listening. Do you understand the pact we're making tonight? If you don't, we should stop now."

"I'm not sure . . ."

"I want you to succeed. Bring back your friends. Bring an age of illumination and truth to this world. Wake it from its stupor, relieve it of its delusions. There will be chaos. Wars. A time of darkness. Many will die. But what is worse—a war for truth, or the slow death our kind is facing now? The dying of the light, the passing of our spirit as complacency turns us into slaves of the Elven?"

Tom shuddered. She knew. Good God, she knew everything!

"The Elven walked among us long ago, with their shining white faces, their gleaming red eyes. We knew them well. And we knew they were not the Lasa."

"The Lasa?"

"The Lasa are the Old Ones. Those who have dominion over the elements. The keepers of the underworld. The beings nature depends upon to ensure that life and death remain in balance, that crops grow and rain falls. The Lasa are the spirits of water. The Linchetto are pretenders. A blight upon this world. That's why the Settiano seek to guide you."

Tom stared at her blankly.

"The Settiano. The spirits of fire."

"That's who's visiting me?" Tom asked. "The burning man?"

"I believe so. But I have no proof. All I can say is that just as the Settiano visit you in your dreams, they too must rest, and when they do, a powerful Strega like me can visit them in their place of repose. It's not wise to confront one openly in such a place. But their dreams play out like the dramas of old all around them. It isn't difficult to reach them in this way. If you like, I can show you how."

"Maybe. I mean—what you're telling me. It's a lot for me to take in all at once."

"Then I'll make it simple for you. You were raised to believe that there were angels for every station, every purpose, yes?"

Tom nodded.

"In my *religione*, there are spirits who command the inner workings of all life, all mortal and immortal existence. Palós are of the north. They help to inspire great thought, individuality, creation. The Settiano are of the south, the Lasa the west."

"I heard Luchia say something about the Lare."

"Spirits who protect the families of the Strega."

Tom shook his head. "If all this is true, if you can do magic like an angel—why didn't you save Juno?"

She shook her head. "Juno did a terrible thing once. The Old Ones have cursed him. There is nothing I could have done for him. That's why I'm grateful to you. Why I want to help you."

"All right," said Tom. "Tell me more. As a matter of fact, tell me everything. . . ."

Kayrlis sat alone. Her brother had gone to sleep. And she had no idea how long Tom was going to be sitting with old Mother Jael, talking with her, gesturing in strange ways. It was as if she was teaching him some whole new language.

"May I join you?"

Kayrlis looked up sharply and was surprised to see Reni towering over her. She stood up and went to her mount. Drawing out the blades she'd been given she said, "Do you want your knives back?"

"No, keep them. I have a feeling that you're more skilled with them than I am."

"I rode with a carnival for a time. The knife thrower taught me a few tricks."

"Is that it, then? The extent of your knowledge?"

"Yes," she said warily. "What else could it be?"

"The Spider and the Fly."

Kayrlis tensed. "You overheard Cameron."

Reni shrugged. "You seemed familiar, even before he spoke. Now I know why. I remember the Spider and the Fly."

"The name for my act with Cameron. That's all. You probably saw it on posters. We traveled all over the Territories."

"What I recall happened before that. I've spent some time traveling. I was involved in that last Crusade in the Yunnan province. I know all about the Spider and the Fly. What they did. How many died because of it."

Kayrlis stared at him silently.

"Don't worry. It wasn't common knowledge. In fact, it was privileged information," he said. "If anyone had known that I'd stumbled across the truth, I'd have never made it to these shores. But I know when to keep my mouth shut."

Kayrlis turned the knife over in her hand.

Once. Twice.

Then again.

"Not really," she said.

She threw the knife!

Ten

Tom Keeper dreamed that he was on the shore of a nightmare black sea. He drifted above it, arms outstretched. The sun blazed in the distance. Tom was not blinded by its brilliance. There was something comforting in its purity.

It wasn't until fiery lashes reached out from the sun and seared his flesh that he began to feel afraid.

"I knew this time would come," said a thunderous voice that came from everywhere and nowhere all at once. Tom felt his blood begin to boil with each word. When the silence came again, he felt a coolness.

"I need to know if it's true or not," Tom said. "Are you the Settiano?"

"You're concerning yourself with immaterial issues. I am your ally. I have helped you time and again."

"You've had me endure trials. You've turned me into something that's not entirely human. I think I deserve some answers. Are you the Settiano?"

Before Tom, the sun suddenly flared. Tom felt daggers of heat move through him.

He didn't close his eyes.

"I choose fire because it pleases me to do so. There is

a certain inner poetry involved. I could just as easily appear to you as ice or wind, music or devastation. Who and what I am should not concern you."

Tom struggled with his next words. "How do I know I can trust you?"

"It is a matter of faith. As it has always been. Now put your fears aside. They are blinding you to more basic truths. Preventing you from acting upon matters that mean a good deal more than the minutiae with which you are obsessed. Behold."

The sun became blinding once more. From its core came a shimmering black diamond that grew until its darkness overwhelmed Tom's perceptions. A chill overtook him as he saw two familiar figures come into bold relief. The former Emissary Grin and the warrior Malkiyyah, the Angel of Blood.

Lord Ainigrim Bosh R'Hayle Skalligrin was heavily armored in the eastern style. He wore a black mask that looked like the traditional embodiment of the Enemy, with narrow slits cut for eyes, nostrils, and teeth. A pair of large golden horns curled upward from the sides of the warrior's helmet. Fabric fanned out on either side of his head, bearing beautiful designs not unlike those found on the wings of rare butterflies. A strange cap adorned with straw-colored "hair" rose a foot above the top of the fighter's skull.

His body was covered in layers of armor and fabric. Pads overlaid with steel and gold protected the shoulders and arms, and his hands were covered by gauntlets. Small lacquered iron plates laced together with silk and leather hung from the armors forming exquisite designs. Skirts reached down to the knees in the front, mid-calf in the back. His sword was black and gold.

Tom knew that the warrior could not take these armors off. He had incurred the wrath of the Vessel he'd served, and the armors were seared into his flesh as punishment.

Malkiyyah, the Angel of Blood, was a supremely handsome specimen with dark eyes and nightmare black hair. Shards of crimson swam in his eyes, and a single red streak rippled through his hair. His leathers were cut away to reveal his muscular arms and legs. He wore a crimson sash around his waist.

Both angels were shivering as they climbed through a passage composed of amethyst shards larger than a man. Each shard burned with an inner glow. Mists drifted between the stones.

"How long do you think we've been lost in this maze?" Grin asked.

"Days, at least," said Malkiyyah. He was trembling. Each step was made with great effort. "I need to stop."

"We can't stop. You know what happens if we stop."

Malkiyyah nodded solemnly and trudged forward.

Tom called out to his friends. "Grin! Grin, Malkiyyah, I'm here! I'm with you. You're not alone."

The voice of the flame guardian seared his mind. *"They cannot hear you."*

"Is this happening now?" Tom asked. "Or is this another prophecy?"

"They make this fruitless journey even as we speak."

"What did Grin mean about stopping? What would happen if they stopped?"

"If they stop, they will be torn to pieces."

"They'll be killed?"

"No."

Tom shuddered, wondering how many times his friends had already endured this punishment. "Where are they? What's happened to them?"

"They are in the Realm of Shadow, in one of its more hospitable lands."

"What about Aitan?"

There was no reply from the flame guardian. Instead, the sight before Tom changed. Before him now was the burning city Abaddon. Tom saw a fissure open in the ground.

Thousands of crimson angels rose from the earth.

Tom recognized them as the tortured souls who'd been imprisoned in the Ring of Punishment. The angels rose to the sky, and fiery light struck them, cleansing them of evil. Circling the great city, the angels linked hands and began to sing. Sigils appeared in the air.

And the city fell.

"No more!" Tom cried.

Abruptly, the vision ceased.

"Why did you show me that?" Tom said, weeping.

"Because you have seen, but you did not understand. The angels rose from the Ring of Punishment. Aitan Anzelm and Komm Kayriel entered that place not long before the angels' exodus."

"You're saying they escaped?" Tom asked.

"No. You saw the crimson taint of corruption that clung to the departing angels. It is true that some of the souls who'd been flung to the circle were evil, but many were not. The wickedness that clung to them was due to Komm Kayriel's presence among them."

Tom shook his head. "Was Aitan corrupted, too?"

"No. He did not seek to take Kayriel's newly acquired power, as they did."

Tom recalled Kayriel's murder of the Second Vessel, the near-infinite power the Lord of Darkness attempted to take into himself. "The angels who fled—they took the power from Kayriel!"

"Much of it, yes. And used it to become openers... Abaddon was not destroyed so much as it was displaced. They cast the city into the Realm of Shadow."

"But what happened to Aitan?" Tom asked. "And Komm Kayriel?"

"There is so much you do not know, so much to teach you," the flame guardian said. *"When you think of shadow, you think only of darkness. But consider, it was the Elven who named this Realm. To them it was a place of shadows.*

A place of analogues. Echoes. A world that was, in its way, a counterpart to their own."

"Like our world."

"Yes. The Ring of Punishment was a portal that lay between the True Lands and the Realm of Shadow. It has, in that Realm, its opposite number. The Abyss of Judgment. The force required to give flight to the angels escaping the Ring of Punishment created an equal and opposite reaction, a backlash, that sent your friend and his enemy into the Abyss. The former emissary Grin and his companion Malkiyyah struggle valiantly to reach the Abyss to free Aitan Anzelm, but they are thwarted by the Keeper of the Keys at every turn."

"My name is Keeper," Tom whispered.

"Yes. You are his shadow. And there is one other. A being from the True Lands who shadows each of you."

"Is there a way for me to reach the Abyss?" Tom asked. "If I find Aitan's Patron, will he have the power to call Aitan back from this horrible place?"

"It will require much of you. A great and terrible sacrifice must be made to open the doorway between this world and the Abyss. For your own sake, it might be better if you turned back now."

"No," Tom said firmly. "Aitan's my friend. I'm not gonna let him or anyone else suffer if there's anything I can do about it."

The flame guardian appeared before Tom. The lad looked down to see that his naked, floating body was again covered in strange runes. The guardian had explained to him before that these runes were important. Tom appraised them with his artist's eye and tried to burn them into his memory. When he awoke, he would draw them and try to decipher their meaning.

"This you must know: Not mere knowledge, nor mere action, but action with perfect knowledge, without any desire for its fruit and consecrated to God, is the path you

must take toward your ultimate destiny. Mark these words well. Your future will depend upon them.''

"What else do I need to know?" Tom asked.

"Much. But this is what I will tell you for now: The Keeper of the Keys is waiting for you. He knows you're coming. He fears you wish to usurp his position, and so he will put you through trials to judge your worthiness. The games he plays are ancient games. Do not play along. If you do, you will be trapped in the Abyss forever...."

Tom woke on the shore of the stream. He didn't remember falling asleep here. It was the first night in weeks that he hadn't spent with Kayrlis in his arms, and he felt unsettled over that.

The runes. He needed to draw them. Already he was losing their image.

Dawn was breaking. The fiery light of morning shimmered on the waters. Mother Jael was gone. His mind was buzzing with all she and the flame guardian had told him. He got up, then crossed the stream without even looking down to see if he was indeed walking upon stones or simply the waters themselves.

He felt that something was wrong even before he saw that Kayrlis and Cameron were missing.

Juno, Mother Jael, and Luchia were gathered around the fallen Reni.

"What happened?" Tom said. "Did someone take Kayrlis and Cameron?"

Mother Jael looked up. "No one took them. They left of their own accord. And left this behind."

Tom looked down at Reni. He was moaning, his hand slowly going to a large red welt on his forehead.

"I thought she was going to kill me," he muttered.

"What are you talking about?" Tom asked.

"Your woman did this," Mother Jael said. "She attacked Reni."

Tom saw the knife lying off to one side of the fallen man. "She hit you? With this?"

"Threw it at me," Reni said. "It was a miracle I was struck by the hilt."

Somehow, Tom doubted that. He saw the way Kayrlis had handled a blade. If she wanted him dead, he'd have been dead.

"What did you say to her?" Tom asked, fury rising up to couple with his concern. "What happened?"

Reni hesitated.

"I'll know if you're lying," Tom said.

"He has been blessed with the Power to tell a lie at fifty paces, old friend," Juno said. "Out with it."

Reni shrugged. "I told her that I recognized her. That I knew all about the Spider and the Fly."

"That you knew *what* exactly?" Tom asked.

Reni shook his head. "Children," he spat. "To put such power in the hands of children!"

Tom surged forward, grabbing Reni by the shoulders. "Listen to me! I don't have one blessing, I have two. The Power to tell when a lie is being spoken in my presence and the Gift of prophecy. I've never tried to use that second Gift on anyone before. But if you don't start making sense, I'm going to start with you."

Reni stared at him with hard eyes.

"Would you really want to know what's in store for you?" Tom asked. "When you'll die? How?"

The lad had no idea if he could really use his Power in this way, but he had to get the truth out of this man.

Finally, Reni's shoulders sagged. "I made her a promise," he said. "I swore an oath to do her a good turn whenever she required it. But that was before I knew who she was. What she was. Once I realized what I'd done, I felt I had to tell her."

"Tell her what?" Tom asked.

"That I would honor my word. I wouldn't relish it. But

I would do as I'd promised. Even for one such as her."

Tom couldn't take any more. "What do you mean?"

"She never told you," Reni said, his dark eyes filling with regret. "Yes, I see that now. I pity you."

"Why?"

"You've lain with evil. You've made your bed with a traitor, a murderer, and a heretic. The blood of thousands is on her hands."

Tom felt the Power rise within him, though a part of him desperately wanted to force it down.

Then he *knew*. To his horror, and he feared, his ultimate damnation, he knew.

Reni was telling the truth.

THIRD INTERLUDE

The Abyss of Judgment

AZAZEL SAT UPON HIS THRONE AND SURVEYED HIS KINGdom. It was a place of strange beauty. Emerald hills and onyx plains. A sky the color of blood.

From his throne he saw something that no other being in the Realm of Shadow could. High above, through a break in the winged, hungry, charred black clouds, there was another land, and in that land was the Other.

Azazel knew that if he could speak with the Other for even a moment, he could withstand any punishment, no matter how severe or long-lasting it might be. He also knew that he would never be granted that chance. The Other was the companion he'd longed for, the understanding embodiment of grace and love that he had dreamed of for so many centuries.

With a touch, the Other could soothe the wounds he felt in his soul, and fill the emptiness he felt in his heart.

With a touch . . .

Azazel shuddered and tremors leaped out to rack his kingdom. His subjects wailed at this new horror, and Azazel took no pleasure in their cries.

A million souls had been trapped here, some righteously,

others not. Many suffered the torments they wished to suffer and would do so for all eternity. And he would be there to see it all. For Azazel was cursed; he could not die.

Far worse, he could not live, either. Only when the thousand-year reign of God's Army upon the world of man ended would he be free of his duties, but that day would never come.

The mortals had been told so many lies. . . .

Azazel thought of his life in the True Lands. He recalled fabulous dances during which lives were ended and others begun, and the fate of entire cities decided by the skill and mastery a lord had over the dance.

He could not dance as he once did because music did not exist in the City of the Abyss. He could not laugh and sing because the land itself did not allow it, and he was bound to the land, and it to him, for eternity. All who came here were bound as such; it was their punishment for coveting this Realm and its vast supplies of magic in the first place.

Only the dead had some measure of freedom, and he both envied and despised them for it.

"Lord Azazel?"

The angel looked down to see Mnensogoth, his greatest lieutenant, standing before the throne. Mnensogoth retained no one shape for very long. One moment he looked like an ox standing upon two legs, the next a spider with a thousand eyes.

Azazel rose from his throne. His dark wings, a last mocking jest from his jailer, scraped along the plain grey rock of his throne, which was carved from the side of a mountain. He stood fully a league, and uprooted the roots that had been snaking out from the soles of his feet.

"Amuse me," Azazel said wearily.

"The angels wish an audience with you. I believe they want to plead for release from the Abyss."

Azazel grinned. This was amusing. "Good. You've done well, humble servant."

"I live to serve."

"No, you live for *this*," Azazel said, raising his foot high above his companion, then bringing it down and crushing him. For several blessed moments, Mnensogoth would know the peace of sleep and oblivion. It could only be granted by the Lord of the Abyss, and it was a favor that was highly coveted among the damned.

His eyes bursting into brilliant crimson flames, Azazel said, "Come."

Because he wished it to be so, a pair of angels appeared before Azazel. One was tall and beautiful, with luminous pale skin, long silken black hair, and dark eyes. He wore elegant black armors but carried no weapons. The other was a creature of shadows. His body undulated and shuddered, then reconciled itself into the form of an angel with charred black skin and glowing crimson eyes.

"Aitan Anzelm and Komm Kayriel," Azazel said. "Do you not like the accommodations? Is there some way I could make your new lives with us more pleasurable?"

Aitan bowed. "Lord Azazel, I beseech you. It's of no consequence to me what torments you put me through, but you must—"

"Ah, two errors in your opening remarks alone," Azazel said. "So you don't care about what's done to you. Well, that's just it, isn't it? I need you to care. If you don't, then what's the point in causing you suffering? As to your second error, you used the words 'you must' while addressing me. There is nothing that I *must* do except to remain in this hole for all time. Anything and everything else is purely a question of desire. And I have little of it."

"I have no wish to offend you," Aitan said. "But Komm Kayriel has declared himself the embodiment of the Enemy. He has made pacts with obscene powers. He has slain one of the Vessels in an attempt to become a god himself. Despite all of this, he is allowed to walk free in this place, where he might win followers and take even your power!"

Azazel frowned. "Have you been practicing that speech for very long?"

Komm Kayriel laughed.

Azazel spun on him. "What manner of creature are you?"

The shadowman stopped laughing. Even he did not wish to incur Azazel's wrath. "I'm sure I don't know what you mean."

"You *laughed*! That is impossible in this place. Or, at least, it should be." Azazel raised his hand. Two streaks of black flame reached down and engulfed the angels. They bellowed and writhed in agony.

"I can see inside each of you," Azazel said. "You are connected in ways that neither of you may ever understand. And though I can do what I like with your flesh, there is nothing I can do with your souls. Not without exerting myself, which is something I've not had the pleasure of doing in a very long time. I can feel the power of the Vessel in not one of you, but both. And I covet that power."

Azazel closed his hand. Aitan and Kayriel fell limply to the blasted soil.

"But I am willing to let you keep it. For a price."

Kayriel raised himself up first. He looked to Aitan. "Cousin, I think I understand. This place is alive. Any who come here are bound to it. But the power that I took from the Vessel now surges through us both, and it protects us."

Aitan tried to rise, but the agonies he had just suffered, so much more intense than anything he'd ever experienced, had left him weakened. "I'll see you dead," Aitan whispered, "for all you've done, for all you would do—"

"Stop talking like an idiot," Kayriel said. "We're staring at an opportunity. If Azazel is powerless against us, we can leave the Abyss and enter the Overrealm of Shadow. I have power there, and I can free us both."

"I'd sooner burn in the Ring of Punishment than see you loosed upon the world."

"Mortals," Azazel bellowed. "You haven't even asked my conditions for allowing you to keep your power. My feelings are getting hurt."

Aitan and Kayriel looked up at the giant.

"Better," said Azazel. "Komm Kayriel, you spoke of your power in the lands without. I ask you to consider my power in this land. It is absolute and unwavering. I could destroy either of you, though I would not. Better to imprison you on the outskirts of my kingdom, to encase you in amber and allow you to stare forever at a freedom that can never be yours. I wouldn't even allow you the luxury of madness. Such is my power. All I have to do is will a thing, and it may happen."

"Except your own laughter," Komm Kayriel said. "Or so it would seem from the way you're acting."

Azazel ignored the taunt and bent low. "I will allow *one* of you to leave so long as the other agrees to take my place here, upon this throne. For I have no more desire to be in this wretched land than either of you."

This time, it was Aitan Anzelm's turn to laugh. "You seemed to have missed something here. Komm Kayriel and I *hate* each other. Neither of us would ever make that sacrifice for the sake of the other."

Azazel smiled. "Then what you propose is a riddle for me to solve. I will find something that each of you cares about. Then I will leave it to the two of you to fight betwixt yourselves as to who will have the honor of taking my place."

"It can't be done," Aitan Anzelm said. "There is nothing here that I would value so highly."

"Nor for me," Kayriel said. "Or so I would wager."

Azazel curled his great wings around his guests, casting them into darkness. "Don't be so sure, little ones. I may have some surprises waiting for each of you. . . ."

A chittering came from somewhere close. Everyone turned to see Mnensogoth begin to re-form.

"Would that I could find *that* disturbing," Azazel said with a sigh. "I'm beginning to think I'm getting used to this place."

And the darkness, suddenly, was all.

Abaddon! cried a familiar voice.

The dark angel raised his head. "Who approaches the Keeper of the Keys?"

Would that I could approach you. But I am trapped, as you well know.

"Azazel," the angel whispered. "It has been a long time since you have cast your will beyond your kingdom. What do you want?"

What I want is immaterial. All that matters is what I have to offer. We were brothers in blood, once. Warriors fighting for the glory of our gods.

"Yes, and see where it has gotten us. You are the ruler of the Abyss, and I am ever the wanderer, keeping safe that which no one wants anyway. Keeper of the Keys. As if it meant anything."

It does. For both of us. Listen closely, for deliverance may well be at hand for us both.

Abaddon listened.

Eleven

CAMERON RODE BESIDE HIS SISTER. "I'M TIRED. We've been riding most of the night."

"I know," Kayrlis said. "Believe me, I'm not enjoying this any more than you are."

"Are you gonna tell me what's goin' on? Why'd we have to just leave like that? Where're we goin'?"

Kayrlis looked around. Where *were* they going? Blessed God, she didn't even know where they were. She had used the stars to guide them west. Now that the sun was up, she could see that the road she had chosen was very well traveled. It wound about so many times Kayrlis had worried that she was being led around in circles, but now she saw that she was following the path of a lake that had been guarded from her view last night by the trees lining its shore.

"You trust me, don't you?" Kayrlis asked.

"Sure," Cameron said. "Always have, always will."

"Then take my word for it that we're doing the right thing."

Cameron nodded. "I do. I just don't understand it, that's all. Did you and Tom have a fight?"

"No," Kayrlis said.

"That's a relief. So he'll be meetin' up with us later?"

Kayrlis hesitated. Finally, she said, "No."

Cameron yanked hard on his reins, and his mount came to a halt. Kayrlis brought her horse around.

"We've got holy work to do, Tom and I," Cameron said. "The angel Zagzagel told us both."

"Who are you . . . Zagzagel?"

"He's the angel who appears to Tom and me in our dreams. The angel of the burning bush, the teacher, the giver of knowledge. He's the one who guided us to Tom when Abaddon was falling."

"The burning man never told Tom his name."

"Well . . . Me either, to be honest. I figure he's just modest. Or he's tryin' to see how smart we are. Tom's a blessed soul, a good fella and all that, but I got him beat when it comes to the teachings."

"All right," Kayrlis said. "But to answer your question, I'd say the work you and Tom have to do leads in separate directions. And as much as I love Tom, you and I are kin. We're all the family either of us got left. So I'm stayin' with you."

"Did Tom send us away?" Cameron asked.

Kayrlis felt light-headed. She didn't know how much more of this she could take. If her brother kept at her, she would end up blurting out something like, *we had to get out of there 'cause that damned Reni knows all about us and is bound to talk. And once Tom knows the truth, he wouldn't want us around anyway. All I'm doin' is sparin' all of us a lot of tears. Don't know what got into me in the first place, thinkin' you and me could ever have a normal life.*

"No, Tom didn't send us away," Kayrlis said. "It was just time to move on, that's all."

Cameron's expression turned solemn. "Wish I coulda said good-bye to Luchia . . . she seemed nice."

"Yeah, she did," Kayrlis said. The decision she had

made was tearing her up inside. She wanted so badly to turn around and go back to Tom, to beg him to love her despite all that she'd done.

But that was crazy.

Suddenly, Cameron looked to the sky. His face went pale, and his eyes glazed over.

"Oh," he said.

Kayrlis placed one hand over her heart. She'd seen her brother act this way before, and she knew what it meant.

"Where?" Kayrlis asked.

"About two miles up ahead. I never felt it this bad before."

"A lot of them?" Kayrlis asked.

"Merciful God," Cameron whispered. "I think *all* of them."

Kayrlis turned her mount and urged him on. The horse was sluggish at first, as if he, too, sensed what lay ahead. Cameron followed her.

"Can we talk some more?" Cameron asked. "You know how nervous all this makes me."

"'Course we can," Kayrlis said.

"I was thinkin' about what you said. About how your place was with me and all."

"Uh-huh," Kayrlis said. She forced a smile. "You got a problem with that?"

"Well..."

Kayrlis glanced over at him. She suddenly felt concerned. "What is it?"

Cameron frowned. "I, uh...I think my place is with the angels, Penelope. I always have."

Kayrlis had known this moment would come eventually. But she wasn't in the least prepared.

"Tom was right," she said. "You can't go to them. You have to wait and let them come to you."

"It's what I've always wanted," Cameron said. "And I feel it more strongly now than I ever did before. When we got back to the colonies, after Mom and Dad . . ."

"I know."

"When we got back, I wanted to go into the service. I wanted to serve God then. But I didn't. I held back for you."

"For me?" Kayrlis said, kicking at her mount, urging him on. "What are you talkin' about?"

Cameron's lower lip trembled. "Well, what's the Spider without the Fly? I knew how much performing meant to you. I wasn't about to take that away from you, not after we'd both lost so much."

Kayrlis couldn't believe she was hearing this. "You did it to help me?"

"Yeah. But you got Tom now. And our performin' days are over. We both know that. This blessing I got . . . It should be up to the wisdom of the angels to see that it's used right. What do we know about God's plans? Who are we to set ourselves above the warriors of the Almighty?"

"Cameron," Kayrlis said, hating herself for the lie she was about to tell. "The Enemy has slipped his chains. Tom told me that."

"He did."

"Uh-huh. That's why there was a war in the Heavenly City. And there's no saying which angels might have become renegades. Would you put the Gifts God gave you in the hands of the Enemy?"

"No," Cameron said.

"Then until Zagzagel comes right up to both of us and tells us that—"

"Ahhh!" Cameron gasped. "We're close. There's so many . . ."

Kayrlis looked ahead. There was a path through the woods to her right. It led away from the lake. "This way?"

Cameron nodded, shuddering.

Easing herself from her mount, she said, "I think we should lead the horses the rest of the way."

"Better to tie them off here. They're not gonna want to go in there."

Kayrlis could sense the truth behind her brother's words. Her mount was already frightened. "I'll take them down to the lake. You go ahead. Do what you have to do."

Cameron shivered as he climbed down from his horse. Kayrlis couldn't help but notice his hands.

They were already wreathed in a fiery blue-white haze.

Tom rode between Mother Jael and Juno. Reni and Luchia brought up the rear. The noonday sun was rising. It was past time to make themselves something to eat. But no one broached the subject.

"You'd ride into perdition itself for her, wouldn't you?" Juno asked, breaking the silence that had engulfed the small group for the last few hours.

Tom said nothing. He was certain that Kayrlis and her brother had come this way. He could feel it.

"That barge of yours is lost. You'll have to find another means of reaching the north."

"Then that's what I'll do," Tom said.

"What about your other friends? The two Mother Jael told us about?" Juno asked. "The angels?"

Tom looked sharply to the old woman. She rode with her gaze fixed firmly ahead.

"I have to find Kayrlis," he said.

"Seems like she doesn't want to be found," Juno said.

"I don't care what it seems like to you. No one asked any of you to ride with me. You just took it on yourselves to follow. If you don't like the road I picked, then go find one of your own!"

Tom pulled ahead of the others. Juno raced up beside him.

"Calm yourself, boy!" Juno said. "I was just trying to suggest that you consider coming up with some kind of plan. Something that you can say to her so she won't bolt on you again."

"It won't matter what I have to say. Just that I'm there ought to be enough."

"You don't know much about women, do you?" Juno said. "There's a difference between what ought to be enough and what it takes sometimes to get the job done."

"Yeah," Tom said. "You know so much. Just look at you and Luchia."

Juno laughed. A strange fire came into his eyes. "You're right. I shouldn't be lecturing you, Tom. Truth to tell, I'm not sure I understand people. There are some, you can take a look at them and right off you know they're in pain. And you can see the simple thing they could do to ease that pain. But they won't do it. Almost as if they like suffering. Think they were born to it or something. But I don't think that's right."

"What are you talking about?"

"People who love each other shouldn't keep secrets, but they do. Sometimes a person's pride gets in the way. Obligations to what they see as their calling. Most times, it's just fear. And the thing about fear is that it can become a living thing. It'll get right inside you and keep you from doing much of anything. You've made a hard decision today, Tom. Whether you realize that or not."

Tom frowned. They rode in silence along the twisting road, following the course of the lake.

Kayrlis had told Tom that the flame guardian had guided them to his side. Sometimes it was in visions, at other times it was nothing more than a feeling about which fork in the road was the right one to take.

Tom suddenly *knew* exactly where to find them.

"Stop here," he said, eyeing a trail in the woods to his right. "They're not far."

Mother Jael laughed. "I could have told you that."

"I need to do this myself," Tom said over his shoulder.

"I appreciate your coming this far with me, but whatever obligation you feel to me for what I did in New Florence— that's over. What I did, I would have done for anyone. I did it because it was right. Not because I wanted anything in return. And I don't feel I deserve anything, either. You folks have new lives to go on and forge. I don't want to be the one stopping you."

"Good plan," Reni said. "Let's go."

Mother Jael glared at him. Reni looked away.

Juno said, "We'll stay with you. For a little while, at least. Who knows? You might find yourself needing someone to watch your back."

Tom wasn't going to waste any more time arguing with them. He dismounted and secured his horse to a tree near the path's entrance. Then he stuffed a few things he might need into a bag and slung it over his shoulders as he walked on.

At first there wasn't much of anything to hear or see. The woods on either side of him were thick—and unnaturally silent. The sun seemed a little dimmer now, but that was probably because of the dense cover of branches and leaves above, a canopy that reached out and filtered the brightest of the light and delivered shafts of gold onto the ground.

The moans and cries of the dying drifted from somewhere not far ahead. Tom had heard those sounds before.

He knew then what he was about to face. The knowledge didn't slow him. He continued on until he came to a small clearing where two men struggled, one with a pickax, the other a shovel. They shook as they worked at the firm earth, desperately attempting to dig a hole with the last of their strength.

He smelled the bodies a moment before he saw them under a blanket, a dozen feet away.

"Who are you now?" the first man asked. He had a ruddy complexion and his upper lip curled in anger and fear. His hair was wild and matted. He was dressed plainly, in a tan frock and leggings. His boots were gone. Sold, Tom assumed, for a meal. His companion was older and thinner. Tufts of white hair lifted up from his chest. His nose was bent a little to one side and his eyes seemed to have a dozen bags of loose flesh beneath them.

Tom found he couldn't speak. He stared at the sweat pouring off them and saw that it was blood.

They were both victims of the Scourge.

"If you're thinkin' of robbin' us, boy, think again," the first man said. "I may not have much strength left, but I've got plenty for the likes of—"

"No, Joseph," the other man said. "Look at his eyes. He's with *them*."

Joseph stared at Tom for a time, then nodded. "You can pass. Pass along to the pit for all I care. You'll find your friends not far along the trail."

"I could help," Tom said.

"Another healer, are you?" Joseph asked.

"No, I meant—" Tom pointed at the earth. "I'll dig for you."

Joseph shook his head. "This is something we have to do for ourselves. Even if it takes the last of what we've got left to give. Those are my daughters under that sheet. There weren't any healers coming around when they were still in the early stages like us. No children quoting scripture and laying glowing hands on the sick. I don't know if it's true, what the boy claims, that he can heal the Scourge. But even if it is, I'm not having him touch me. It's too late for that. I want to be with my family."

The older man nodded. "With my child, and grandchildren. That *is* what's best. . . ."

Tom nodded grimly, and walked on. He saw a light ahead, something he took for a fire at first. It led him the rest of the way.

He found Cameron knelt over a child his own age. It

wasn't Cameron's hand that was glowing now. His entire body was suffused with a brilliant energy that made his body shimmer like that of a divine being.

"The angel's messenger will save you," a woman said to the child, sobbing. "God is just, God is good. He sent us salvation."

A dozen other people had gathered around. A few regarded the scene before them with fear and mistrust. The others were clearly convinced that they were in the presence of an Avatar of the Almighty.

Kayrlis was not among them.

For several long moments, Tom felt overwhelmed by the sight before him. He had been delirious when Cameron had taken the disease from him. There was a vague recollection of a glowing hand, then darkness. But Tom had thought that to be nothing more than a part of his fever dream.

He'd never expected the act of Cameron performing a healing to be such a majestic sight. Tom thought that Cameron simply *touched* the people he saved. The transformation of the boy Tom had known into this beautiful creature made of light and love was breathtaking—and alarming.

Concerns that hadn't arisen in Tom's mind before now suddenly threatened to consume him.

"Tom?"

He turned to see his beloved.

"You know, don't you?" Kayrlis asked. "Reni told you what he knew." She looked devastated—and relieved—all at once. "Then say what you need to say. Tell me how awful I am. Say whatever you need to before you go. I shouldn't have taken the opportunity away from you."

"Are you done?" Tom asked.

Kayrlis nodded.

Tom led her deep into the woods, away from the spectacle of her brother and his work with the dying. "It doesn't matter," Tom said. "There isn't anything you could tell me about your past that would change the way I feel about you."

"I doubt that," Kayrlis said.

Tom found a place for them to sit and set down the sack that was slung over his back. "I want you to tell me everything," Tom said, "and then we'll see. Sound fair to you?"

Kayrlis nodded and began her tale.

Twelve

"CAMERON AND I STILL REMEMBER OUR PARENTS, even though we were both pretty young when we were taken," Kayrlis said. "I was six when the angels came for me. My mother was pregnant with Cameron. It wasn't until five years later that I got to meet him—but now I'm getting ahead of myself.

"I knew how unhappy it made Mom and Dad when I was taken away. That's how I felt, too. And it happened because I was a darn show-off. When I played hide-and-seek with my friends, they'd never catch me because I could squeeze myself into the tiniest, strangest places. Just double myself up—or whatever it took.

"And I loved to climb. There wasn't a house that didn't have my footprints on its roof at some time or another. Everyone just thought it was kinda cute, what I did. There I would be, climbing trees that everyone knew weren't safe, but that didn't matter none to me. I never got hurt. Never got a scratch. I fell once, too, just like Juno's beloved Luchia, but I didn't have any one to catch me. No divine intervention. Nuh-uh. What I had was my hands, my feet, and my wits.

"About a dozen people saw it. As I fell, I just stayed

cool as could be. I saw a branch that might slow my fall and I reached out and grabbed it. Then I caught hold of a vine and ended up swingin' out of that tree, flyin' about a hundred feet in the air, before I landed in a grove. Everyone talked about it. The Curacas told the angels. Word traveled. And pretty soon, I was traveling, too. . . .

"I don't remember much about the boat ride to China, except that it took forever. I had this boy named Bo as my companion. He was nice-lookin', and decent. Twice my age, twice as strong. He coulda done things to me, bad things, but he never did, and after a while I came to realize that he never would.

"Bo was sorta my first teacher, though he never *made* me do anything. I think he realized that I hated the gifts God had given me. When I was put on that boat I was thinkin' about how the last thing I ever wanted to do again was climb or run or jump . . . But just before my father said good-bye he told me to make him proud. So I didn't see as I had much choice.

"I watched Bo as he prayed in the morning, as he limbered up and trained. He did things that made me hurt just watching him. And at night, he put on shows for the crew of the ship we were on. I couldn't believe the things he did."

Kayrlis frowned. "Did I mention that he was a juggler?"

Tom shook his head.

"Well, that's what he was. But he didn't juggle just anything. The first time he did it, he juggled knives. The next night it was torches. The night after that, he did 'em both at once. I'll tell ya, the crew might have been entertained, but the captain was scared the whole time that Bo was gonna drop one of those torches and set the ship on fire. It never happened, though.

"I came to understand that the old saying 'less is more' just didn't apply to entertainers. It's always more is more. By the last night of our journey, Bo was juggling swords, torches, knives, lanterns, and more. And he'd tell stories while he did it.

"I couldn't help but watch him. And I also couldn't help but notice the way the crowd was just taken away from everything that might have been worrying them whenever Bo came out to perform. I felt it, too. It was like stepping outside of reality. Do you know what I mean, Tom? Or does that just sound stupid?"

"No," Tom said. "I know exactly what you mean. It's what I feel when I'm drawing. I can do it all day, all night. Just get lost in it. Nothing else matters. Nothing at all."

Kayrlis nodded. "So before that journey was done, I had Bo showing me a couple of things. He was funny, too. What most people didn't realize was that a trained juggler who's tossing knives or something like that around can see if something's coming down at them the wrong way. They can just get out of the way, they're not in real danger so long as they stay alert. 'Course, the other thing people don't realize is that most of us would rather take a *knife* than let one fall in front of an audience. Kinda crazy, I know, but that's how it feels when you're out there performing. You just don't think like you would at other times. It's like you're trying to be perfect. Trying to be something a lot more than human. I dunno.

"Anyway, like I was sayin' before, he'd tell these funny stories. They all pretty much had the same plot. A big battle was just about to start up, and just before the two sides could start goin' at one another, a juggler would appear on the field. In one it was Xiong Yiliao of the Chu State. There was a war with the Song State and what he did was, he walked right past all those spear-wielders and archers and axmen, walked right past 'em, and he juggled nine balls. The Song warriors were so shook up by it all that they just ran in every which direction."

As Kayrlis spoke, Tom drew his sketchpad out of his sack and started to create an image. It was something he hadn't done in so long, and it felt wonderful.

"You don't know how grateful I was for stories like that," Kayrlis said. "I was so scared."

"You?"

"Yes, *me*. What do you think, that I don't get scared of anything?"

"Now that you mention it . . ."

"Well, I do," Kayrlis said. "When we left last night I was scared of never seeing you again. Even more scared of what would happen if our paths did cross. You knowin' the truth about me . . ."

"I love you," Tom said. "Nothing else matters."

Kayrlis sighed. "You're either the sweetest thing that's ever been, or you're a fool."

"Or both," Tom said, sketching away.

"Don't get cocky, old son," Kayrlis said.

"Heaven forbid."

"As to why I was scared . . . I didn't like not knowing what was coming next. What was going to be expected of me. But even though I was scared all the time, I was determined not to show it. So I liked Bo's little stories. He made me laugh when no one else could.

"He also taught me a little of his language, but it was hard. In Chinese, you might have one word that means a dozen different things, and it all depends on how you use it. If you say it soft or loud, if you drag it out or you're really abrupt. You get the idea."

Tom nodded.

"Once I reached Peking, I realized that I didn't need to worry about anything anymore. I never had enough time on my hands to be bored or scared, and there were always enough people around to tell me or show me what to do. When I wasn't training, I was taken to the countryside to see how people lived under the angels. It wasn't long before I realized that a lot of what we did as tumblers and acrobats pretty much came out of the lives of everyday people. Folks climbing trees and bamboo poles inspired our Pole Climbing; and folk games and sports was where Balancing on a Bamboo Pole, Shuttlecocks, and Diabolos started.

"You should have seen me do the Rolling Cups. I'd lie on my belly and hold up four cups each with my hands and feet, then I had a bit in my mouth that led to two more stands with four more cups on each side. Then I'd let them roll... The ones in my feet went to my hands, the ones in my hands to the platform I held up with my teeth, and those went to my feet. I do it faster and faster and I never dropped a bowl.

"I learned all my masters had to teach me. Plate Spinning, Hard Qigong, Drawing Five Bows... everything. And I loved pleasing the crowds.

"The years flew by. I was taught to read and write in four languages. I was taught history and worship. It got so that all I wanted to do was learn, and I got frustrated, because I always had the feeling that my teachers were holding back. One night, Bo told me about the Forbidden Libraries. I didn't understand then that it was a challenge, I just rushed ahead and found out where the libraries were, and one night I broke into them. Getting around the guards was easy. In fact, I don't think that I would have been caught at all, except that Bo was already there, waiting for me.

"At first I was scared. I didn't know what he might do, and I was worried that my actions might reflect badly on my folks. But he didn't turn me in. He shared a lot of the books with me."

"What kind of books?"

"Most of 'em were just stories. Things the angels found subversive. One book was all about God and the angels and heaven and a place called hell... It talked about a man who died for our sins and was God's own son..."

Tom nodded solemnly. He'd never heard of such things,

and he could see why the angels would want things kept that way.

"Pretty soon it became a game for us," Kayrlis said. "Sneaking out at night. Racing over rooftops. Spying on people. Taking things—little things. A hairbrush, a fan..."

"It was all part of your training," Tom said.

Kayrlis nodded. "Then one day everything changed. Cameron came to stay with me. I loved him right off, 'cause I could see some of my mom and dad in him. It made me feel like I'd gotten 'em back."

"Your parents never came to visit?"

"They weren't allowed. I kept hoping, but..."

"I understand."

"Cameron was amazing. He was five and he could bend over backwards and touch his head to his tailbone."

"Really?"

She nodded. "I was worried that he'd be scared of me at first, but he wasn't. He said I looked like Momma. That made me sad in a way—but proud, too. A year later, the Spider and the Fly were born. We were headliners, traveling all over China. The angels loved to watch us. How it turned out, of course, was that they'd been watching us all along. And making plans."

"What did they make you do?" Tom asked, laying his sketchpad aside.

"Lemme see," Kayrlis said, reaching for it.

"After. I want to hear the rest of the story."

She frowned. "All right, all right. Bo stayed with us. He didn't have a problem with Cameron being a part of the games we played at night—y'know, sneaking into places, borrowing stuff... What started changing was the kinds of things we took. I don't know how long it took me to realize that it wasn't just for fun anymore. We took maps. Battle plans. Sacred wedding gifts.

"It was kind of fun, seeing the chaos we caused. People

blaming one another for taking things we did. At least, it was fun at first. Then something terrible happened. We took a ring that two brothers had been fighting over. Naturally, each of the brothers blamed the other for the ring being gone. They fought a duel, and both of them died."

"Kayrlis," Tom said, reaching out for her, trying to draw her into his arms.

"Wait," she said, shaking her head and pushing him away. "You don't understand. It was terrible that they both died. But what was worse was how it made me feel inside. I was . . ." She swallowed hard. "I was happy about it."

Tom said nothing.

"Didn't you hear what I said?"

"Go on."

Kayrlis shuddered. "I was damned glad. I didn't know until that moment how much hate I had inside me for what the angels had done, taking me away from Mom and Dad, taking Cameron, too. After that, it didn't take much to get me motivated. Bo never pushed me. Half the time, I had to go to him. Tell him I was bored. That I wanted some excitement.

"That I wanted to sin.

"Because, that's what it was, you know. I was a sinner. I *fomented* disaster and death. That was the word the Emperor used later . . ." She hung her head. "There I go, getting ahead of myself again. What you need to know is this. Cameron and I, we were guests in the Forbidden City all the time. The Emperor liked to watch us perform, and we played games with his children. I never really questioned who was behind all the mischief I caused with my brother. I mean—really, I thought we were. But it was Bo who made up all the schemes. And it was the Emperor, and the angels behind him, who were really the ones thinkin' all this stuff up.

"The Emperor called for us one night. He had a task for the Spider and the Fly. At first I thought there was a celebration, but he admitted that he knew about all our little games. Our ancient games, he called them."

Tom flinched at that. The same words the flame guardian had used.

"But what he wanted us to do now was different from any of our other 'missions.' He said that to do what must be done would be the ultimate proof of our loyalty to him.

"Anything, I told the Emperor. Anything at all..." Kayrlis hung her head low.

"You don't have to tell me if you don't want to," Tom said.

"Does that mean you don't want to hear?" Kayrlis asked without looking at him.

"I just meant—"

"I want to tell you," Kayrlis said sharply. "I want you to know everything."

"All right."

Kayrlis hugged herself. "The Emperor had bastards all over. One of them was feared by the Emperor. His astrologers had told him that a great threat had arisen. The bastard would destroy the Emperor within a year if his light wasn't snuffed out now.

"He wanted us to kill for him. I said we would. It didn't seem real to me at the time. Before I left, Bo told me that this killing would be kept a secret, but the Emperor would cherish me and keep me in his heart for this service.

"I was sent to a remote village in the Yunnan province. Finding the threat wasn't hard.

"He was curled up in his mother's arms. Just a baby." Kayrlis shook her head. "Why they sent me, I'll never know. But I was damned that night. Cameron and I both."

"What did you do?" Tom asked quietly.

"I took the child and brought him to one of the Emperor's greatest rivals. I told him who the boy was and why the Emperor wanted him dead. I knew that he would be the only one who could protect the infant."

"You did the right thing," Tom said. "You couldn't have just killed—"

"A war broke out," Kayrlis said. "All in the name of the holy infant. A hundred thousand people died, and their blood was on my hands. Do you understand that? It's what Reni was trying to tell you."

Tom considered what she'd told him. Finally, he said, "I'd have done the same thing. How'd you escape?"

"I didn't. The Emperor was going to have Cameron and me put to death. But Bo and a few of the angels reminded the Emperor that we were just children and that sending us had been his own 'fatal error.' He was reminded of all the times we'd brought joy to his heart, of the gifts we had to share. So he sent for a ship to take us home. Our parents were on it.

"Everything I felt—all the hatred, the anger—I was ashamed of it. I was ashamed of myself. I could only barely look at my parents. The day I'd finally screwed up enough nerve to talk to them was the day our ship was attacked."

"I thought Cameron said there was a storm."

"I've seen storms. What hit us that day wasn't natural. Not anywhere near. And when it was over, an angel rescued us. Just Cameron and me. The only survivors."

"You think the angel brought the storm."

Kayrlis nodded slowly. "But I could never tell Cameron that. He'd never believe it. I need him. He's all the family I had. Until you."

They sat alone in silence for a time. Tom could sense that everything Kayrlis had told him had been true.

"I can just imagine what you're thinking of me right now," Kayrlis said.

"No, you can't." He picked up his sketchpad and handed it to her. The image Kayrlis saw was her own. In the drawing, an aura of fiery light played across her breathtaking but hard features. Only her eyes showed a vulnerability, a softness that made her weep when she looked at it.

"It's beautiful," Kayrlis said. "This is what I look like to you?"

Tom nodded.

"Even now? Even after everything I told you?"

"Yes."

"God's love, Tom, you are a good man. More than I deserve."

"No," Tom said, brushing the tears from her eyes. "You're more than I deserve. I love you. Don't you get what that means? No matter what."

She smiled. "Really?"

"Yes."

They were about to kiss when Juno interrupted. "Sorry," he said, "but we have visitors."

"Who?" Tom asked.

"Angels," Juno said. "And I think one of them's dying..."

Thirteen

TOM LEAPED TO HIS FEET. "WE CAN'T LET CAMERON anywhere near the angels. I thought the burning man had given him a Gift like mine, one that no one can see. But Cameron, when he lays on hands, he looks like—"

"I know," Kayrlis said. "It's just a matter of time, isn't it?"

"If he keeps healing," Tom said. "Rumors spread, stories go around . . . The angels are gonna hear them. It's a miracle they haven't found out and come after Cameron already."

"You can't ask him to let an angel die," Kayrlis said. "Not if he has the power to help."

"We don't know that he does," Tom said. "If he tries—"

Juno, who'd stood nearby, all but forgotten, cleared his throat. "I neglected to mention that Cameron's *already* with them."

The fight drained out of Tom. It was over.

Kayrlis touched the side of Tom's face. "Get out of here. I'll make sure Cameron doesn't say anything about you."

"I'm not leaving you," Tom said.

"I can't leave my brother. Tom, please. If you love me, like you say you do, don't make me choose. I can't."

"I won't make you choose," he said. "Come on then." He started walking back to the group of plague victims.

"Tom, don't!" Kayrlis said, racing after him. Juno stepped out in front of her.

"You wanted him to make the decision for you, he did," Juno said. "Now abide by it."

She pushed past him. Tom was already in the main clearing, where a pair of angels consumed the attention of even the most wretched of the dying.

The angels wore golden armor. *A rarity from Tom's experience*. Each had flowing chalk white hair and coal black eyes. One lay in the other's arms, his head lolling back, dark tears flowing from his eyes. The breastplate of his armor had been mangled and caked with blood. Tom saw the trail of angel's blood that led from the woods. Only a few drops stained the earth, but they smoldered with crimson mist.

Cameron was near them, but he had not yet openly approached them. His flesh was not yet shimmering with the incredible forces locked within.

He seemed exhausted, his legs about to give way at any moment.

"I am Ophiel," the angel who was uninjured said.

Cameron fell to his knees. "He whose name appears on the Bell of Giradus, one charged with the knowledge to raise the dead."

The angel nodded grimly. "Some portion of that knowledge. There are seven of us in all. For the incantation to succeed, we must all agree to work together, and such a thing has not yet happened, nor will it ever if some of my brothers have their way."

"Ophiel, do not . . ." the wounded angel said.

There was an undisguised bitterness in Ophiel's next words. "Why should I not? Because these beings surrounding us are mortal? Because they may carry my words to the ears of those who would punish me for my outcries? Let them."

Cameron shuddered, clearly unprepared for such a vehement display from a warrior of the Almighty. Several of the plague victims wept openly. Others huddled together in fear.

Ophiel went on, "My friend is Gabuthelon. Know you his designation, boy?"

Cameron nodded. "His name was revealed to Esdras as one of the nine who will govern at the end of the world."

"And the others?"

"Michael, Gabriel, Uriel, Raphael, Aker, Arphugitonos, Beburos, and Zebuleon."

Ophiel nodded with satisfaction. "You have studied well. Few know of us unless they are scholars or priests. Are you from a School of Light?"

"To my shame, no," whispered Cameron.

"Come closer anyway, boy," Ophiel said. "The sight of you alone seems like enough to raise the spirits of my dying friend."

Gabuthelon nodded and reached out his hand.

Tom took a step forward, but Kayrlis stopped him, digging her fingers into his arm so hard that it hurt. He winced with pain and stood his ground.

A curious thing happened next. Tom watched as Juno looked to Mother Jael. She nodded slowly. Tom thought that Juno seemed different somehow. His back was as straight as ever, but his bearing was no longer that of a proud, swaggering ass. Instead, he seemed curious and hopeful, yet wary at the same time.

Cameron took the angel's hand. There was no sudden flaring of the blue-white fire that had engulfed the boy earlier. Even so, the wounded angel's shoulders sagged some in relief.

"Know you any scripture?" Gabuthelon asked.

Cameron nodded. " 'Thy word is a lamp unto my feet, and a light unto my path.' "

Gabuthelon smiled. "Would you like to know how I was hurt?"

"I would hear whatever you would tell me, lord," Cameron said. " 'Yours is the one wisdom which is perfect.' "

"Hah!" Ophiel cried. "Clearly the lad has never gambled at your table. Wisdom is the last thing you possess."

Gabuthelon frowned and looked away.

"I'm sorry," Ophiel said. "Forgive me, old friend. Humor is like a sword that I wield poorly, cutting myself and those I care most about."

"No forgiveness is needed," the bleeding angel said. "Boy, what is your name?"

"Cameron."

"I'm not afraid of death," Gabuthelon said. "For soon I will be in the Kingdom of Heaven. But even now, the sound of your words brings comfort. It is, to me, the music bordering nearest heaven. Pray, go on."

" 'I mourn death, I disperse the lightning,' " Cameron began.

Next to Tom, Kayrlis tensed. She whispered in his ear, "I've heard him say these words when the Power's upon him."

"But nothing's happening," Tom said.

" 'I announce the Sabbath,' " Cameron said, " 'I rouse the lazy, I scatter the winds, I appease the bloodthirsty—' "

" 'This is the substance of things hoped for, the evidence of things not seen.' "

Everyone turned in surprise. It was Juno who had spoken.

Cameron seemed worried. He looked at his hand, which was still only flesh. " 'I am the resurrection and the life.' "

Gabuthelon smiled serenely. "Brother?"

"I'm with you," Ophiel said.

"I can be at peace in company such as this. Tell them

of my folly. How I flew higher than any angel ever dared on this mortal plane, and how I met ill fortune with a flock of blackbirds flying south.''

Tom looked again to the ravaged breastplate of the angel.

Ophiel grinned despite himself. He started to laugh, and Gabuthelon laughed with him.

"No," Cameron said, falling back, his hand pulling free of the angel's warm touch. "There can be no humor found in tragedy, lord."

"I was mauled by a flock of birds," Gabuthelon tittered. "It's absurd!"

Tom looked around. A few of the dying were smiling now, though their smiles were thin. He noticed the trail of blood that the angel had left and saw that it ended suddenly. They hadn't come from the woods at all, he now realized. They descended into this clearing from the skies above.

"Brother," Gabuthelon said, leaning up a bit. "The bleeding has stopped. I'd say the faith of this good lad has given me a strength I thought lost to me when I demanded you put us down among these people."

"You have given us inspiration and hope," Cameron said.

"And a comforting and rather silly story," Juno added.

"Indeed," Gabuthelon said. "Ophiel, lift me up. I would die in the skies if I am to die this day. Yet, by my faith and the blood of the Vessels I think that I will not. Get us to the gates of the Heavenly City by nightfall, and I promise I will break bread with you at the dawn."

"Yes," Ophiel said. "I will."

Ophiel closed his eyes and strengthened his grip on the other angel. Then he lifted Gabuthelon from the ground and leaped into the air. They rose high above the tallest tree in seconds, then were gone from sight in a blink.

"I failed," Cameron said. "I couldn't bring healing to the angel."

"Well," Juno said. "For one thing, he wasn't dying of

the Scourge, which your Power seems to have been given you to cure. For another, you did heal him. But not in so grandiose and revealing a manner. You have the Blessed Gifts of Mother Jael to thank for that."

Cameron looked over at the old woman, who nodded.

"You put out the fire of Heaven?" Cameron asked.

"Its visible aspect," Mother Jael said. "That glow would have gotten you in trouble sooner or later. But the Power that is yours and yours alone will not be stilled, not even by your death."

"And third, and last," Juno said, taking a step away from all others, "very little in this life is truly what it seems."

Tom watched in wonder as Juno's body began to shimmer.

"Juno!" Luchia cried.

"Have no fear, daughter," Mother Jael said. "Our Juno is well, I can sense that. But this is not he."

Juno's body was engulfed in a light that was all the colors of the spectrum and more. It seared itself into the minds and hearts of all present, even when they tried to close their eyes or otherwise shield themselves from its brilliance.

Tom felt that he should be doing something. He recalled the many agents of darkness that Komm Kayriel had sent against him and Aitan. Yet... Something deep within told him this was not a transformed being. That the figure who was slowly revealed as the light faded was far from being a damned soul.

Soon, a figure who couldn't have been more different from Juno Meazzi stood in his place. He wore the black armors tinged with crimson that were like those of Aitan Anzelm. His body was lean and heavily muscled, his hair wild and black, his eyes crimson, and his face...

His face was the most beautiful sight Tom had ever beheld. Looking upon the luminous features of this being caused Tom to drop first to one knee, then the other.

It was a gesture repeated by all present.

"Rise," the newly revealed angel said. "Rise, for you are in the presence of one who loves you all, and should indeed fall upon bended knee to ask your forgiveness."

"Lord?" Cameron asked in confusion.

"I am Mithra, Patron of Aitan Anzelm. An Angel of Truth, who has been with you in lies. But all for a good cause."

Tom stared at the angel in disbelief. "You're the angel we were traveling to meet?"

"Indeed," Mithra said, "guided to you by visions of a burning man who has graced my dreams for half a lifetime. I loathed the deception, but I had to know if you were worthy."

Tom was shocked. Why hadn't his Power revealed this to him sooner?

Then it came to him. His Power had been granted by the burning man. A being with whom Mithra was in league.

"Where's Juno?" Luchia asked, tears forming in her wide dark eyes.

"Alive, safe, and waiting for the four of you to join him."

"The four of us?" Reni asked. "But there are only three. Mother Jael, Luchia, and me."

"One more must go with you," Mithra said, pointing at Cameron.

"No!" Kayrlis cried.

"It is the only way," Mithra said. "Mother Jael has the power to keep Cameron's Gifts a secret. He can continue God's work in peace until such time as his other blessings are revealed, and he will stand with us all upon the Night of Glory."

"I'll do it," Cameron said. "Penelope, please, let me do this. You should be with Tom. We both know that. Please."

Kayrlis went to him and wrapped her arms around her brother. "This is what you want?" she asked.

"Please," he repeated.

She kissed his cheek. "Then I guess you have my blessing, too. Don't know how it'll stack up next to the blessings the angels gave you, but for what it's worth—"

"It's worth everything," Cameron said.

Tom turned to the angel. "Lord—"

"I know you have questions, Tom. And the answers will be in your hands soon enough. But for now, understand that there is a war brewing in Heaven. And the rumors of war, and the leanings toward war and strife, extend in all directions, from the highest and brightest residences of our kind, to the darkest pit where innocents will suffer if you do nothing."

"Me?"

"I deceived you all because I had to know that Aitan had chosen well—especially as he was unaware at the time that he was choosing at all."

"Choosing what?" Tom asked.

"A warrior who would stand before the Vessels on the Night of Glory, who will give all he has, his heart, his soul, his life, and that of all he cares about, to stop a creature whose madness threatens two worlds."

"Komm Kayriel," Tom whispered.

"No," Mithra said. "He is not the true threat."

"Then who is?" Tom asked. "Please, I've got to know."

Mithra shook his head. "You have a journey to make, Young Master Keeper. When it is over, it will fall to you to name that enemy. I can't do it for you."

Tom looked to Kayrlis, but she was still talking with her brother. He glanced about at the plague sufferers. "Will they die?"

"Some," Mithra said. "The cure young Cameron imparts takes strength to withstand. Some of these are too weak to survive it. But most will live."

The angel raised his hand. Fiery Sigils gathered round it,

flaming symbols that burst into existence in the air near him.

"Left to their own devices, they would carry word of Cameron's miracles to those who would destroy us all. And so they will not get that chance."

"What are you doing?" Tom asked.

The angel's hand became a golden fire.

"No!" Tom shouted.

But it was too late. The flames fanned out in every direction, striking each of the afflicted, searing their flesh with the Sigil that quickly vanished from them.

"What did you do?" Tom asked in horror.

"A simple magic," Mithra said. "To make them forget. It will protect their lives as well as ours. You know what they say about killing the messengers."

"What about all the others Cameron already cured?"

Mithra smiled. "You haven't wondered why no angels have come to hunt you down?"

"I have," Tom said. He knew that Cameron's fantastic displays would engage the attention of the angels at some point.

"I have repeated this ritual with all he touched," Mithra said. "It was one of the reasons I was not there for Aitan when he needed me—or thought he needed me. In truth, there was little I could have done for him that he didn't do himself. It was all part of the game, in any event."

"The game?"

"The most ancient of games. And there is one facet of these games that we must concern ourselves with immediately, if we are to have a hope of rescuing Aitan from the pit."

"What's that?" Tom asked.

"Do you know a woman named Lilith? We must go to confront her. And we must go *now*."

Tom shuddered. He remembered her icy touch and the words she spoke when she spared his life.

I don't share the fondness for our liege that my fellows did. Besides, you and the child have potential. Another time.

If what Mithra said was true, that time was practically upon them.

FOURTH INTERLUDE

THE VOICES WOULD NOT LET LILITH SLEEP. SHE HAD WELcomed them into her, begged for the wisdom only they could provide. At the time, she had no idea what price she would pay for the knowledge.

The voices spoke of Mithra, Patron to the angel Aitan Anzelm. They warned that he was near and that preparations must be in place before he traveled much farther with the boy and his lover.

She lay beside Matthew, her body pressed close to his; it was a place she was loath to depart, but she had to think of the future.

"Sleep," she whispered, kissing his ear.

He mumbled something, then dropped even deeper into the depths of his slumber, where he would remain until she either summoned him—or died.

As she rose from the bed they shared and quickly dressed, she thought of her lord, Komm Kayriel. She knew that he would consider her actions a betrayal, but he could burn for all she cared. The only reason she was willing to carry the plan to its logical, if slightly altered conclusion, was because he intended to bring both pain and truth to the world.

She loved Matthew, but could not be honest with him about who and *what* she was. The truth would put their love to the test, but when compared to the greater darkness that had silently, invisibly enveloped their world in the guise of God's love and eternal light, she was certain that she would earn his forgiveness.

To her, it seemed like the only way.

She hurried from their bedchamber. After retrieving a scroll that she kept hidden among her few belongings, Lilith quietly slipped from Matthew's house into the street. She followed the directions given her by the voices and was guided to a remote stable more than a mile from the settlement. Within, three young men were contemplating an act that would damn them in the eyes of every god both dark and light.

"We know the path she takes, and the time," said one of the feral young men.

"And look at the way she dresses," said another. "Shameful."

"Inviting," added the third.

The first sat back and laughed. "Is it a sin to be accommodating? To give a harlot the treatment she deserves?"

Lilith watched them from the shadows, her heart filled with loathing. She considering murdering them now and finding others to take their place. It wouldn't be difficult, she was certain. But the voices had chosen these three, and she had sworn to follow them.

As the leers and boasts of the men grew more hideous and graphic, Lilith took out the scrolls she had recovered. On them were words that had been copied from the forbidden book, the Mysts Arcana. The spell of transformation would work upon any who secretly longed to become one with depravity and evil. But with examples such as the men before her, its effects would be startling.

Lilith recited the incantation in her mind. When she was done, she had only to utter a single word and the full power of her dark sorceries would be unleashed. It would be a painful thing; since she had become more than human, magic of any kind was a source of great agony to her.

She focused her will and tried to think of the greater good. Then she burst from her hiding place, running to the door with terror stamped upon her features.

The trio was startled at first, but they were quick to respond, capturing her before she could escape.

"Gentlemen," their leader said as he clutched Lilith's trembling face within his viselike grip. "This isn't the prize we spoke about, but why wait until tomorrow when opportunity is before us now?"

All three were upon Lilith, tearing at her, stripping her of her clothes, then apparently her dignity and maidenhood. At the height of their wickedness, Lilith said the word that bound them to her and delivered them to their fate.

Then all they could do was scream.

Fourteen

THE ROAD TO GENESIS WAS LONG AND WINDING. They had been riding all day and into the night. Mithra had worked a magic upon Tom and Kayrlis, removing their fatigue, satisfying their hungers, ending their need for sleep. The lovers said little to one another; a glance was all that was needed to indicate their love and commitment to one another.

And their fear.

Mithra broke the silence. He gestured at the moonlit trail and the ridge of mountains ahead. "The road will bend around the rises in the distance. If we follow it, we'll need two more days to reach Genesis. But if we take a path I once found through the mountains, we'll be there by dawn. *That* is what we'll need to do."

"Lord Mithra," Tom said, "I don't understand why we have to confront Lilith. Can't you take us to where Aitan, Grin, and Malkiyyah are being held?"

"If I could, I would have done it by now," Mithra said. "She alone has the means to open a portal to the Realm of Darkness. We have to be there when the portal is open to stop her from going through and rescuing Komm Kayriel. His evil cannot be unleashed on the world. Aitan was willing to give his life and his soul to bind the darkness that was once his friend. But that may not be enough. Kayriel has to be expunged. His darkness has to be burned away by the light of decency."

"Do you know the claims he made?" Tom asked.

"Yes," Mithra said.

"Do you believe them to be true?"

The angel's expression never changed. "I believe that what matters most is that Komm Kayriel is on a quest for power. He hopes to throw two worlds into chaos so that he can ascend to ultimate power. Human beings cannot stand and fight against the warriors of God. Not without facing slaughter and defeat as they did in the Thirty Years War so many centuries ago. You have no idea of the cost of Komm Kayriel's truth."

"But I'm learning the Ways," Tom said. "If I can, then other people can, too."

Mithra pulled on his reins and turned his mount to face Tom. "What we are discussing is fire and destruction and fields flowing with the blood of the innocent. Is that what you want?"

"No," Tom said.

"Then what else is there to discuss? Komm Kayriel needs something that is within Aitan Anzelm so that he can become whole and mount his final crusade for power. So long as Aitan is trapped in the Realm of Shadow with Kayriel, there is a chance that he may acquire that which he seeks. The burning man told you that there would be a cost if you desired to press on and help your friend. A terrible cost. And you said that you would pay any price to save your friend.

"I ask you again, Tom Keeper, is it really in your heart to go on? Because if it's not, then I have wasted the time I spent observing you and judging your character. And my student, Aitan Anzelm, has similarly thrown away his life."

"Blunt, aren't you?" Kayrlis said.

"Honest," said the Angel of Truth. "It's not something I can do much about." He looked back to Tom. "You're angry with me. Why?"

Tom lowered his head. "You're an Angel of Truth, but you lied to me."

"I deceived you so that I could test—"

"Now you want me to follow you, to do whatever you tell me to do. Between you and the flame guardian, I don't feel like I've got any control at all over my own life."

Mithra's expression softened. "You have more control than you know. All of this is about the choices you make. You have far more control than I—or even the burning man—over what fate is to befall those who are mortal or divine. All we can do is shepherd you, and try to teach and protect you."

Tom nodded, taking in the angel's words.

Mithra held out his hand. "I wish only to be your friend. If you will let me."

Tom took his hand and bowed his head. " 'Faith is courage. It is creative where despair is always destructive.' "

"I'll take that as a yes," Mithra said.

They rode on to the mountains, reaching them in a matter of hours.

Standing before a stone wall, Tom said, "I don't see a trail."

Mithra gestured. "It's right before us. Is the moonlight really so dim?"

Kayrlis looked to Tom. "I have no idea."

"It's a matter of faith," Mithra said. "The oldest of mortals have said that faith moves mountains. If we are to continue, the two of you must put that faith to the test."

"Pardon me?" Kayrlis asked.

"What I want you to do is simple," Mithra said. "Ride back far enough so that you can break into a gallop. Then charge this large stone here in the center. See it?"

Tom nodded. "But—"

Kayrlis shook her head in disbelief. "And what are *you* going to be doing while we're either knocking ourselves senseless or having our mounts toss us like rag dolls the moment they come to this stone wall?"

"Watching," Mithra said.

"Did you hear that, Tom?" Kayrlis asked. "He'll be watching. Tom?"

She turned and saw that he had ridden a quarter of a mile distant. She went to him.

"This is insane," she said.

Tom shook his head. "No, I see his point. There has to come a time when we're not afraid to give ourselves over to something greater."

"I didn't come all this way and part with my brother just to ride beside you and throw my life away with yours!"

"I know. I love you," he said. Then he spurred his mount on, and raced headlong for the wall.

"Tom!" Kayrlis shouted, kicking at the flanks of her mount and leaning forward as it broke into a gallop. She was vaguely aware of passing Mithra along the way, but although she was the more experienced rider, she could not force her mount to overtake Tom's. He rode head down, his purpose indivisible from that of his mount.

Why wasn't the creature stopping? she wondered. She didn't want to see Tom thrown from his horse. Visions of him lying on the ground, his bones shattered, raced through her mind.

"Tom, on your love for me, don't!" she cried.

He didn't stop.

Kayrlis raced on, no longer worrying about what might happen to her if her mount struck the wall or threw her as it reared up before the solid stone. She caught a glimpse of Tom's face. He was resolute.

Then the wall was before her. Her instinct was to brace herself. But she knew that the best way to take a fall, any fall, was with her body relaxed.

"You're the dumbest animal I've ever known," she whispered to her mount as she realized that it was *not* going to stop.

A darkened blur raced up before her. A shimmering black mass tinged with moonlight.

They passed through the wall.

The stone seemed to close all around her like a cool but gentle fist. It eased into her body, her mind, and she *understood* it, she felt its patience, its strength, its slow but inevitable acceptance of change.

The stone disappeared and she was laughing, her hair wild and free, whipping about her in the night winds. She saw that she was riding behind Tom along a narrow trail. The walls of the mountain rose up on either side of her.

"What just happened?" she asked.

"Magic," Tom cried simply.

"Was it an illusion?" Kayrlis asked. "Or did we really pass through solid—"

"Magic!" Tom shouted again, with a joy she hadn't heard from him in so long.

"All right, then," she said. "Fair enough. Magic it is."

They turned a corner and a horse whinnied a few hundred yards before them. Tom pulled on his reins and Kayrlis eased her mount to a stop.

Mithra sat tall upon his mount, the moonlight framing him. "Good," he said, nodding to Kayrlis. "I was afraid we were going to end up leaving you behind."

"No," she said. "That'll never happen."

"Then let us continue. We have a long and difficult journey ahead of us."

The trio passed through several dark tunnels, with only the light of a shining sphere Mithra called into existence to help them find their way. The ride went on for hours, and Kayrlis had a sense that they were constantly rising.

Finally, they emerged from the darkness. Kayrlis breathed in the thin night air and sighed.

Then she looked down.

Mithra had guided them onto a narrow stone bridge connecting two towering rises. The drop on either side was dizzying.

Kayrlis laughed. She looked ahead and studied Tom's face. "You're not gonna get sick on me, are ya, Tom?"

"No," he said, unconvincingly.

Mithra took in the lead in their procession. Kayrlis brought up the rear.

From the rocky crag on the other side of the bridge came the sound of falling rocks. Mithra looked up sharply.

"It's begun," he said.

A creature plucked from a nightmare disengaged itself from the wall before the angel. It had the wings of an insect and the body of man. Pincers took the place of hands, and mandibles jutted from either side of the creature's jaw. Its eyes were bulbous and its legs, all ten of them, were sharpened spikes.

Kayrlis heard movement behind her. Two more creatures appeared. One had the twisting, slimy torso of a slug, with the arms and legs of a man reaching out from its flanks. Its mouth was a jagged cavern, which stretched open wide to show the fabulously distorted features of a man's face. The monstrosity rose up and slammed itself down, shaking the narrow stone bridge and causing rocks to fall to the abyss below.

At first glance, the last of the transformed beings appeared human in all respects. However, he stood upon the air, his feet together and pointing downward, his arms crossed over his chest, his head wobbling back and forth on a neck that seemed devoid of bone. His flesh began to shudder and ripple, as if hundreds of smaller, vile creatures were anxious to escape from his mortal prison.

"All you need do," Mithra said to the monster before him, "is stand aside and let us pass."

"She promised us," said the winged creature, its words coupled with the clicking of its mandibles.

"Her promises are meaningless," Mithra said. "This will be your final warning."

"She promised that if we did this thing, she would make us human again."

"You can't regain what you never had in the first place," Mithra said. "The spell she used only works on those who are first damned."

"Lies," the winged man said. "She told us you would lie!"

"I wonder if she also told you that we would be the death of you," Mithra said as he unsheathed his sword. "Let's find out...."

Fifteen

Kayrlis leaped from her mount, snatching one of her saddlebags in the process. She'd seen all manner of deformed beings during her travels with the Carnival of Wonders. But she always knew that she could look into their eyes and see that in their minds and hearts they were no different from her.

These creatures were something else entirely. Even so, the sheer magnitude of their hideousness did not overwhelm her. She felt the old fires rising up within her. Opening her bag, she pulled out a black truncheon and whipped it to one side. The motion caused a mechanism within it to release, and suddenly the truncheon was twice its length, and twice that again. It expanded into a staff, a steel blade sliding from one end.

Though she had brought misery to thousands, and engineered the deaths of many, unwittingly or not, Kayrlis had never actually *taken* another's life.

Tonight, she vowed, that would change. Because she would not allow these monstrosities to harm the man she loved.

Nearby, Mithra held his long sword before him. Tom saw

that he wore a short sword as well, and cried, "Give me your other sword!"

"Would you know what to do with it?" Mithra asked.

Practically no idea, Tom had to admit, if only to himself.

"Kayrlis," Mithra said. "Stand down. There will be no need."

"What are you—" Kayrlis began.

Before she could finish, Mithra spun his sword once over his head and cried a word that had no equivalent in any human language. Crimson lightning struck out from his sword. It enveloped the winged creature in blood red bands of energy that squeezed tighter and tighter still until the damned thing screamed in agony and was crushed into a fiery ball the size of a man's fist.

Then even that light flickered out.

Mithra didn't even bother to look over his shoulder at the other two transformed beings. "Have I made my point?"

Kayrlis watched as the sluglike creature and his hovering companion drew back.

"Good," Mithra said. He rode ahead across the bridge. "Tom, Kayrlis—to me!"

Kayrlis reclaimed her mount. She watched the creatures over her shoulder as she followed Tom across the bridge. Once all three were safely across, Mithra aimed his sword back at the bridge. Fissures appeared across its length. They grew, crackling like ebon lightning, and tore the bridge apart. The pieces plummeted downward, smashing as they struck the floor of the chasm.

"Lord, wait!" cried the hovering man.

"What is to become of us?" called his companion.

All three turned to look at them.

"What do you mean?" Mithra asked.

The hovering man slapped at the *things* writhing within his chest. "Stop," he hissed. The undulations ceased.

"Where are we to go?" the slug creature asked. "Lilith

promised to change us back. Could *you* change us back? *Would* you?"

The hovering man opened his arms imploringly. "Like this, we have nowhere to go. We can't show our faces in the company of mortals. And the guardians of the Heavenly Cities would burn us to cinders if we dared approach. How are we to eat?"

"I'm already hungry," the slug creature moaned.

"Who are we to talk to?"

Mithra shrugged. "You have each other."

"You don't understand, this isn't—" the hovering man began.

"You want mercy," Mithra said. "All right. Tell me what you were doing before you were changed."

"We—"

"And don't lie," Mithra said. "I'm an Angel of Truth. I will know if you are lying. And *if* you dare lie to me . . ."

They explained what they had planned to do with the woman from Genesis who came once a week to school their neighbor's child, and what they instead did to Lilith, thinking her unable to defend herself.

"Mercy," the man with shuddering flesh cried.

"Lord, we beseech you," his companion said.

"Look down there," Mithra said, pointing with his sword to the abyss.

The transformed beings did as they were told.

"If you wish mercy, you will cast yourselves into that darkness."

"We don't want to die!" the sluglike man said.

The hovering man shook his head. "To take our own lives would be a sin!"

"You've already sinned. You could make your crimes no worse by ending your miserable lives. But the choice is yours," Mithra said. "You are abominations, and I will have no more to do with you."

He turned and led his charges into a darkened tunnel.

The screams of the damned echoed for a time behind them, then faded completely. Mithra created another fireball and spun it over their heads to light their way.

"What will happen to them?" Kayrlis asked as she carefully twisted and turned the various segments of her staff, hiding the blade and restoring it to its original size and shape.

"So long as they don't trouble us again, I really don't care," Mithra said. "If they're foolish enough to try, I'll take their lives."

"Didn't it *bother* you?" Tom asked.

"What?"

"Killing that . . . that *thing*. I mean, I—I helped Aitan destroy a transformed being. It was—"

"They're damned," Mithra said. "Taking their existences from them is an act of mercy. But to answer your question, of *course* it bothered me. The day taking the life of even something as wretched as *that* no longer makes me feel sick at heart is the day I will leap off a cliff."

"I'm sorry," Tom said.

"Don't be. You had every right to ask. Aitan asked it of me more than once. In ways, you remind me of him."

Tom's momentary surge of elation over Mithra's words pushed away his sad recollections. "Why do you think Lilith sent those . . . beings?"

"To kill you, of course," Mithra said.

"She knows we're coming?" Kayrlis asked.

"Apparently. But she didn't know that you were traveling with *me*. If she had, she would have sent more transformed beings."

"How do we know she didn't?" Tom asked.

"I'd have sensed them by now."

Kayrlis was startled. "You mean you *knew* they were waiting for us? Why didn't you warn us that we were walking into a trap?"

"Because you were never in any danger," Mithra said.

The Elven Ways: Ancient Games 175

"As I mentioned before—you're traveling with me. I was trained in battle by the Angel of Violence. So, for that matter, was Komm Kayriel. We lived in the same house for a time."

The trio rode through the darkened tunnels and winding paths of the mountain, occasionally entering larger chambers, where armor and swords gathered rust and blankets holes.

"What was this place?" Tom asked, pointing at a well in the center of the room.

"A place of worship," Mithra said. "Warriors came here once to sacrifice themselves to their primitive gods. The well is so deep it is considered bottomless. But, I assure you, it's not."

After another hour of slow travel and descent, they emerged from a narrow tunnel on the other side of the rise.

Tom could see the settlement called Genesis in the distance. Its most prominent feature was the tower at the edge of town.

"The Spire of Truth," Mithra said. "That's our destination."

The angel looked to the sky. There was no hint of approaching daylight as yet.

"We have a little time," Mithra said. "The two of you may wish to spend it together. I'll ride ahead. You'll hear my call when it's time to rejoin me."

Without waiting for a reply, Mithra rode off.

Tom glanced over to his lover. "That doesn't sound good, does it?"

They climbed down from their horses and came together slowly, approaching one another as if they were strangers. The moment their hands met, the instant flesh touched flesh, their worries faded, while their need to be together grew greater.

"Are you scared?" Tom asked Kayrlis as he held her.

"Are *you*?"

"Asked you first."

"A little." She swallowed hard. "A lot."

"Me, too." He stroked her hair. "We could just leave."

"But Aitan and Grin—"

"I'm not saying it's what we should do, I'm just saying . . ."

Kayrlis shuddered. "I know. We could be together, we wouldn't be hunted, we wouldn't have to worry about anything." She pulled away from him and looked deeply into his eyes. "You'd end up hating me."

"That's not—never," he said.

"You would. Because you'd always wonder what would have happened if you'd gone on. You'd always feel like there was something you could have done about everything that's wrong with the world, only you didn't. All because of me. Well, I don't want that responsibility. I don't want to be the one who did that to you."

"But what do you want?" Tom asked.

Kayrlis shrugged. "To make love with you. To lie in your arms. To have friends. A normal life. That's what I want. But what I *need* is for you to be the man I fell in love with, not a boy who's acting on his impulses. Do you understand?"

Tom nodded slowly.

"Whatever's waiting, we'll face it together. That's how it'll always be. Nothing can change that."

He wanted to believe her. But a part of him understood how fragile their lives were.

"I'm curious, Tom. When were you born, anyway?"

"You know how old I am."

"I'm lazy. And I *ain't in no mood to do arithmetic,* okay?"

Tom grinned. Kayrlis's accent always became more pronounced when she was relaxed. He told her the year and the day he'd been born.

"Now that's interesting," she said.

"What?"

"When I was in China, I learned a bunch of things about what they call astrology. According to my old friend Bo, the year you're born sets your character."

"Not me."

"You were born in the Year of the Tiger," Kayrlis said. "They would call you the delightful paradox. A trailblazer. Your destiny is to go after the impossible and try everything new. You're meant to be a performer. To dance to life's music. Every color of the rainbow is inside you.

"But you're not just the tiger. You're also the rabbit. You like the quiet. You like being alone and dreaming of other times and places. You don't want to be like everyone else. You want harmony and inner peace. You want to see and feel and be a part of everything in the world.

"I felt that, too. When we passed through the stone wall, I knew what it felt like to be stone. To be patience and acceptance. And it was a real eye-opener because that's not what I am. I was born in the Year of the Rat. For me, every search has to end with a new quest. I aim high and never miss my target. I love life. I'm all *about* life."

"Kayrlis—"

"I'm not conflicted like you are, Tom. I know what I am, what I'm meant to be, and I'm happy with that. You know who and what you really are, deep down."

"And what's that?"

"A kind and gentle soul. A good and loving friend. Someone who might be afraid to die but wouldn't let that stop him from doing what needs to be done. Just accept it, and we'll both be better off."

She went to her horse and took something from one of her bags. Then she held it out to Tom.

"Take it," Kayrlis said.

He stared at the small carving resting in the palm of her hand. It was a jade figure of a woman reaching outward, her back arched like a crescent moon. There was a chain secured to it.

He took the necklace from her. She opened her other hand to reveal its mate, a male in the exact opposite position. Only this figure was crimson.

"Now watch," she said, putting the two halves together. They formed a whole in perfect harmony. "Yin and Yang."

"Two halves of a perfect whole," Tom whispered.

"Us," Kayrlis said.

Before Tom could say anything more, a voice whispered to them on the winds.

Come. Now. We must be ready.

Tom kissed Kayrlis. Then they got on their horses and rode on to meet with the warrior angel.

Sixteen

LILITH SAW THE DAWN OUTSIDE HER WINDOW AND knew that the time was at hand.

"Matthew," she whispered, shaking her lover by the shoulder. "Wake up."

He rose slowly from his slumber. "Lilith?"

"A messenger came in the night," she lied. "You were so exhausted, I didn't want to wake you."

"I would have heard," he muttered, then shook his head. "A messenger? It's Jumping Dan Hatch, isn't it?" he asked. "Despite it all, he reached the spire."

"No," Lilith said. "Hatch is not a concern. Your men have seen to that. But it does involve the spire."

He stretched and ran his hands through his hair. "How?"

"Avram Luvonic, the Curacas's son, is waiting there for you."

"Him?" Matthew said with open disdain. "What would he want with me?"

"Your blessing, I would assume."

Matthew sighed heavily. "Yes. I sent a letter. My response was . . . Unfortunate. Hardly enthusiastic. Which is about how I'm feeling now."

"You have to go," Lilith said.

"I know. But to have to see him the same day I've got to tell John that the position isn't his after all . . . I don't know, it grates."

"Of course," Lilith said. Her blood was in him now. It would be a simple matter to tweak his annoyance into hatred, and from there, to transform his hatred into a murderous rage. All she would need to do then was put the actors on the stage, stand back, and allow Matthew to damn himself by hurling the fool off the tower and claiming he fell by accident.

She did nothing.

"Come on," she said, noticing the way he was eyeing her naked form. "Time enough for *that* later . . ."

They dressed and ate, discussing trivial matters. Lilith had made the acquaintances of several local ladies of prominence. She was well traveled, and had been able to instruct them in the subtle differences between the clothing of the Lahu people, which had been in style a year ago, and that of the Deang. Though both cultures had come from provinces of China, and the styles of both depended heavily on the proper usage of the color black with brighter colors as highlights, the Deang women wore hoops in a tradition that went back for a thousand years.

"In their fairy tales," Lilith said, delighting in the unwavering attention she drew from her beloved, "women could fly when the angels first made them. In order to live with them, men created the rattan hoops to weigh them down and keep them closer to the earth."

"Only angels can fly," Matthew said wistfully.

Not so, Lilith thought, but she held her tongue. *I could make you soar through the heavens, I could make you so much more than just a man—*

—but then, would I still love you?

"Lilith?" Matthew asked.

She pushed away her daydream of flying through the

The Elven Ways: Ancient Games 181

clouds and making love like gods. Touching his hand, she said, "A flight of fancy. Nothing more."

"You've barely eaten anything," he said, nodding toward her plate.

"I have other appetites," she said, easing her shift from her shoulder.

Matthew was pleasantly surprised. "But you said—"

"I changed my mind," she said, rising and clearing the table with a single swipe of her arm. Plates and glasses shattered as they hit the floor.

He grabbed her, kissing her hard, his tongue exploring her fiery mouth. He pushed her down onto the table and took her fiercely.

Clinging to Matthew, Lilith suddenly found her hands sinking into his flesh.

"Ah!" he cried at the sudden chill.

She withdrew instantly, realizing that she had almost no control whatsoever where this man was concerned. Fear had touched her heart a moment earlier, and she needed to drive it out, needed his fire inside her.

For a brief time, it was enough.

Tom was surprised to find that Mithra had made himself look human once more. He hadn't resumed the form of Juno Meazzi. Instead, he looked pudgy and nondescript. His bald spot glowed in the intense light of morning.

"Well, you've changed," Tom said.

The angel didn't answer him. His gaze was fixed somewhere in the distance.

"Mithra?" Tom asked.

The angel shuddered, wiping the sweat from his eyes. "My apologies for seeming distant," he said. "We should go."

"What was it?" Tom asked. "A vision? Are you like me, do you have visions?"

"All is in readiness," Mithra said. "Lilith is about to open the portal to the Realm of Shadow."

They rode on to Genesis. Tom and Kayrlis flanked the warrior angel.

"What'd you see?" Tom asked.

Mithra found that he couldn't answer. He had seen the vision that had been granted to him before. Lilith and two men standing upon the Spire of Truth. One of the men was strong and handsome. The other was pear-shaped and younger, a look of superiority on his rather plain face. Lilith did nothing but watch. And why not? Her work was done.

And as Lilith looked on, the man she'd seduced and corrupted surged forward and pushed the pear-shaped man from the observation tower. The man fell, his arms and legs pinwheeling, a scream torn from his lips. He struck the ground with a sickening thud. Then Lilith's victim turned to her. The rage had fled from him. Damnation was in his eyes.

She said a word. A single word.

And the portal opened.

That had been the vision.

"Mithra?" Tom asked again.

The angel smiled wanly. The scene he'd witnessed was about to play itself out. Mithra would be there to witness it. So would Tom and Kayrlis.

They would want to do something about it. Prevent the murder from occurring. This was the right thing to do. This man Matthew did not deserve to be transformed into a killer any more than his victim deserved to die. It was simply the way of things. And it was inevitable. Any attempt to alter the future he had been shown would end in tragedy.

Their appearance had to be timed exactly right. Tom had to see the murder take place but not have a chance to do anything about it.

It had all been foretold—and *agreed upon*.

"Lilith will recognize me," Tom said as they traveled the the solitary road leading to Genesis.

"She won't even see you," Mithra promised. "Not until it's too late for her."

"Do you think Kayrlis should wait for us in town?"

"Oh, right," she said. "As if you could keep me from climbing that tower with you."

"I'll leave that up to you," Mithra said with a slight smile.

"Not another word, Tom Keeper!" she cried.

"But you don't know what this woman's like," Tom said. "She's not human."

"No, Tom. I'll be at your side, and that's the end of it."

So it was. The trio rode into Genesis. The settlement was a collection of buildings reflecting architecture from a handful of diverse sources: stone buildings with steeples sat beside wooden rectangular warehouses. Pagodas and buildings patterned after ancient Indian temples or Mayan altars of sacrifice were interspersed with liveries and barns.

A good number of people were out and about, but few paid any real attention to the trio riding in from parts unknown. Visitors were welcome here, as were all who were one with God.

"We'll tie our horses there and walk the rest of the way," Mithra said.

"But we could reach the tower faster—" Tom said.

Mithra shook his head. "I am powerful, that is true, but my resources are far from unlimited. Our horses are strong and have minds and wills of their own. I may cast a cloak about the three of us, protecting us from view, with some effort, but not so much that it will leave me drained and wanting in the battle to come. To do any more—"

"Sure," Tom said. "Sorry." He relaxed, because he had faith in the angel leading them.

When Mithra was certain that no one was watching, he

cast a spell that rendered all three travelers invisible to one another—and even themselves.

"How are we supposed to keep from walking into each other?" Kayrlis asked nervously.

"Don't let the use of magic unsettle you," Mithra said. "I know you didn't grow up with it, but—"

"Lord, please just answer the question," Kayrlis said, her panic over her unnatural state rising.

Then she felt Tom's hand close around hers. "I won't let you get lost," he said.

It took about a hundred yards for her to realize that all Tom was doing was watching their footsteps in the dusty earth. But she liked the feel of his hand in hers. It made the fear gripping her heart settle just a bit.

The tower loomed before them. A spiral staircase led to a deck at its farthest reach. Two men could be seen near a rail. One leaned against it. Another was farther back from him. They seemed to be having a heated discussion.

Mithra could feel that the time was upon them. Nevertheless, he decided that he would go first. The wide deck at the top of the spire cast a shadow at its base. Mithra had no sooner placed one foot upon the first of the spiral steps when a sudden wind kicked up. A blinding cloud of dirt rose up and covered the travelers, defeating the spell of invisibility Mithra had cast. His form, and those of Tom and Kayrlis, were mercilessly revealed by the earth cast about on the winds.

Mithra thought that was a natural occurrence. He realized his error a moment too late. Kayrlis let out a cry of terror that was quickly cut short.

"Kayrlis!" Tom screamed.

"No one moves," a voice called.

Mithra knew that voice. He'd heard it in his dreams. "Lilith."

The winds died down. Mithra released the spells he'd cast. All were visible, and he now looked once more like a warrior angel. Lilith stood with a blade to Kayrlis's throat.

"Don't," Tom whispered. "I love her."

"I know," Lilith said. "And you want to hear the damnedest thing of all? I understand . . ."

Seventeen

"STOP HER," TOM SAID TO MITHRA.

The angel shook his head sadly. "There's nothing I can do."

"She's vulnerable to magic," Tom said. "Any magic. I've seen—"

"Tom?" Kayrlis said, the terror only barely masked in her voice. "I think she wants something."

Mithra stared at Lilith, trying to understand how his vision could have been wrong. Had his allies used him? Deceived him?

No. This was something unforeseen. Something that could never have been anticipated. "You fell in love with the mortal."

"It happens," Lilith said.

"Not to beings like you. You're damned. You have no soul. What do you know of love?"

"More than you, I'd wager," Lilith said.

"I've stood in the fires of God's perfect love," Mithra said. "I have spoken with the Vessels. I have—"

"Enough," Lilith said, pulling the blade close enough to Kayrlis's throat to draw a drop of blood.

Mithra looked up suddenly. "Should I summon the man so that he can witness this?"

"Only if you want the girl to die."

"Please," Tom said.

Lilith regarded him. "You're looking fine, Tom! Even more of a man than when I last saw you. Eating well, I hope?"

"Tell me what you want," Tom said.

"That's simple," she said. "I'm going to open the portal to the Realm of Shadow. I want you to go there for me and bring back Lord Kayriel. That's all."

Tom stared at Kayrlis's darting eyes and looked away. "I can't do that."

Something in Lilith's expression softened. "I don't want to take her from you. I don't. But this thing has to be done."

"Why?" Tom asked. "You said you weren't Kayriel's most loyal follower."

"I'm not."

"Then prove it."

"All right," Lilith said, taking the knife from Kayrlis's throat and backing away from her.

Kayrlis took a few steps forward, then doubled over, screaming in pain. Tom went to her side. He knelt beside her, and held her hand. She squeezed so tightly that the blood drained from his face.

"What'd you do to her!?" Tom screamed.

"To her, nothing," Kayrlis said. "To the child she carries? *Your* child? I have condemned him to damnation. I have corrupted his soul."

"Yes," Mithra said. "The corruption of an innocent who is bound to a prisoner in the Realm. The only way to open the portal."

Tom struggled to understand, but the sight of his beloved's face, wrinkled up in pain, was all-consuming.

"It was meant to be Matthew," Mithra said. "The

innocent, brotherly love that Kayriel shared with him that had never been tainted. Instead, it is your child. He is, of course, linked by flesh to your wife, who was once raised from the dead by the Emissary Skalligrin. It is those links in the chain which serve us now . . ."

"A baby?" Kayrlis whispered, gasping for breath. "Can't be. Oh God, it hurts . . ."

A sudden, shocking image leaped into Tom's mind: Kayrlis falling back, her head rolling from her shoulders . . .

"No!" he cried, prying his hand loose from her grip and leaping back from her.

"It's starting," Lilith said. "The doorway's opening."

Tom looked to Kayrlis again. This time, she was being hacked to pieces by creatures out of a nightmare. He closed his eyes and fell to his knees.

"Stop it!" he cried. But the images would not cease.

"The Realm's calling to you," Lilith said.

Tom could feel the doorway beckoning. It was less a physical thing than a state of mind. A darkness deeper than any he had ever believed existed called for him, a swirling cavern of madness and depravity.

He looked up and saw Kayrlis staring at him. She appeared normal. The visions had ended.

Through gritted teeth, she cried, "Go."

"Yes," Mithra said. "Seek out the Keeper of the Keys. Your shadow. He will guide you. Do what must be done, Tom. Consider the cost to all who live, not just your child . . ."

Lilith turned to the angel and smiled. "I see. You seek to counsel the boy to betray me. To take Lord Anzelm in my master's place." She glanced back at Tom. "You may do as you like. I can't enter shadow, I would never be able to leave again. The same as Mithra and anyone who wasn't standing in the presence of the Vessel when Kayriel struck him down. But Aitan Anzelm cannot cleanse the spirit of your unborn child, Tom. Only a Vessel could do that. Or Kayriel.''

"Go!" Mithra urged. "The time is at hand, go!"

"I love you," Tom whispered, staring deep into Kayrlis' beautiful eyes.

He didn't hear her reply.

An instant later, he vanished from view.

Sounds came from above. Heavy boots slamming on iron steps. "Lilith are you all right?" Matthew cried.

"Behold," she said. "An angel come to free us of our earthly torments."

And with those words, she began to laugh. . . .

Tom Keeper opened his eyes. A vision of damnation pressed in upon him. He stood upon a rocky mound, looking out at a twisted and charred black landscape. Something like an obscene, gelatinous belly loomed above, filling up the sky. Screaming creatures, some made of flesh, others of vapor, were trapped within it. They beat at its walls for escape. The grotesque *thing* drifted over him, rising now so that he could see more of this nightmarish place.

Before him was an achingly beautiful array of lavender spires that seemed to be alive, rising and singing a hymn that had no words and made no sound, but could be heard only with the inner powers of the soul. Beyond, in the far horizon, was a dark, round shape, like the tail of a beast the size of a mountain. The tail lazily slapped back and forth.

Balloons drifted through the air, carrying chittering, malignant creatures that rained down buckets of blood and acid upon howling, tormented figures rooted in the black earth, only their torsos, arms, and heads exposed.

Tom could not abide these horrors. He knew his duty, but his fear propelled him to the brink of turning back to the world he knew. This he could do with only a thought.

Suddenly, the nightmarish vision faded. The land was

revealed to be a beautiful place of rolling fields and emerald mists. Grinning, white-robed figures with long, doelike features and eyes much larger than any human's opened their arms and sang. Only the music that Tom had somehow *felt* instead of *heard* remained the same.

"Yes, it . . . tries to be accommodating," said someone behind Tom. He whirled and saw Grin and Malkiyyah standing before him.

Tom dropped to his knees before the angels.

"Now I thought we had an understanding about that sort of thing!" Grin said.

His trembling hands covering his face, Tom began to weep. Grin went to his side.

"Don't be afraid," Grin said.

"He's right," added Malkiyyah. "This place isn't so terrible. Not unless you will it to be so."

"I don't—I don't understand," Tom said.

Grin looked around. "The land's alive. It will shape itself to be whatever you expect it—or wish it—to be."

Shaking his head, as if those words simply held no meaning for him considering the horrors that were still fresh in his mind, Tom allowed the angel to help him to his feet. "It's Kayrlis . . . she's—what was done to her . . ."

"Who?" Grin asked. "Someone was careless? I don't understand."

"Kayrlis. The spider of the Spider and the Fly. You saved her life," Tom said. "The carnival. She and her brother were performers—"

"Ah!" Grin said. "The woman who fell. Then you and she—"

"Yes," Tom said.

"Well, good!" Grin cried.

Tom shook his head. "She's with child. Mine. And one of Komm Kayriel's soldiers . . ."

"You don't have to talk about it," Grin said. "I'm here if you need me, lad."

"Perhaps it would be best for all of us if we talked of escape," Malkiyyah said, eyeing the land warily.

"Good point," Grin said. He patted Tom's back. "You're becoming quite the wielder of magic, aren't you? I'm not even going to *ask* how you got here."

"You mean you don't know?"

Grin stared at him blankly.

"You're not aware of what must be done to open the doorway from my world to the Realm?"

"Again," Grin said, "we can trade incantations when we have more time. What's important is—do you have a way back?"

Tom nodded. "But I can only take one person with me."

Grin and Malkiyyah stiffened at this. Then they looked at each other and lowered their gazes as one.

"Aitan," Grin said.

Tom said nothing. He had no intention of rescuing Kayriel. And yet... His *child*. The very concept of becoming a father, and having a son whose soul was damned before birth...

"I think it *does* matter how he got here," Malkiyyah said. "Tom, who sent you?"

"Aitan's Patron."

"*Mithra*," Grin spit. "Even more of a cold fish than Aitan on his worst day. God love his soul. Well, Mithra didn't help you out of love for his student, that much is certain. He has none to give. Aitan resides with Kayriel in the Abyss. There must be some danger involved in the two of them being bound together. If that wasn't the case..."

"I agree," Malkiyyah said. "Look around you, Tom."

Tom did as the angel commanded. He saw that the robed figures now looked like emerald butterflies with human features.

"You were expecting a place of horror and torment when you first arrived here, and so it gave you that. When you reacted badly to the images it presented, it gave you something that it knew you would find more pleasing."

"It's in my mind?" Tom asked. "This place?"

"More than a place," Malkiyyah explained. "It's alive. And it wants to keep us here."

"I had a vision of the two of you," Tom said. "You had to stay in motion all the time, if you didn't—"

"It's what we expected," Grin said.

"What we felt we deserved for letting Abaddon crumble around us," Malkiyyah added.

"From what we've been able to gather by talking with the Emissaries from this land, it has been waiting a very long time for guests who won't just melt into its depths and become a part of it," Grin said. "Why we are different from all others—"

"You were around when the Fourth Vessel was destroyed," Tom said.

Malkiyyah shuddered. "You mean to say some fraction of the Vessel's Power is within each of us?"

"Part of His Power," Tom said, "part of Him . . . I don't know." He looked to a darkness that was gathering on the horizon. "Is that the way to the Abyss of Punishment?"

Grin nodded. "It's a land not far from this one. But there's no way to reach it."

"Show me," Tom said.

With a shrug, Grin threw open his arms and called out, "We'd like to visit the end of the world once more!"

Suddenly, they stood in a far different place. Tom looked out on what seemed to be an endless sea of darkness. He heard something moving, drifting his way.

"That light in the distance," Grin said from behind Tom. "Can you see it?"

Tom strained his eyes and saw a single star in the field of blackness. Then he realized that the darkness was also a living thing. Undulating.

Hungry.

"That speck of light is the Abyss," Malkiyyah said. "As

you can see, there's simply no way to get from *here* to *there*."

"Sure there is," Tom replied. "You said the land wants to make us happy, right?"

"I would call that an understatement," Malkiyyah said with a grunt. "You should have seen the *females* it threw at us—"

"It would make me happy if the border of this world was only a little closer to the Abyss," Tom said.

All three felt a trembling beneath their feet, and suddenly, the distant star burned a little brighter.

"Now if only it was a bit *closer still*," Tom said.

Again, the rumbling, and the Abyss was now brighter than ever.

Tom continued to wish for the land to extend until finally all three could see the City of the Abyss clearly. It was surrounded by glowing white mountains with jagged peaks. Beyond those heights, fortresses, domed buildings, and razor-sharp spires could be seen, along with glimpses of strange creatures that sprang furtively from its heights and plunged downward yet again.

"Not far now," Tom said.

Suddenly, from all around, a booming voice called, *"You know I could never allow this, don't you?"*

The land that had been reaching toward the City of the Abyss suddenly burst into flame!

Eighteen

SURROUNDING TOM AND HIS COMPANIONS WERE WHAT seemed like millions of creatures impaled on spears of fire. Some appeared to have the features of humans or angels. Others were strange amalgams of beast and man, while yet more were wholly bizarre and unfamiliar meldings: opening flowers and oily black tentacles lined with blood red eyes; trees that became prisons in which other sentient creatures pleaded for release.

It took Tom a moment to realize that the flames could not harm him. The fires did not touch the land.

"More illusions," Tom said finally. And with his words, the terrible sights went away and the darkness resumed.

All three looked around for any sign of the being who had spoken. But there was nothing.

With a jarring, thunderous roar, the voice came again. *"Now, what was that about presiding over the death of my city?"*

"Abaddon," Grin said.

And in naming the hidden angel, the being appeared. Or more to the point, his shape, which had been in plain view at all times, came together in a form that Tom and the angels could recognize. The darkness coalesced into a figure with eyes like suns and a body crafted from the rolling clouds of night surrounding the City of the Abyss.

"I am Abaddon," the dark angel said. *"If you would seek to bind me by the ancient ways, you would need to know more than just my name."*

"You are the angel of the bottomless pit," Grin said. "Known also as the Destroyer."

"Oh, good," Abaddon said. *"Someone who can read. And here I thought it was a lost art. What volume of the Great History am I listed in now?"*

"You're also known as the Angel with the Key to the Abyss," Tom said. "The Keeper of the Keys."

Abaddon almost laughed. *"Very good. Especially for a mortal."* He sighed. *"I was told you were coming, whelp. Look about you. While it is true that I have no power over the Hungry Lands, this paradise in which you find yourself, I can do much to keep you from fulfilling your quest. For you wish to visit the City of the Abyss, and I am that Abyss. To reach the city of the creature I have bound, Azazel by name, you must first pass through me. You cannot do that without losing the exact measure of power and spirit that you would need to leave the city once more. So long as you stand upon that holy ground, you are protected. Your soul is in no jeopardy. But in other ways, you are damned, for there is nothing you can do to reach your friends."*

"Not without the Keys," Tom said.

"Are you challenging me?" Abaddon cried.

"No," Tom said. A sudden notion had seized him during Abaddon's rant. He had nothing to lose by giving it voice. "Challenging you is exactly what you want me to do. I can see it now . . ."

Tom's Power of prophecy, which he could never before control, flared within him. Visions came. Not of a future that had to come to pass, but instead of the future Abaddon desired.

"You planned on sending me on a quest. Turning me

into an old man while I navigated labyrinths and solved riddles..." A ragged gasp escaped him. "I've been tested enough—and I've had a really lousy day. You don't seem to understand what you're up against, Abaddon. I can tell when people aren't telling the truth. Angels, too. Or whatever God's seen fit to make you. And much of what you said is nothing but bold-faced lies."

"You have no idea what you face if you truly mean to pass through my essence," Abaddon said, with a slightly less confident tone. *"You are in the Realm of Shadow. Do you have any notion of what that means? What this place is?"*

"I've been told that it's a reflection," Tom said. "And I think I understand now why the Elven call their world the True Lands. *They* named this place the Realm of Shadow. To them it was an evil, unholy place, because it could see into their hearts. But I can feel what it really is."

"And what's that?"

"Alive. And filled with magic." Tom's power flared again. Knowledge that he shouldn't possibly have possessed flooded through him. "Your people came here hoping to conquer these lands and take their magic. But they failed. *You* failed, didn't you?"

Abaddon's body grew larger, more substantial. Rippling muscles formed out of blackish grey clouds that were his body. Lightning flared to reveal his chiseled form.

"We're taught that you bound the Enemy and would keep him imprisoned for a thousand years," Tom said. "The Millennium, the rule of God's Army upon the earth."

The hidden knowledge was being revealed to him through a means he didn't understand, but he knew enough not to fight what was happening. He wondered if this had something to do with the fact that he and Abaddon were shadows of one another. Then he had no more time to think. Knowledge was racing into him.

"Bound for a thousand years..." Tom said. "That's what they teach. But that's not the way it happened at all, is it? This Azazel you spoke of... The Abyss is his city? I wouldn't be surprised if Azazel was the one who came up with the brilliant idea of trying to conquer this place. Were you his lieutenant? His dog soldier? What?"

Abaddon was silent. Then his rumbling voice came again. *"I will never give you the Keys."*

"Of course you won't," Tom said. "That doesn't mean I won't get my hands on them one way or another. So far as I can tell, there's only one Key that matters, anyway."

Abaddon tilted his head slightly to one side, like a wolf. *"You are more than you seem, aren't you? I will enjoy making you suffer."*

"Tom," Grin said, coming forward and seizing the lad's arm. "What are you doing?"

"Let him be," Malkiyyah said. "I'm enjoying this."

Tom shrugged off the angel's hand and took a step forward to Abaddon. "You're not the real power here."

"Would that this damnable place had not robbed me of my ability to laugh at your pitiful efforts," Abaddon said.

Tom cleared his throat. " 'The learned student who guards the secrets of the gods will bind his favored son with an oath before Shamash and Adad and will instruct him in the secrets of the gods...' "

For an instant, Abaddon's form shimmered and lost its shape. The mammoth angel trembled. *"Who taught you those words?"*

"The Vessel," Tom said, final understanding dawning on him. "This was the Vessel's gift to each of us when he died. He didn't want Kayriel to possess all his knowledge—"

"Because knowledge is power," Grin said.

"Yeah," Tom said. "Every one of us who was there when the Vessel died inherited knowledge *and* power. That's what keeps us from becoming part of this land. And it's what'll protect us when we go through Abaddon to reach the City of the Abyss."

"You can't mean it," Malkiyyah said. "He knew you were coming! He's planned something."

"Not this," Tom said. "I can feel it. This spell is terrifying him." Tom steeled himself. He had no idea what would happen when the incantation was done. " 'Thus was the line of priests created, those who are allowed to approach Shamash and Adad.' "

"No!" Abaddon cried. Suddenly, a storm ripped through him. A blinding, raging wind tossed Tom and his companions to the soil of the Hungry Land and whistled in their ears as it took the air from their lungs and pressed down upon them.

"YOU HAVE CALLED US FORTH!" cried a pair of voices within the angry winds. "APPEASE US OR BE RENT LIMB FROM LIMB FOR AN ETERNITY!"

"Shamash and Adad," Tom cried, gasping for air.

"The gods of this place," Grin hissed.

"The rest, say the rest of the spell!" Malkiyyah wailed.

But Tom couldn't. He'd spoken all of the incantation that he knew . . .

Aitan Anzelm raised his head. "Tom."

"The boy's near, yes," Kayriel said. "It would take a mortal to anger the spirits of this place so much. Listen to the storm out there!"

Aitan and Kayriel were in a chamber with grey and black furnishings. A painting hung upon one of the far walls, a blinding white cube that hurt Aitan to look upon, though it surprisingly cast no illumination upon the room. Only the pale light from the shining city itself allowed Aitan to separate Kayriel's constantly shifting form, one made entirely of darkness, from that of his surroundings.

The storm was unnatural, and surely alive, like everything else in this realm. Aitan worried about what promises

Tom might have made to secure passage to this terrible place. To whom had he gone? Who would help him open the door to nightmare?

"I like this room," Kayriel said, his form darting like the living shadow that he was from table to chair, to jagged outcroppings leaning down from ceiling or inward from floor. "I find a comfort in the darkness, a stillness that exists nowhere else."

"There is no stillness here," Aitan said, nodding toward the window and the gale outside.

Kayriel laughed. "I also like the storm. The madness of it. The fury and passion. I used to tease you that you were too serious, remember? That you needed to go insane once in a while, allow your instincts to rule. *Passion* is what you lacked. Now it's something you can't escape!"

Aitan turned from the window. "Explain."

"You're passionate about destroying me, even though we were once friends. Doesn't *that* seem a bit evil and shortsighted?"

Looking back to the window, Aitan said, "Save your rhetoric. You won't make a convert of me the way you have so many others in this place."

"Did it ever occur to you that there might be a *reason* why people are willing to listen to me?"

"You are chaos incarnate, and this is a place of restraint. It's natural that you would hold some allure to the damned."

"No," Kayriel said, springing to Aitan's side like a spider. "They listen because, deep down, they *know* I'm telling the truth. And you know it, too."

"All you want—" Aitan began.

"How would you know what I want!" Kayriel railed. "You've never taken the time to ask me, though you stay as close to me as any guardsman."

"You *murdered* a Vessel," Aitan said.

"Yes, but not the one who needed killing, I'm afraid," Kayriel said.

"You're insane."

"Think about it. You saw the abomination unleashed by the lord of creation. A human made to look like the ancient conceit of an angel. What's next? That we should all have rosy flesh and soft feathery wings? That we subvert all that we are and all that we will ever be to the service of the Great Lie?"

"You're no savior," Aitan said. "No words that leave your lips or acts you may perform will ever make me see you in a flattering light."

Kayriel looked away. "There was a time when things were not so strained between us. When there was joy and hope."

"Yes. But we were children then."

"There was also a time when you would have gladly given up all for me, as I would have for you."

"I know what you want," Aitan said wearily. "Within me there is a part of you that has never been corrupted. And so long as that fragment of your spirit exists and does not surrender to your depravities—"

"*Depravities,*" Kayriel repeated bitterly.

"Then you are powerless to make your final ascension. No matter what power you gain, you will be less than one of the Vessels. And so they will be able to destroy you."

Kayriel said nothing. He looked up at the eternal darkness with a strange, indescribable longing.

"You want me to take Azazel's place, to become a part of this land," Aitan said. "It would corrupt me, and you would be free."

"As a matter of fact," Kayriel said, "no."

Aitan looked at him sharply.

"You've misjudged me," Kayriel said. "You see, I feel a certain kinship to this place. I think I can restore its dead heart."

"Ridiculous," Aitan said.

"Truth. I was born in darkness, and to darkness I wish to return. Believe me, I've seen enough suffering. My communion with the Vessel changed me. I now understand what it's like to be as one of them, and that is no longer my desire."

Aitan waited.

"I've also seen the horrors Azazel has prepared for you."

"Tom," Aitan said. "His plans center on Tom, don't they?"

"Actually, no. There is a greater hurt inside you that he has found, a wound he would exploit to torment you. I'd rather that you were spared such agonies. So I've decided to take Azazel's place. When Tom arrives, you may leave with him. I will offer no resistance . . ."

Nineteen

TOM FELT *PRESENCES* WITHIN HIM THAT HE COULD NOT define. They were neither good nor evil. Instead, they seemed to be the embodiments of that which was otherwise missing from the Realm of Shadow, the full kaleidoscopic range of emotions from rage to tenderness, love to seething hatred.

"WITHIN HIM—" one of the voices cried.

"BUT HE KNOWS NOT, LET US AWAY WHILE IGNORANCE MAY YET SHIELD US!"

As suddenly as these living winds had descended upon Tom Keeper and his companions, they withdrew.

Tom rose unsteadily and turned to see Grin and Malkiyyah slowly stirring.

"That's an experience I'd prefer not to have on a regular basis," Grin muttered.

Malkiyyah drew his fiery blade. Shuddering, he held the weapon before him in a two-fisted grip. "They were inside my *mind*. I felt them closing on my soul, learning everything about me..."

"It's over now," Grin said gently. "They've fled."

"They're not the only ones," Tom said, raising one hand to point at the sky. "Look!"

The darkness that was the body of Abaddon had vanished. An abyss remained, but it was one of searing light. The city at its heart was now only a speck of darkness.

"The Key to the Abyss," Tom said.

"What?" Grin asked.

"Fear," Tom said. "The key was fear, but not *our* fear. We had to summon something that would frighten Abaddon away. And we did that."

"*You* did it," Grin said. "You also made those creatures leave. How?"

"I'm not really sure," Tom said. "I have ideas, but..."

"The gods spoke of something that's within him," Malkiyyah said. "Something that made *them* afraid. What could make beings like that afraid?"

"I don't know," Grin said. "But I think we're going to find out, sooner or later."

Tom looked to the city in the distance. "I'm going there."

"Yes," Grin said. "If we move quickly enough, we should be able to move the land once more, re-create the bridge—"

"No," Tom said. "No time. Abaddon's not going to be away for long. I can feel him starting to re-form. He's not far from us."

Tom turned and started walking toward the sea of ivory before them.

"Wait," Grin said. "You'll fall!"

"I have *faith* that I won't," Tom said. He touched the necklace Kayrlis had given him. He could feel her in the Human Worlds. The love she held for him was an anchor that would always bring him back. He understood that now.

"Tom, don't!" Malkiyyah cried.

Ignoring them, Tom stepped off the edge of the land. He kept his gaze firmly trained on the prize up ahead. The floating city that was his destination.

And he did not fall.

"You have to have faith," Tom said, his thoughts dancing upon images of Mother Jael walking across the waters, and of the stone wall he passed through because his faith was strong.

"All right, then," Grin said, following Tom into the abyss. "I'm not about to be left behind after all this."

Malkiyyah approached the edge warily. He whispered, "Faith in all that is holy," and stepped into the abyss.

All three felt a tremendous sense of loss at leaving the Hungry Land. There was a comfort that could not be denied in its all-consuming desire to please them. As they approached the City of the Abyss, an altogether different sensation radiated toward them.

"It wants our souls," Malkiyyah said. "I've never felt anything so empty before in my life."

"What it wants and what it's *getting* are two different things," Grin said.

Ahead, a peninsula of crackling black stone reached out for the trio. Tom walked upon it first. He winced as invisible tendrils reached up and snaked over his body with an obscene familiarity. They quickly withdrew.

All three gazed up at the rocky wall ahead. It stretched high enough to blot out the sky, which was quickly returning to darkness.

Abaddon had returned.

"So how do we get inside?" Tom asked.

A dark flash came from beside the lad. Tom turned to see an angel standing before him. The angel's flesh was grey, his eyes white. His armor was composed of constantly shifting gobs of darkness broken up by strikes of lightning.

"Abaddon?" Grin asked, unsheathing his sword. Malkiyyah surged to his side, weapon at the ready.

"No," the angel said listlessly. "I'm called Furfur. In the True Lands, mine was the dominion of lightning, storms, and strong winds. In shadow, all I can do is *long* for such things."

"But what about the storm that just hit?" Tom asked.

Furfur looked at him strangely. "I don't understand."

"The storm. The skies were ripped apart!"

"No," he said. "Not to the best of *my* knowledge. Perhaps you're making a jest at my expense. If so, that is fine, just fine. But I cannot accommodate you with laughter. Or joy. Such things are all but forgotten in this place. Or, I should say, they are not forgotten, but the means to produce them is."

"I see we're in for a fun afternoon," Grin said.

Furfur opened his arms. "I will take the three of you over the city gates. There is much you will wish to see, I am sure."

"I'm looking for someone," Tom said. "He's like me, apart from all this."

The angel nodded sadly. "Yes, I thought I was apart from 'all this' too when I first arrived. But the land will teach you otherwise...."

"Just take us inside," Grin said. "We'll find our own way."

"As you wish," said the laconic angel. With a gesture, he lifted into the air. Sudden winds came and carried Tom and his companions along.

The walls fell away before them, and the city was revealed. It was far more, and far *less,* than Tom had expected. The city was made of stone. It was ill conceived, with additions stacked on top and beside one another. It had none of the beauty and grandeur of the Heavenly City that Tom had visited before its fall. Was the city shaping itself to his perceptions?

Tom had a sense that it was not....

The trio was set down in a wide courtyard where other angels wandered about.

"Where are the pillars of fire ripped from the heart of the penitents?" Malkiyyah asked, falling to his knees. "I don't understand. This is where the oldest and most evil of our kind have always been sent to be purified of their wickedness—or to be bound as in the Ring of Punishment. Is it all lies? Everything we have believed?"

"I'm beginning to think it is," Grin said. "But I had suspected as much for a long time."

"All I want to do is find Aitan," Tom said. He turned to the Angel of Storms. "Where are prisoners kept?"

The angel shrugged. "Everywhere." Sadness creased his features once more. "By the Vessels, for even the slightest breeze or to be able to fly once again . . ."

"You just flew," Tom said.

Furfur looked around. "If only that were so." He wandered off, downtrodden.

"There *is* punishment here," Malkiyyah said. "Your senses and your sanity seem to leave you if you stay too long."

"I think it's worse than that," Grin said. "The torments simply aren't so readily seen as we might expect, that's all."

Suddenly, a ring of fiery red beings exploded into view. They were nothing like the flame guardian Tom had seen in his visions. Instead, they looked more like logs that had been charred without and hollowed from within by flames. Yet they twitched and writhed and cried out in untold agonies.

"So you were thinking that we'd see something more like *that*," Grin said, gesturing at the wretches before them.

"Like what?" Malkiyyah asked. He looked around. "I see nothing."

Grin looked over his shoulder at Tom. "We'd best leave this place quickly."

Tom nodded.

They avoided the smoldering men and approached another angel. He was handsome, with raven's hair, and skin as cold and smooth as marble.

"You do my work for me, and yet I take no pleasure in it," he said with a deep sigh.

"Pardon?" Tom asked.

"I am Olivier, and my task is to tempt people to be cruel and unfeeling. It once gave me such joy to see horrors such as *those* ignored," he said with a flourish of his hand to indicate the ring of charred men. "Now all I have to comfort me are my memories, and even *they* grow dim."

"We need to know where—" Tom began.

"Do something for me, would you?" the dark angel asked. "Kick one of them. I would know if there is even a spark left of my old power."

Tom turned from the angel. Were they all mad?

Grin walked over to one of the charred men and knelt beside him. "Were you angel or mortal?"

"Heavenly," the charred man said. "Divine."

"And your name?"

"I know it not. It's lost to me."

"Do you know why you're here? Or what this place is? What purpose it serves?"

"Yes!" the charred man cried. "I am damned. I was a scribe. I spoke out against the words of a critic. I felt I was unfairly judged. One night I came to my rooms, and I saw the *twins* waiting for me. I tried to run, but they caught me, took my life, and cast my soul here."

"How can I free you?"

"You can't," the charred man said. "I am here as carrion to Haborym."

"Who?" Malkiyyah asked. "The name is familiar."

"Haborym," the charred man repeated.

Tom looked down at him. Years of despair had settled on this man, perhaps even centuries. Yet there was something else in his voice. . . .

"He thinks he deserves his punishment," Tom said. "They all do. They're creating it." He looked around. "The Hungry Land and this one . . . They're the same. Or they were. I can feel it. The lands want to take hold of anyone who comes here and never let them go. But something happened in this place. A war was fought."

"There are many wars, many crusades, in our history," Malkiyyah said.

"Not like this one," Tom said.

"What are you talking about?" Grin asked. He rose from the charred man, who seemed content to drift back to his own private torment.

Tom felt his power rising within him once again, illuminating the darkness. "The Elven came here to take these lands, to bind them to their power and take their magic. But they lost. This land was changed. It died screaming and became something else."

"What?" Grin asked.

"A means to an end," Tom said. The words simply came to him now as his Power allowed him to untangle the web of dark secrets that had been placed within him when the Vessel died.

"You're not making any sense," Grin said.

"It makes perfect sense," Tom said. "The True Lands are dying. And the Scourge is beginning to take our world. Both our worlds."

"Yes," Malkiyyah said.

"And the reason for it is here," Tom said. "Somewhere in this city . . ."

The darkness that was his body was again powerful and capable of assuming any form he so desired. Abaddon had conspired with Lord Azazel to trick the child from the Human Worlds. They had created plan after plan, considering every possible contingency except one: the summoning of the beings who held ultimate power in the Realm.

Judging from their response when touching Tom Keeper, it was good that all of Abaddon's scheming with his former friend had gone to waste. Otherwise, Abaddon might have lost the only thing that mattered to him—his existence.

Until the moment the gods set upon him, he'd been certain that he had wanted to die. Anything would have been better than this solitary *amorphous* existence. But when faced with the very real possibility of oblivion, he suddenly began to cherish his life in a way he never did when he was flesh and blood.

Did Azazel know that the boy could destroy him so easily? It was clear that the *boy* did not.

That meant that either Azazel had played Abaddon for a fool with hopes of destroying him and linking his cursed land to all the others in this ancient plane, or he was simply a fool who would soon encounter a Power greater than even he could possibly have imagined.

"What to do, what to do," Abaddon whispered. Warn his former friend? Or sit back and wait to see what would happen if the Lord of the Damned was destroyed—without first transferring his duties to another?

His inclination was to sit back and revel in whatever happened. What did he care, so long as it no longer affected him?

The question that burned within his consciousness was a simple one: *Would* it affect him? Could he *afford* to stand by and do nothing?

As Abaddon weighed his options, a rumbling sounded within the heavens that were his body.

Far below, standing ever vigilant, though he scarcely knew or cared why, the Angel of Storms heard the sounds and reveled in them.

A moment later, they were forgotten, and his longing returned.

Twenty

AITAN AND KAYRIEL STOOD BEFORE LORD AZAZEL once more. This time, thousands of creatures crowded in to watch.

"Good day to you," Azazel said, nodding at his guests. "Not that the concept has any *meaning* in this place, but I don't wish to appear uncivilized, or uncharitable. Have you considered my generous offer?"

"We have," Aitan said.

"And I have an announcement," Kayriel added.

Azazel nodded. "Tell me."

Kayriel was about to speak when Aitan cut him off. "We decline your offer," Aitan said.

Azazel's tail rose and slammed against the dark earth. The ground shuddered and quaked for several long moments afterward.

Kayriel looked to Aitan in surprise. The shadowthing spit, "I thought we were *agreed.*"

"You were wrong."

"The time for discussion between the two of you is long past," Azazel warned. "I promised that I would give each of you reason to beg for the honor of taking my place.

Anzelm, since you are the one who seems to stand so firm in this, I will start with you."

Azazel opened his massive arms and drew a fiery Sigil in the air. He did this many times, until finally almost two dozen strange symbols hung in the air.

"Recognize any of these?" Azazel asked.

Aitan did not.

"Lord Azazel, please," Kayriel said. "There is no need for this. I am willing—"

"Of course there's a need," Azazel said. "I desire it."

Azazel gestured and the Sigils began to writhe in the air. Their odd lines and strange curves reconciled themselves into the bodies of golden angels.

"*Now* do you know what I have done in your honor, Aitan Anzelm?" Azazel asked. "Look closely. Listen to the timbre of their screams."

Azazel bathed the golden angels in a crimson light. The sound that came from them did not, at least to Aitan, seem at all reminiscent of wails of the damned. It was more like music, and the tune was familiar.

"Listen well," Azazel said.

The chorus rose up and suddenly Aitan knew where he'd first heard this arrangement. It had blessed the corridors and chambers of House Anzelm when he was only a child.

He looked up sharply at the two dozen angels who hung suspended in the air above, Azazel's light bringing them untold agony. He gasped, "My family . . ."

Azazel almost smiled. "Finding them among the millions who've been sent here wasn't easy. I know your story. You committed a great sin. Fell in love with the spirit of a woman brutally murdered. A human woman. Then you defied an edict to leave the killer to God's punishment. You took the murderer's life and his soul, sending it to the Torture Garden, a domain far darker than the Realm of Shadow. Your family paid the price for your indiscretion. But not the price you were told. . . ."

"Aitan," Kayriel said. "Let me end this. I am *willing* to take Azazel's place. He only needs one of us to agree to his terms. You can leave with him. See this nightmare no more!"

"No," Aitan said.

"The noble house of Anzelm," Azazel said. "Stripped of name and divinity, with no knowledge of who they were before. Tragically scattered throughout the Human Worlds to suffer lives of hardship. That is what they told you, isn't it?"

Aitan nodded.

"They lied. Sending them here, to me, was far easier. How would *you* ever learn the difference?"

Aitan stared in horror at those he'd loved so dearly. He could feel in his heart that these tortured beings were indeed his kin.

"I wanted to warn you," Kayriel said. "I tried."

"Now," Azazel said, "do you still think my offer so very cruel? I could give you the power to ease their torment, to defy the land. *Or* I could make you officiate over their damnation. I wonder how you would feel to have them staring at you, despising you for an eternity as you hurt them again and again."

Aitan sank to his knees despite himself, the sheer weight of the madness before him more than he could bear.

"*I* would take your throne," Kayriel said, stepping forward. "And I would do so gladly. I am of shadow. This land doesn't frighten me. It doesn't deaden my senses. It invigorates me." He turned to Aitan. "Have no worries, your kinsmen will be unharmed under my rule."

For a moment, Aitan couldn't bring himself to speak. Finally he rose to his feet and said, "There will be no rule for you. Not even in this place. I will fight you. No matter the cost."

"You can't mean it," Kayriel said. "You've already

won. Don't you see that? Leave me to this domain. I will make of it a heaven. That *is* in my power."

"You would say anything," Aitan said. "Anything at all, so long as it served your ends."

Kayriel turned to the Lord of the Damned. "Lord Azazel, I beg you. Your power is absolute in this place. Make him stand down. It's for his own good. And yours."

"*I'll* decide what's best for me," Azazel said. "Besides, this is amusing. You wish to be a ruler, Kayriel. Impress your will upon your first subject."

The shadowlord turned back to Aitan. "I've explained my ambitions to you," Kayriel said. "Let the worlds without wallow in ignorance. Let them all kill themselves and each other for all it matters to me. Don't you understand the cost of the burden I undertook? I read the forbidden tome. The secrets of the Mysts Arcana are mine, and I wish to God they were not!"

Aitan brandished his sword.

"Allow me some measure of peace," Kayriel pleaded.

"I intend to," Aitan said. Then he lunged at Kayriel!

Tom and his companions journeyed through the city. No one tried to stop them. Walking through a narrow alley, they turned and came upon a fantastic onyx waterfall. It took them a moment to see that the waters were actually being dragged backward and were climbing toward the walls of a fortress.

A voice came from behind them. "*That* is the palace of Azazel."

All three turned as one. An unholy creature stood before them. It had the curved tail of a scorpion, the body of a man, and the head of a goat. Armors made of silver covered its lower body and reached up to its ribs.

"Don't let my appearance disturb you," the creature said, gesturing at his strange body. "Formal wear. There's an event going on today, and I'm *loath* to miss it."

"Who are you?" Tom asked.

"Nybras, the unfortunate fool who accepted the thankless and unfortunately *impossible* task of dispensing pleasure in the pit."

"Azazel is the ruler of this city," Grin said.

"So he is," Nybras replied.

Malkiyyah gestured with his sword. He hadn't yet sheathed it in this darksome place. "Is this the way to Azazel's fortress? The waterfall?"

"Yes," Nybras said. "Step beneath the waters, and they will carry you into his presence. But you will not be doing that anytime soon."

Grin took a step between Tom and the creature.

Nybras didn't seem at all worried. "What you don't seem to realize is that despite what you might perceive as a kind of lethargy and chaos, there is an order and a purpose to this place. The land shares its desires with us. In return, we share a vision of what the city must remain."

"And what's that?" Grin asked.

"A prison. One in which dreams and hopes and distant memories torment us all. For we are the fallen, each and every one of us. We are the damned. And what would be the point of it all if we didn't inflict pain on the spirits entrusted to us? Then there is the matter of ravaging our own souls, in the vain hope that we might yet achieve a higher plane of existence."

"You wish to be free of this place," Grin said.

"We seek to *educate* it. To prove that we are worthy in sharing in the delights that are forbidden to us. Laughter, love, brotherhood . . . True, we may have embarked on an impossible enterprise, but we are immortal. What do we have to lose?"

"Let us be on our way and no harm will come to you," Malkiyyah said, his gauntleted hand coming to rest on the hilt of his sword.

"We seek what you seek," Nybras said, ignoring Malkiyyah's warning. "And that is *enlightenment*. But we do so in very specific ways. Come, that your lessons may begin!"

Suddenly, the waterfall vanished and the trio found themselves standing in a nightmarish grove. A collection of dark angels stood among twisting crimson vines, occasionally removing them from around their throats.

Tom could see the vines bulging in places, the subtle forms of hands or faces pushing through their surfaces.

Nybras went to the dark angels. "Gentlemen! Tell me of today's business."

"We must never forget to look at things from the point of view of the damned," a tall, thin angel said. "The *truly* damned, that is."

A colleague nodded grimly. "Our subjects expect much of us."

"Disappointing them is unthinkable," the third said.

Nybras shrugged. "I *have* sensed a certain ennui."

"No!" said one of the lesser angels.

"You do not say!" cried his companion.

"Really, I'm afraid it *is* so," said the tall angel. "There is a comfort in predictability. We must not allow our subjects a moment's release." The tall angel looked over to the visitors Lord Nybras had brought to them. "I see that we have been rude. Let us gather to welcome Lord Nybras's guests."

The dark angels bowed, one at a time, and began to introduce themselves, giving their names, ranks, positions, and latest achievements.

"This could go on all day!" Malkiyyah cried. "We have no time for this foolishness. We have dwelled too long in this place as it is."

"I agree," Grin said. "I can feel the land attempting to reach inside me."

"How do we get back?" Tom asked.

Nybras and the dark angels looked crestfallen.

"Don't they understand?" the tall angel asked. "We have forsaken the call of Azazel himself so that we would not fall behind in our duties. Ours is a sacred calling!"

"They understand," Nybras said petulantly. "But they don't *care*. I wonder what should be done about that?"

"We must punish them," the tall man said, a blade suddenly appearing in his hand. Weapons manifested from the darkness for each of the warriors.

Tom knew *exactly* what was happening. Nybras had been sent to keep them away from whatever was happening in Azazel's fortress. And forcing them to stay in the city even a moment longer than was necessary gave the land a better chance to lay its claim.

"At last," Malkiyyah said, brandishing his shining blade. It had been forged to burn brightly in even the darkest region of the pit and to forever sear away corruption in any form—or so the weaponsmaster who forged it for him swore. Over the years, the second statement had been put to the test, and had proven quite true. Now, it seemed, was the chance for Malkiyyah to test the first.

The warrior didn't notice the odd black tendrils reaching down from his boot and snaking into the ground.

"Grin—" Tom said.

"I saw it, too," the former emissary snarled.

"Malkiyyah wasn't with us when the Vessel died," Tom said.

"No, but he was in Abaddon, and that has served him well— until now."

Ahead, the tall angel used his blade to sever a handful of vines that had wrapped themselves around him. Shrieks sounded in the darkness as the crimson vines fell to the earth and slowly inched toward one another again.

Malkiyyah looked down and saw the roots that sought to bind him to the land. He swept at them with his sword, severing them, and teetered slightly as a strange weakness overcame him, if only for a moment.

"Go," Malkiyyah said. "I'll hold off this lot. By the blood of the Vessels, it'll be a pleasure..."

The dark angels surged toward Malkiyyah. He dived into their midst, slashing and thrusting with consummate skill. He fought with a ferocity born in the darkest and most dangerous corners of the True Lands and quickly cut the competition to pieces.

They re-formed.

"Hah!" Malkiyyah cried, parrying a thrust while striking with his gauntleted fist at the face of an opponent. "Do you really think *tricks* will stop me? I could battle the lot of you for *eternity*!"

The warrior angel laughed as he tore into his prey.

Grin turned to Tom and held out his hand. "We have to go now, while we still can. The way has been shown to us."

"But Malkiyyah—" Tom began. Then he saw it. The roots were springing from the warrior's legs and plunging deeply into the ground.

Malkiyyah made no move to stop them. He was so consumed by his passion for this endless battle that he no longer seemed to notice the vines linking him now and forever with the damned.

"How do we leave here?" Tom asked.

"The same way one gets from place to place in a Heavenly City. By wishing for it to be so. Nybras left a pathway open that we can follow if we move quickly."

Tom took one more look at Malkiyyah. The warrior was moving slower now. His lust for battle—and for life—was being drained from him. Soon, he would be like the rest of the damned, unable to experience anything that gave him pleasure in the outer world. Already, one of his enemies was practically past his defenses, and would soon be upon Grin and Tom.

"Now," Tom said, unable to watch this another moment.

Grin closed his eyes and willed it to be so.

* * *

In the darkness surrounding the City of the Abyss, thunder sounded. It rolled and pealed, sounding strangely like laughter....

Tom felt a sudden chill. He looked around and realized that they hadn't materialized near the upside-down waterfalls. Instead, they were in the middle of some grand courtyard. A darksome figure that was not quite so huge as Abaddon stood before a cold grey throne. But unlike the lord of the outer dark, *this* creature was made of flesh. And he seemed startled.

"Tom, look out!" someone cried.

A feeling of elation overcame Tom as he realized that Aitan's voice had been the one he'd heard. But suddenly, ice ripped through his chest, followed by an explosion of burning pain and a pressure on his skull. His legs refused to hold him upright any longer, and yet he didn't fall. Something was keeping him from falling. What?

Every instinct he possessed warned him not to look down, but he did it anyway.

An ebon sword jutted from his chest.

"Tom, no," a voice whispered from behind him. Komm Kayriel's voice. "I didn't mean—"

Tom fell forward. The lad sank to his knees, not really believing that this was happening. Hands were on him, keeping him from falling forward and impaling himself worse on the blade.

He thought of Kayrlis. Of the child she carried.

Then he thought of nothing at all....

Twenty-One

WHAT HAVE YOU DONE! THUNDERED AZAZEL'S voice. HE CAN'T DIE IN THIS PLACE!

Abaddon laughed. *Of course he can. And far better for him to do it in your city, a place from which I can withdraw, then here in my domain. To think that I was going to challenge him as the Keeper of the Keys.*

HE IS YOUR SHADOW, Azazel roared.

The latest standard-bearer to hold that title. And not the last. But certainly the most dangerous one to date.

MY CITY! Azazel screamed. EVERYTHING HERE WILL BE DESTROYED.

Only if you sit back and do nothing.

WHAT ELSE CAN I DO?

Give him to the land. It's the only way. He has the true blessing that Haborym once possessed. The land may well let him leave so that he can spread its darkness. In any case, it certainly can't hurt, now can it? Not compared with the alternative, that is.

IF THE END EVER COMES, I WILL FIND A WAY TO MAKE YOU SUFFER—

Spare me. You knew what he was. That's why you wanted me to engage him. To see me suffer in your place.

NEVER, I—

You can't lie to me, Azazel. You never could. Give him to the land. It's your only recourse. Now leave me. I have lands other than yours that are in need of a little attention . . . .

Aitan knelt beside Tom. The blade was out of him, but the wound it had left was terrible.

Grin stood above them. He had willed that he and Tom be taken from the shadowy grove to the waterfall. Instead, they'd been brought into the heart of a pitched battle between Aitan and Kayriel. Some other force had interfered with the magic he'd tried to employ.

Grin had an idea of who *must* be responsible. . . .

"What in the name of all that's holy did you do?" Grin asked, staring at the living shadow that was Komm Kayriel.

Kayriel nodded at Aitan. "He started it. Look up there."

Grin turned his gaze upward and saw the array of tortured angels.

"His family," Kayriel said. "The sight of them made him snap. He attacked me." The shadow looked down sadly. "Why would I want to hurt the boy? It's innocence like his that I want to protect."

"By becoming a god," Aitan murmured.

"If that's the only way, yes," the shadowthing said. "A god of even this Realm might well suffice for the challenge I must make."

"I knew you hadn't given up," Aitan said bitterly.

Kayriel pointed at Tom. "Forget about that for me. Don't let the lad suffer. End it quickly. Cleanly."

Aitan looked up to Azazel, who stared off at the darkness that was the horizon. "Lord Azazel!"

Azazel seemed startled. He turned his full attention to the little angel below.

"You said that no one could die in this place," Aitan said. "Is that true of Tom Keeper?"

"No," Azazel said. "He's not of this land. It's not a part

of him, and he is not a part of it. But if you consecrate him to the land, he will live."

"How do I know you're telling the truth?" Aitan asked.

"Because I wish for you to be grateful to me," Azazel said. "Or have you forgotten that I want something of you?"

Aitan Anzelm called upon an ancient incantation that he had learned in his youth. He touched his fingers to his lips, then placed them on Tom Keeper's forehead.

"To have you," Aitan whispered. "To keep you."

And it was done.

Komm Kayriel felt something flare within him. The last part of his essence, which had been granted to Aitan Anzelm in his youth so that he would live after a terrible fall, had just darkened. It was not fully corrupted. Not yet. But the act Anzelm had just performed had set him down the path to damnation.

Why that was so, Kayriel had no idea. But as much as he truly regretted whatever pain Tom Keeper still had to suffer, whatever travails he still had to endure, he was grateful to the boy. For without even trying, Tom Keeper had done something Kayriel had been unable to do despite all his machinations.

"You are consecrated to the land," Kayriel whispered, eager to see what would happen next.

Tom woke with a start. He looked down at his chest. There was no wound.

Bright sunlight bathed him. He looked around and saw that he was back in his old room.

In Keeper House.

In Hope.

"It's not real," Tom whispered. "None of this is real."

But God help him, it felt real. And he wanted it to be real.

His door opened and his barrel-chested father came blustering in. "There you are!"

"Papa," Tom said, the word leaving him like a living thing, with a yearning and a heartbreak all its own.

"So," Saul Keeper said. "Do you mean to sleep all day while the rest of us do your share of the labor?"

"I thought it was worth a try," Tom said, falling back into the old patterns with an ease that was both comforting and alarming.

"Well, too bad for you," Saul said, surging forward and grabbing Tom by the ankles.

"What—" Tom began. But then he was dragged to the end of the bed and hauled up in the air. His father shook him, and Tom laughed uncontrollably.

"I'm going to shake some sense into you!" Saul said.

Tom couldn't stop giggling. His father started singing an old tune and dancing around the room with him. Tom's hair dragged along the floor, but his head never touched the hard wood.

"All right, all right!" Tom shouted, grinning ear to ear.

His father stopped dancing around and held him still for a moment.

"An honest day's work for not a bit of pay!" Tom said. "That's what seems fair to me."

"I can accommodate you, lad!"

Tom put his hands on the floor. His father released his ankles. Tom walked on his hands to his bed, then tumbled into a sitting position.

"Seriously, now," Saul said. "I have to go meet a few of my friends. I need you to go down and help your brother and sister."

The words stung Tom. Before he'd left Keeper House, his father had revealed that he was a member of the Protestant underground.

"I don't think you should go," Tom said.

Saul Keeper's smile faded. "I love you, Tom. But I

won't have you telling me what I can and cannot do."

"No, I mean—" Tom groped for words. "I'm not feeling well."

Fear etched itself upon Saul's face. "You don't have a fever, do you?"

Tom's mother had been taken by the Scourge; its first sign was a fever.

"No, it hurts right here," Tom said, touching the spot where a sword had run him through. And suddenly, he felt the same agony that he'd endured when he'd been pierced by Kayriel's sword. Something hot and wet leaked from his chest, and suddenly he couldn't sit upright.

"Looks like you have a little cut," Saul said, kneeling over his son. "Nothing too serious. You had me worried for a moment."

Tom felt his blood draining away and knew in that instant that he was dying. The walls of his room became dark. He saw his father reaching for his chest.

"Is this where it hurts now?" Saul asked. His hands became long twisting roots which shot forward and pierced Tom's chest!

Tom screamed as his father became something *else*. Something that was stone and earth, tree and vine.

He was becoming the land.

Tom tried to force away the *thing* that was attempting to get inside him.

"No sense fighting," the land's Avatar said. "You were given to me. The angel who watches over you has been very generous indeed, pledging you to my service without so much as asking you first. Still, a promise is a promise, and it really doesn't matter who made it."

Tom felt his power rise up within him. The Avatar was telling the truth.

Suddenly, the creature screamed and withdrew from Tom. It looked down at its hand, which was withered.

"Another," it whispered. "Another like Haborym."

Tom wondered who the creature was talking about. He felt stronger now. His chest was whole once more. He sat up and the Avatar continued to back away from him.

"Haborym," it whispered, then it was gone.

The walls around Tom vanished. A near-limitless void surrounded him. A darkness that was almost alive.

"Abaddon?" Tom said.

There was no answer. Tom touched his ravaged chest. The wound remained, but the pain and weakness he'd felt were gone. He stood up and saw that a streak of crimson lay on the horizon. Tom looked down and saw that the land beneath him was shifting and changing. Wherever he stepped, the healthy soil turned black.

He took another step, wishing that he was not in any way touching the land that was, he suspected, the body of his enemy in this place.

And suddenly, he found himself walking on air. His heart felt light. Almost as if Kayrlis were near.

"Tom?"

Kayrlis's voice. It had come from behind him. He'd known, deep down, that the land would next try to use her as a weapon.

"What is it you want?" Tom asked. He didn't slow.

"If you'd turn around, I'd show you," Kayrlis said. Her voice was low and throaty. Playful.

Tom touched his chest again. The chain that had not been around his neck a moment ago was now in place. He touched the pendant his beloved had given him and felt the strength of their love course through him.

"You're not Kayrlis. You fooled me once because I wanted to be fooled," Tom said. "No more."

The voice behind him changed. It settled deeply in his mind. *There is no place for you to go. The light you see will never come any closer, nor will you ever reach it. This is your punishment. Your torment.*

It had been the voice of the flame guardian. But Tom

knew that it was not the being who had guided him. It was merely yet another of the land's desperate tricks.

"I don't want to be here," Tom said. "And you don't want me here. Do you?"

Silence.

Then the ground below him started to shake. Jagged lines appeared and sections of the land strained upward toward Tom. He rose higher in the air by simply willing it to be so. He kept himself apart from the land without difficulty.

Suddenly, the strange Sigils that had been painted upon his flesh in so many of his dreams appeared on his chest and arms.

NO! the land screamed. DO NOT TURN US AWAY. COME UNTO US, PLEASE. WE WERE WRONG TO TURN YOU AWAY. COME UNTO US THAT WE MAY SHARE THE FINAL SILENCE.

"I'm not ready to die, if that's what you're getting at," Tom said.

The land roared with rage. Fissures opened and boiling lava spit up at him. Tom rose higher still until the land could do nothing to harm him. The Sigils on his flesh grew more distinct. They burned bright red, like crimson coals.

Then another of Tom's Powers flared within him. The fire of truth could do more for him now than ever before. Rather than simply telling him when someone spoke a lie, it could reveal secrets, as well.

The land *wanted* to die. And if it couldn't have that, it wanted to strike back at any who would deny it release.

"Tell me about Haborym," Tom said. He'd heard this name so many times and sensed its importance.

THE ONLY ONE OF OUR KIND WHO EVER ESCAPED, WHO EVER BECAME MORE THAN AN ANGEL, YET LESS THAN A GOD. . . .

"What do you mean, 'your kind'?" Tom asked. "You're the land. How can the land become an angel?"

WE ARE NOT ONLY THE LAND. THOSE WHO

CAME. THOSE WHO DESTROYED. THEY ARE ONE WITH US NOW.

"The Elven," Tom whispered. "The ancient conquerors. Their souls are a part of you. How could that have happened?"

He kept walking. The glow in the distance was becoming brighter. He could see something at the center of it. An object that was shining and white.

A sword.

His heart felt about to break as he realized that it was his friend Malkiyyah's sword. The warrior was damned to live forever in this place.

The land spoke. IN THE WAR, THERE WAS PAIN AND DESTRUCTION. ALL WERE DYING. TO JOIN WAS THE ONLY WAY TO SURVIVE.

"But Haborym broke free," Tom said. "And he took a part of this land everywhere he went."

YES.

"Oh God," Tom said. "The Scourge. It's because of Haborym, isn't it? He took the poisons that are inside you, and he's spreading them."

THE DYING OF THE LIGHT IN THE WORLDS WITHOUT. THAT IS RIGHT.

Tom approached Malkiyyah's sword. It was close now. Close enough that he could take it, if only he reached for it.

But he couldn't. The voice of the land had fallen silent. Tom could feel that something had stilled it. Looking down, he saw that the land was now a withered husk. The part of it that was alive had retreated.

What could the land itself be afraid of?

A wind howled in the distance.

"You're here, aren't you?" Tom asked.

The wind kicked up and seemed to come alive in response. It hadn't occurred to Tom that there had been no air in this place or that he wasn't actually breathing until this very moment. He was not in a physical place. This was a domain of the mind.

Raising his hand before him, he realized that he wasn't even flesh. The skin he beheld was only an illusion. He was nothing but spirit. But to be able to conceive of himself as something more, he needed to see flesh, and so flesh had covered him.

Just as whatever was coming needed air to convince itself that it, too, had some kind of body.

"You're here, aren't you?" Tom asked. "Show yourself, Haborym. It's time."

The burning man appeared.

Twenty-Two

"So," Tom said. "What happens to me when I take the sword?"

The flame guardian opened his arms. *"You gain your third and final power, added to your ability to divine truth and see the future: The ability to burn away corruption in any form."*

"In other words, *Haborym*, you want me to take care of the mess you made."

"You know less than you think you do, Tom Keeper."

Tom felt his Power stir within him. The knowledge given to him by the Vessel about this angel was finally ready to give voice. "Haborym. Angel of Fire and Holocaust." He laughed. "I don't know what you're worried about. Spreading the Scourge. Destroying two worlds. It sounds to me like you're living up to your title."

The burning man was separated from Tom only by the sword. He flew forward in his anger, stopping inches before the weapon.

"This isn't just Malkiyyah's sword anymore, is it?" Tom asked.

"No," the flame guardian replied. *"No more than I am*

who and what you wish to call me or you *are what you believe yourself to be."*

Tom considered the flame guardian's words. "You said that if I was to do what needed to be done, I'd have to make a sacrifice. What is it—exactly—that I give up if I take the sword?"

"Your son," the flame guardian said, *"and any chance you might have had to save his soul."*

Tom recoiled. "But you said I'd get the power to burn away corruption. He's been corrupted. You said—"

"You will only be able to purify those you can touch. If you take up the sword, you won't live long enough to see your son."

Trembling, Tom said, "And if I leave the sword here for someone else?"

"There may not be anyone *else. There may not be time."*

"If I leave it," Tom repeated, "for somebody else..."

"The soul of your child may be saved. But the world he will inherit may not."

"Well," Tom said, hugging himself, trembling in the sudden cold of the void. "At least you don't make it hard on a fella." A ragged gasp escaped him. "I guess I only have one more question for you."

"Ask it."

Tom stared into the burning man's face. "Are you the land?"

Around him, the land exploded into flame. The burning man lost his shape and fell away.

Tom understood exactly what was happening. He had walked through the gauntlet of deceptions and seen through each one. But the final deception had contained enough elements of truth to deceive even his Power to divine honesty. Somehow, the land knew a great deal about the flame guardian's plans. And that in itself was terrifying to Tom.

TAKE THE SWORD! the land roared.

"Seeing as how it's causing you so much pain," Tom

said. "I don't mind if I do." His hand closed over the sword. Its power raced into him. But it was not the power the burning man had promised.

The power of the sword dragged him back to the physical world as it dissolved within him, sealing his wounds, and breathing life back into his cold body.

Aitan Anzelm gasped as he watched Tom's wounds heal. The boy shot up into his arms with a sharp intake of breath. They stared at one another for a moment, then Tom gripped the angel's arms and tried to stand. Aitan helped him to his feet.

"You're alive," Grin cried, shaking with relief.

Even Kayriel seemed pleased.

Tom surveyed the nightmare land into which he'd been delivered. All manner of man and beast—and some who were a little of both—stood at the outskirts of the arena. The towering giant Azazel had settled onto his throne, his massive wings outstretched. A chain of burning angels was drawn across the air above. Whenever Aitan looked to them, unimaginable grief creased his handsome features. Grin stood near Kayriel, watching the shadowthing anxiously.

"Are you all right?" Aitan asked.

Nodding, he pointed at the burning angels. "Those people . . ."

"My family," Aitan said.

"But you told me—"

"Lord Azazel says that I was lied to. My people were exiled here, where they will be tortured for an eternity. All for my sins."

Tom turned to Azazel and called to the behemoth, "*Is that Aitan's family?*"

Azazel merely smiled. "*An angel of truth come to test me. How quaint.*"

An angel? Tom thought. But he was human.

Wasn't he?

Tom leaned in close to Aitan. "He didn't answer my question."

"Of course not," Azazel roared. *"True torment comes from uncertainty, does it not?"*

"Tom!" Grin called. "Don't waste time here. Take Aitan and go!"

Tom shuddered. He had been warned that only Kayriel could take the stain of corruption from his unborn son. The land, pretending to be the flame guardian, said that even when—and if—Tom gained the fires of purity, he wouldn't live long enough to use them upon his child.

His Power to divine truth had revealed to him that neither of these statements were lies.

And yet . . .

Mithra had deceived him. Aitan's Patron had worn the flesh and form of another in order to test Tom in the use of his Powers. Mithra claimed this was possible because the flame guardian had appeared to him, and granted him the Power to deceive Tom, all in the name of the greater good.

Tom was no longer certain he believed that statement.

It was possible that some of what his Power had told him was truth was indeed lies. But as the flame guardian and Mithra had told him, faith was all important now. Faith . . . and the choices Tom would make.

Tom turned to Azazel. "I'm here to take someone back with me."

Azazel shook his head. *"No one leaves the Abyss of Punishment."*

"I can," Tom said. "And I will."

"Then stop talking about it and get on with it," Azazel said. *"You're beginning to bore me, and I* hate *to be bored."*

"I want an answer to my question first. The angels above. Are they Aitan's family?"

Leaning forward, Azazel plucked one of the angels from the air—and ate him.

Tom recoiled in horror. Aitan stumbled backwards and fell to one knee.

"Merciful God," Aitan whispered.

"There are no merciful gods here," Azazel said. *"But I can think of one that's feeling hungry. You'd best take your friend and leave while you can."*

Tom hesitated. It was almost as if Azazel wanted Tom to open the doorway to his world.

Why?

Suddenly, a vision overwhelmed Tom. He saw—

—the City of the Abyss enveloped in chaos. Azazel was gone, his throne empty, but Aitan and Kayriel remained. Untold suffering spread through the land. Aitan held his hand out to Kayriel. The shadowthing's essence flowed into Aitan. They became one.

And something more fearsome than Azazel took his throne. . . .

Tom forced the vision away. He understood its meaning. Lord Azazel meant to escape with Tom. His power in this place was second only to that of the land. Tom thought that he could choose whom he would take back with him. Aitan or Kayriel. But that choice was now beyond him.

He saw Azazel reaching for another of the burning angels and screamed, "Stop!"

The Lord of the Damned hesitated. *"You're still here?"*

"I challenge you," Tom said.

Behind him, Aitan, Grin, and even Kayriel chorused, "What?"

Azazel's smug expression faded. *"By whose authority?"*

"In the name of Shamash and Adad, I challenge you," Tom said.

"Don't do this," Azazel said, rising from his throne. *"You don't understand—"*

The Elven Ways: Ancient Games

"In the name of the land, I challenge you," Tom said evenly.

"Foolish child, you must not invoke the land. You must not!"

"Tom, you're not a warrior," Aitan said. "You can't—"

But it was too late. Both Azazel and Tom Keeper had vanished.

The war went badly. The land that more than a thousand warriors of God had come to bend to their will was ravaged. The great twisting walls that rose from the winding lush mountains in the distance were now shattered ruins. Castles and cathedrals had fallen, their defenders powerless to stop the land from shaking them to pieces. Torrents of burning lava had been spit from fissures in the earth like blood gushing from wounds. Some angels had been able to fly high enough, and quickly enough, to escape fiery deaths. Others had been reduced to charred husks. And those who had escaped did not avoid their destiny for long.

Yet . . . No one had *truly* died. That had been the greatest horror of all.

Despite the most grievous of wounds or even the complete immolation of their bodies, the warrior angels still lived, still moved—though many could do little but will their ashes to coalesce or flex the fingers of severed limbs.

The land that had been lush and green, the paradise long promised in the angels' holiest scripture, was now charred black. The sky, once a perfect blue with clouds formed from the breath of angels and rains that came from the tears of the Vessels—or so the conquerors had at first believed—was now a pale, lifeless backdrop, a canvas painted pure ivory so that a new image might grace it one day.

Screams rose up from all around. The land was *screaming*. And the tortured souls of those who should have been dead echoed the sounds.

Then a new sound came.

Footsteps.

Someone was still *alive* . . . .

Tom Keeper waited until the horrible wailing sank to a tolerable level, then he began walking. He felt a strength within him unlike any he'd ever known. Fire coursed through his veins. His heart was stone. His limbs fluid as the most gentle waters, and as powerful as the fiercest wave, leveling everything in its path. He saw with eyes that were green as the emeralds buried deep within the land.

And when he spoke, he knew, his words would have the force of the raging wind.

He was the land.

Tom walked through the wreckage of a war that should never have been fought. Greed and shortsightedness had fueled this conflict. There was a magic in these lands, a magic the Elven had desired.

They had come through a rippling portal high above, a gaping, blood red maw whose teeth were the banished, tortured souls the Elven had condemned.

The Ring of Punishment.

Tom crested a rise and saw a lone warrior standing in the valley below. The warrior stared up at where the portal had been, a look of betrayal and longing stitched across his luminous face.

Azazel.

Only here, he was different. He was not a god. Not yet. His skin was not charred, he had no wings, and he stood no taller than an average man. He wore emerald armors highlighted by crimson and gold. A pair of swords had been dug into the land at his feet, their hilts within his grasp.

Tom approached.

Azazel did not look at him. "What are you? The land? The land come to gloat? Come to make me like they are?"

Looking down, Tom saw the remains of Azazel's fellows. They were neither dead nor alive; even so, they continued to writhe. It was like this everywhere upon the small isle that had separated itself from the larger mass of which it had once been a part. The dark magics, the *disease* that infested it, would not spread to the outer regions thanks to its sacrifice. But the land had been left with a longing to be a part of something greater than itself once more. . . .

"Do you know why I was chosen to be an Emissary to these lands?" Azazel asked. "Because I counseled restraint. I suggested that we set aside lands of our own, where magic wouldn't be allowed for a hundred years, a thousand—whatever it took to restore to them what had been taken. My words were branded heresy, and I was made to come here."

Tom waited.

"And do you know the first thing that happened when our soldiers arrived in this place?" Azazel asked. "We encountered a female. Each of us saw her differently. She was the embodiment of beauty for us all. Hope and love . . . Why am I telling you this? You're the land. You know full well the story."

"Go on," Tom said, his voice causing thunder to rumble from all around them and harsh breezes to blow.

"She told us that all we could ever desire was here. This land would be our new home, grant our every wish. It asked only one thing in return: That we never leave."

"Yes," Tom said.

"The warriors I commanded laughed at this. They could feel the great magics of these lands. And they drew upon them." Azazel hung his head in shame. "I drew upon them, as well. We took the woman. And when we were done with her, we cut her body into pieces and ground her bones to dust. The pieces turned into golden and crimson fish. We were hungry. We ate them."

Azazel gestured at his emerald armor and the streaks of crimson and gold that lay upon it. "The land was inside of us. And that was when it began to rip us to pieces. All but me."

"*No,*" Tom said with the voice of the land. "*Another was spared. The warrior Abaddon.*"

"Spared," Azazel said, his dark eyes suddenly becoming fiery and alert. "Why?"

"*Do you really have no idea who I am?*" Tom asked. "*Or why I am here?*"

The angel stared at him blankly. Then he picked up one of the swords dug into the earth before him and tossed it to Tom. He retrieved the other sword.

"To grant me peace, I can only hope and pray," Azazel said.

The angel surged forward, sword flashing.

Twenty-Three

Tom raised his sword, fending off Azazel's attack with the power and finesse of one who'd been fighting all his life. He understood now that when he had taken Malkiyyah's sword and been healed by it, he'd also gained the warrior's knowledge and fighting spirit.

Azazel was a fine swordsman and a worthy opponent. Tom darted back, parrying thrusts, and deflecting carefully constructed attacks. He pressed forward and found it difficult indeed to catch Azazel unprepared for any of the stratagems he employed.

Their swords crashed together and their dance was more a celebration of life than an invitation to death for either warrior. Azazel spun and drove his boot into Tom's midsection. The lad fell back. Azazel brought his blade down, as if to cut Tom in half, but Tom raised his sword in time to deflect the blow.

Tom grabbed up a handful of dirt and tossed it into Azazel's face. The warrior angel stumbled back, and Tom barreled forward, butting him headfirst in the chest like a ram. Azazel's arms went back and Tom brought up the hilt of his sword, smashing it across Azazel's face. The angel's head snapped back. Tom pressed his advantage, bringing his sword across in a fast, sweeping arc that tore a bloody gash across the warrior's chest.

Azazel fell to the ground. Tom held back, waiting for the warrior to rise again upon his trembling legs.

He had called upon the power of the gods of this land, and now he wasn't quite sure how they had responded. Was the land around him nothing more than a phantasm created from Azazel's memories? Or had he actually been taken back to a point in history just after the fall of this land? Had he assumed the role the land itself had risen up and played long ago?

He didn't know. But he had to break Azazel's spirit. He had to convince the warrior angel not to interfere with his attempt to leave the Abyss.

"You won't show me mercy, will you?" Azazel said.

"What mercy would you have me deliver unto you?" Tom asked.

"Let me leave here."

"No."

"Then let me be alive and whole. Let those who accepted my command live once more, and not in this tortured half-life they endure now."

"They can have the existences they desire," Tom said. *"Lay down your sword and vow that you will never attempt to leave this place. Bind your soul to the land so that no matter your will, you can never leave."*

Azazel faltered. The sword fell from his hands and he clutched at his skull. "This is not as it should be."

Tom waited.

"A pact was made. I would sit upon the throne until I could find another foolish enough to take on that duty."

"That says nothing of ever leaving *the land."*

"No," Azazel said, his shoulders falling, his fiery soul surrendering to the charred spirit of the land. "It doesn't, does it? I will do it. I will give myself to the land."

Tom rose from the land. The strength it had given him

fell away. He understood now that his body had not been changed. He had worn something like a suit of armor constructed by the land, of the land—but it, and its corruption, was *not* within him. He was flesh and blood now, a mortal as he had been before.

Azazel was on his knees, clutching at the earth, tears— his *final* tears—leaving him as the land wove its way into his heart and soul. He didn't look up again until Tom was practically out of view. Then he saw some kind of portal open above Tom, and a land much like this one, only filled with a quiet that seemed like Heaven compared to the unending cries of this place, appeared and took him away. The portal closed, but Azazel imagined that he could still see it. In his mind's eye, the other land transformed into a world of light and life and beauty. He could hear nothing, but he was certain that there was laughter and love in that other land.

And soon, all he could remember of his battle with Tom Keeper, who had worn the armor of the land and had been protected from its hungers by the power of this world's gods, was that some Other existed in that mirror land high above in the sky.

If he only he could reach up and be with that Other, his torments would be over.

If only . . .

Tom felt reality close on him. He found himself standing in Azazel's courtyard once again. The Lord of the Damned had returned as well. Azazel sat upon his throne, brooding over the knowledge he had just gained.

"What happened?" Grin asked.

Tom shook his head.

Azazel finally spoke. *"It's all been a lie. What little hope I had . . . The Other . . . All a lie."*

Tom had his answer. The land had taken him back to the very beginnings of Azazel's torment and allowed him to alter the bargain Azazel had made with the land to serve as the city's ruler. Then, Azazel had been allowed to hope that perhaps someday he would leave this place. Now he understood that it was impossible.

"Leave here," Azazel said. *"I want you gone."*

Grin clasped Tom's shoulder. "You've won."

Tom looked up at the chain of burning angels. Aitan's family. Or was that another lie?

The choice was finally upon Tom. Would he take Aitan or Kayriel back with him? He'd been told that Kayriel had a way of saving the child within Kayrlis. But the shadowman was now in a fitting prison. It seemed that it was only a matter of time before the land sank its roots into any who stayed here, even those who had an element of the Vessel's power to protect them. Once Kayriel and the land were bound, there would be no hope for Kayriel of ever leaving this place. His madness would be contained.

The words of the flame guardian rose in Tom's mind.

"Not mere knowledge, nor mere action, but action with perfect knowledge, without any desire for its fruit and consecrated to God, is the path you must take toward your ultimate destiny."

But who was the flame guardian? The land had told him the story of Haborym, the angel who had somehow escaped this prison and gone abroad to spread pestilence and corruption wherever he went.

No. That could not be the flame guardian. Tom would never believe it.

The Strega taught that the guardian resembled the Settiano of their religion, a figure consecrated to activity, motivation, vitality, and the like. He was not a figure like the Lasa, dedicated to inner motivation and the subconscious. This was a being whose lifeblood was action and *feeling*. Emotion. Like that Tom held for his beloved Kayrlis and the child growing within her. To make the right choice,

Tom would have to put all logic, all reason aside, and act purely out of love.

And faith.

Tom turned and offered his hand to Komm Kayriel. The shadowthing was startled, actually at a loss for words.

"What are you doing?" Grin howled.

Aitan looked away sadly.

"Kayriel," Tom said, "your emissary, Lilith, put a spell of corruption on an unborn child. She said that you could lift that spell. That you could save the child. Is that true?"

The shadowthing spoke. "Yes."

"And will you?" Tom asked. "If I take you back, will you *immediately* perform this service for me?"

"To escape this place?" Kayriel asked. "Yes. Anything."

"A child," Grin whispered.

Aitan nodded. "The sacrifice of innocence. How they came to this land. My Patron would have known...."

Tom looked to his friends. "I have to do this."

"Yes," Aitan said.

"Forgive me?"

"I forgive you, Tom."

Tom looked to Grin. "And you?"

"I can't," the former Emissary said. "Not now. Not ever."

Tom turned his gaze away. He felt Kayriel's icy touch. Closing his eyes, he willed the two of them away.

Twenty-Four

IN THE WORLD OF MEN, ONLY SECONDS HAD ELAPSED since Tom Keeper left Kayrlis and the others. Lilith was laughing. Her beloved, Matthew, stared in shock at the grim face of the warrior angel Mithra, and the pained expression of the woman who knelt, doubled over, in the dirt.

"What's happening?" asked the fool who had followed Matthew down the tower.

"A Mystery Play!" Lilith said. "Don't you think it's a glorious day for a little entertainment?"

"Lilith, we must bow before the divinity," Matthew said imploringly.

"No," Mithra said. "That will *not* be necessary." The angel walked close to Matthew. Another stood behind the Curacas.

"But what's going on?" asked the jowly Avram.

"Silence now and forever," Mithra said.

Avram fell silent. Trembling, he turned and ran away. No one bothered to stop him.

He would never speak again.

Matthew did not look up at the angel. Instead, he recited, " 'In whom the god of this age hath blinded the minds of them who believe not, lest the light of the glorious gospel of the Vessels, who are God, should shine upon them.' "

Mithra laughed. "So *this* is the man for whose love you destroyed perfect innocence," Mithra said. "He seems ... pious. But other than that, hardly worth the effort. Perhaps I should take him to the Kingdom."

"No!" Lilith cried. "Get away from him! There's more I can do. More havoc that I could wreak, more pain that I could bring. So much more!"

Matthew looked up at the woman he cherished as if he was seeing her for the first time. "Lilith?"

"You would threaten me?" Mithra asked. "You flatter yourself, Lilith." Mithra shrugged and a dozen fiery blades burst into reality and sailed toward Lilith. She screamed as they came within inches of her flesh—and stopped, forming a cage about her.

"Divine magic can kill her," Mithra said to Matthew. "You're a man of the word. Perhaps you can tell me why this is so."

"Their magic can kill anyone," Lilith protested.

Mithra shrugged. One of the fiery blades leaped from her and sailed toward Matthew's chest.

"Don't!" she cried.

The blade stopped. "Ah," Mithra said. "So you *did* work some element of your corrupted essence into him, after all."

"I'll touch the blade," Matthew said. "I'm not afraid."

"Now there's an adventurous spirit," Mithra said.

"No," Lilith said. "You don't understand."

Matthew reached up and wrapped his hand around the blade. Pain exploded within him! He shuddered, but he did not let go of the fiery weapon. Then its light faded and his agonies ceased.

He thought of the acts he'd committed with Lilith, which he'd been musing over with secret pleasure only a few moments before, and felt sickened.

"No," Lilith said. "You love me. You said it."

Mithra turned to her. "I had to burn away the corruption you'd placed in him. Now he sees—"

"NO!" she screamed.

"Silence. Now he sees what you are and what you sought to make him. It had to be done."

Kayrlis looked up. "Can you save my child?"

Mithra shook his head. "Matthew's corruption was very slight. Your child has no innocence left within him. All I could do is end his life."

Matthew began to weep. "Forgive me, lord. Forgive me..."

Casually, Mithra said, " 'That ye may be blameless and harmless, the son of God, without rebuke, in the midst of a crooked and perverse nation, among whom ye shine as a light in the world.' "

"Thank you," Matthew sobbed. "Thank you..."

Mithra smiled. "Honestly, Lilith. I don't know what you saw in him anyway. Except, perhaps, what you *wanted* to see. Hmmmm. I wonder if you were guided, as well. Tricked into feeling something for this man. We have enemies. That is possible."

"I love him," Lilith said. "No one made me feel anything."

"Perhaps. Perhaps not. It doesn't matter, everything worked out in the end. The portal was opened, just as had been foretold, and Young Master Keeper went through to perform a task that was inevitable, no matter the circumstances or the motivation. Fate cannot be altered."

"What are you saying?" Kayrlis whispered. "Kill her for what she did to me! Damn you, kill her!"

Mithra smiled. "Watch *who* you say those words to. They could lead to even greater troubles for you." He looked back to Matthew. "Honestly, Lilith, I just don't see it. He is an unremarkable specimen, other than his innocence, which I *could* view as a feast for one like you."

"If she may not, then I'll damn you," Lilith said.

"Amusing," Mithra replied. "Just keep in mind, your part in this is done. Whether you live or die is inconsequential to what happens next."

"What are you talking about?" Kayrlis asked. The pain within her was ebbing. All she felt now was a dull ache.

"What am I talking about?" Mithra asked with a grand flourish. "That!"

Suddenly, a light began to shine beside Kayrlis. . . .

Tom found himself enveloped in shadow.

"I'll spare you the worst of this," Komm Kayriel whispered. "It's the least I can do."

The lad could remember nothing of his journey to the Realm of Shadow. But leaving that place was proving to be agony. Why? He was certain that he had taken none of the land's corruption with him. And the land had not yet been able to dig itself inside the body of Kayriel. Why was this happening?

"Where are we?" Tom asked.

"Between the worlds." Kayriel hesitated. "I have a confession. I've slowed down our little journey so that I might have a word with you before we return to your land."

"Just take me there," Tom said. "I don't want to hear anything you have to say."

"Of course you don't," Kayriel said. "That's why I can't afford to give you a choice in this. You either listen to me, or we will never reach our destination."

"Say what you have to, then."

"You think of me as evil, don't you?"

Tom was silent.

"I wish to spare the world suffering," Kayriel said. "I don't want the Human Worlds to become like the Abyss. And that will happen, given time. Your world was once filled with magic. Impossible creatures roamed the lands. All the old stories, the myths, the fables . . . All were *true*.

"Then a time came when the land had to sleep. And the

creatures you would think fantastic faded, one by one, and the magic seemed to wane. An age of reason was dawning. It would have been bloody, horrible, yet marvelous. But my people came. And they sent your race rolling back in the years instead of forward. Worst of all, they woke the land from the slumber it required. It's too soon for a second age of magic in your world. The land isn't ready yet. And even if it were, the magic belongs to mankind. It is man's to share—or to withhold. Man's decision. Not ours.''

From somewhere close, Tom heard Lilith's voice.

"Behold," she said. "An angel come to free us of our earthly torments."

"You're saying that you care about our world, our people," Tom whispered. "What's to stop all that from changing when you become a god?"

Komm Kayriel laughed. "You."

Another voice came from the darkness. It was Tom's beloved. "Can you save my child?"

Tom gasped.

"Don't worry," Kayriel said. "I will honor my promise to you."

Suddenly, a shimmering light burned away Kayriel's darkness. Tom raised his hand to shield himself from the light—

—and then he was back in the mortal lands. Harsh winds closed on him. The glare of the sun was in his eyes. But he could see the spire before him. And other shapes.

He had returned to Genesis.

Tom's vision cleared, and he saw the living shadow approaching his beloved.

"I don't believe we've ever met," Kayriel said. "I'm the one who will take your husband from you."

Kayriel's hands shot out. One grasped Kayrlis's shoulder, anchoring her in place. The other touched her belly. Tendrils of darkness disappeared inside her.

"Tom, it's so cold, so *cold!*" she screamed.

Kayriel withdrew. He turned to Tom and said, "Remember that I have *not* lied to you."

Tom knelt before Kayrlis and drew her into his arms. "Are you—"

"It's better," she whispered. "What Lilith put in me is gone. I can feel that it's out. It's gonna be all right. It's—"

She drew back from him suddenly. "Kayrlis, what's wrong?"

Then he felt it. His body was burning up. He raised his hands before him and they burst into flame.

Kayrlis screamed. The others could do nothing but watch as the fires raged through Tom. But he felt no pain. The god that Tom had always believed in was *not* a cruel god. He was instead a god of love, who demanded faith, but would never ask for a sacrifice from His follower as proof of fealty.

That was the lesson Tom had to learn so that he could inherit his final Power. But with that Power came duty.

The shadowthing laughed. "Oh, you *do* have a choice on your hands, don't you?"

The fires went out and Tom looked down to see that he was holding Malkiyyah's sword.

Kayrlis came to him. "Tom, what happened?"

"The third Power," Tom said. "To burn away corruption in any form. It's mine now."

He looked to Kayriel. The sword Tom carried was nothing more than an extension of his will. He could destroy Kayriel with a touch.

"I won't run from you," Kayriel said. "Do it, if that's what it takes to satisfy Him. Kill me even though I behaved honorably to you and saved the soul of your child. End my existence when you *know* that all of what I said to you on our journey here was true. Go on. Do it."

Tom felt overwhelmed. To be given a Power such as this—to win it by surrendering himself entirely to love—and then to be expected to do something like this . . .

The lad looked to Mithra for guidance, but the warrior angel was watching him warily.

Why?

Tom felt a horrible suspicion rise up within him. He raised the sword and took a step toward Komm Kayriel.

Mithra gestured quickly, and a fireball exploded into existence over Kayrlis's head.

"Far enough," Mithra said. "Stay where you are, or your beloved dies."

Twenty-Five

Tom felt a desperate need to make sense of Mithra's betrayal. "The burning man appeared to you. You told me that!"

Mithra nodded. "But I don't have to do what he says, now do I? I have my own goals. Much as it repulses me to join forces with a creature like Kayriel, that is what I must do."

"But I had a choice," Tom said. "I could have brought back Aitan. You said that you wanted me to bring him back!"

"Had you tried it, you would have found the task impossible. That's my fault, of course. The true reason why I masqueraded as Juno Meazzi? To have time near you when you suspected nothing of my true nature. So that I could work my art upon you."

"You're a renegade angel," Tom said. "One of the damned."

"Nothing so simple as that," Mithra said. "You'll understand one day. For now, stay where you are and *don't* interfere."

"This is for the best," Kayriel said. "I don't think

you're ready to become a murderer yet, Tom. No matter how righteous the cause."

The shadowthing turned his back on Tom and gazed at Matthew.

"What are you?" Matthew asked.

Kayriel's shadowy form vanished for only a second. He allowed Matthew to look upon him as he had once been.

"Komm," Matthew whispered.

"Yes," Kayriel said. "The one who guided you through the True Lands and shared adventures with you that eased the pain and loneliness we both felt. Komm Kayriel. Now, I have a question for you. Do you trust me?"

Perfect innocence still shone in Matthew's eyes. "With my life."

Lilith screamed, "Matthew, you don't know what you're saying!"

He fell to his knees and closed his eyes. "Of course I do."

"Matthew," Kayriel said. "I thought we had an understanding about this kneeling business."

"Of course," Matthew said. He rose to his feet.

"If you're on your knees, it's harder for me to do *this*," Kayriel said. He reached out with his shadowform, transformed his hand into a scythe, and raked the weapon through Matthew.

"NO!" Lilith cried. "Keeper! Do something!"

Tom wanted to. But he knew it would mean Kayrlis's death. He was trapped.

Ahead, the Curacas stood before the shadowlord, trembling with untold agony.

"How could you?" Matthew whispered. "You were my friend. I dedicated my life to following your edicts, to reflecting your purity—"

"And now you can reflect my darkness," Kayriel said, tearing the scythe through him again.

"Kayriel!" Tom screamed.

The shadowthing looked back. "I know you're upset. But I had to do *something* with all that corruption dear Lilith placed inside your son. Now didn't I?"

Tom realized his mistake. Kayriel's goals might have been noble enough. But he was insane and would stop at nothing to achieve those goals.

Not even the destruction of the worlds he said he wished to save. . . .

Tom watched as Matthew fell to the ground, shaking. When he looked up again, his eyes were black and his face was blistered. Lilith screamed, but could not move from the cage of fiery blades that Mithra had built around her.

Kayriel muttered a few words in an ancient language, and the portal to the Realm of Shadow opened once again.

"Don't worry too much about this, Tom. You have another task before you," Kayriel said. "Retrieve Aitan Anzelm."

Tom stared at it the portal in horror.

"Come, now. You know I need him. If he stays in Shadow, I can never attain my goals."

"Aitan would never want me to bring him back just to help you."

"Good point." Kayriel looked over to Mithra. "Old friend, do you have any ideas?"

"I do," Mithra said. He gestured and the portal vanished.

Relief flooded through Tom. "I knew you couldn't be with him. Not really."

"Really?" Mithra asked. "Look up."

He did.

"Heavenly mother," Kayrlis whispered.

The portal had fled to a place in the sky, and it was growing. In seconds, darkness stretched over the land as the portal descended greedily upon the entire settlement of Genesis.

Mithra tapped on the steel spire next to him. "You're

not a stupid lad, Tom. I believe you can figure out what you must do. And what will happen if you don't.''

The angel gestured again. The ball of flame hanging over Kayrlis's head vanished. Another gesture, and the daggers holding Lilith in check also disappeared.

"I believe it's up to you to get us out of here now," Mithra said to Kayriel.

"Of course," the shadowlord said, touching Mithra's shoulder. Darkness enveloped them, and they were gone.

Lilith ran to Matthew's side. He was laughing now. A chattering, insane laughter. The laughter of one who was damned.

Tom tugged at Kayrlis's hand and took a step in the direction of the tower. "Come on," he said. "We don't have a lot of time...."

In a simple house on the main street of Genesis, a man sank to his knees and prayed for deliverance. His name was Robert Maslin. He had been among the first to see the darkness approaching from on high. It had come without warning and blotted out the sun.

Judgment was upon them. There could be no other explanation.

When Robert had looked into the darkness he had seen shapes that nearly made his mind collapse. He knew then that descending upon Genesis was a thing filled with unimaginable evils. He'd *felt* those evils, too. They whispered to him. Taunted him.

The angels send the damned to us. We punish them. Brand them with eternal flames. Have you sinned, Robert Maslin? Do you feel a need to be cleansed of your own darkness through pain? Let us into your heart. We will see that you suffer well for your crimes....

Robert had sinned. He had coveted the wives of others, he had cheated and stolen.

But he didn't want to die. And he didn't want to burn in the pit.

In fact, Robert wanted nothing more than to hide in the cellar of his home. To pray that he would not be found by the darkness. But he couldn't. An urge had risen within him that was stronger than the fear brought about by the loathsome voices reaching down from the darkness.

He left his house and found dozens of other people who had also taken to the street. In minutes, there were hundreds.

Each felt a compulsion they could not understand or deny. They walked, as one, toward the great spire in the distance.

The Spire of Truth.

All could see the two figures who raced up its stairs, toward the darkness that had settled almost to the spire's apex.

In the coming days, only a few would deny what they knew in their hearts to be true. Those few would argue that it was a pair of angels who ascended the spire and fought the darkness that had come to claim them all. It couldn't have been a simple man and his wife.

Magic had been wielded. The angels had sworn that mortals could never wield such forces.

But the others would know the truth. And they would speak.

Of this, and of other revelations. . . .

Tom and Kayrlis ran up the stairs.

"The only way to close the portal is to fulfill the charter for which it was summoned," Tom said, calling again upon the reserve of knowledge the dying Vessel had granted him. "We have to go into Shadow and bring back Aitan and Grin."

"But—"

"If two of us go in, we can each take one of them out. It's the only way to keep the portal from taking us *and* everyone in Genesis."

"I figured all that," Kayrlis said. "Why do you think I'm so damned scared?"

They reached the deck at the top of the spire. The darkness was closing fast.

"Whatever you do, whatever you see," Tom said, *"don't* let go of my hand."

"Don't worry," Kayrlis said, her entire body quaking with anticipation of what would happen next.

The darkness descended upon them and swallowed them whole.

Tom opened his eyes. This time, he'd been taken directly to the City of the Abyss. The courtyard of Azazel was empty but for the Lord of the Damned and Nybras.

Kayrlis clasped Tom's hand so hard that it hurt.

"Master Keeper!" Azazel said. *"You've decided to come back and grace us with your presence one last time! To what do we owe the honor?"*

"I've come for Aitan Anzelm and Lord Skalligrin."

"Of course! But first... Who's your lovely companion?"

"She's—"

Azazel forced a smile, revealing caverns of sharpened, needlelike teeth. *"You did tell her what generally happens to females in this land, didn't you?"*

Kayrlis trembled, but to her credit, she did not turn her gaze from the dark lord, nor did her defiant expression falter.

"Aitan and Grin," Tom announced. "They're near. I wouldn't have been brought to this place if they weren't."

"Of course," Azazel said triumphantly. *"Behold."*

The angels appeared. Aitan stared at Tom with hollow

eyes. Grin sat upon the ground, head lolling, the life all but gone from him.

Twisting roots had grown from their flesh and sank deep into the ground. Tom felt a cold fist of terror close on his heart.

"What's going on?" Kayrlis asked.

"The land," Tom whispered. "It's alive. And it's inside them. It's corrupted them."

"Your Power's to burn away corruption," Kayrlis said. "That's what—"

"I know," Tom said.

Azazel unfurled his wings. *"Perhaps I should tell her, Master Keeper."*

Tom was silent, desperately attempting to judge if the power within him could meet this challenge.

"You see," Azazel said, *"Tom's power is untried. He may be able to burn away the corruption that is now inside his friends, but at what cost to them? Or himself?"*

Kayrlis turned back to Tom. "You have to try. I'm with you. I won't ever leave. Just try."

Tom shuddered. "This is where the Scourge came from. If I take Aitan and Grin back, and they're carrying any part of this place with them—"

Kayrlis looked up at the dark lord. "Why are you doing this?"

"I'm doing nothing," Azazel said. *"Mithra set this into motion. I'm merely enjoying the diversion."*

She pointed at Aitan and Grin. "You gave them to the land."

"The land is hungry. I couldn't stop it from taking those two any more than I could ever bring myself to leave this place. Not after the conditions placed on me by your beloved."

"Tom?" Kayrlis asked.

"Not now," he said, struggling to make his decision. He

looked to Azazel. Then he gazed at the sky. Rolling ebon clouds coalesced into the form of Abaddon. Both breathlessly awaited his decision.

"She's right, you know," Abaddon said. *"You really must try to save your friends. It's not a simple matter of sacrificing only the people of Genesis. The portal won't be satisfied with simply consuming one settlement. It will spread until its darkness overcomes your world and the True Lands. Beyond, as well."*

Azazel nodded. *"Both worlds will be cast into the pit either way. One will take longer than the other, that's all."*

It was a trap. Tom *knew* that. Even if he succeeded in freeing Aitan and Grin from the corruption of the land, he would be punished in some way for his trespasses against the lords of the inner and outer Abyss.

"Just remember," Kayrlis said, her hand resting in his, "that I'm with you. No matter what happens, how I feel about you won't change. My strength with yours. Do what you have to do."

The ground trembled, anxious for the chance to feed on the hopes and fears of the newcomers.

Tom took a step in Aitan's direction. "Don't touch either of them," he warned Kayrlis.

"Like I said before, don't worry . . ."

Tom settled his hand settled against the cool flesh of Aitan Anzelm's cheek.

Then he felt it—the cold fire rising up within him. His flesh burst into flames. Kayrlis gasped.

"It won't hurt you," he whispered, though honestly, he wasn't certain of that.

Tom felt the final Power he'd been granted. It overwhelmed him. Someone else touched his hand.

Grin.

Suddenly, memories that were not his played out before him. He was born, he lived, and he died a dozen times over, then a dozen times after that. He was

—*a warrior who sired a child named Aitan*

—*an artist whose work was destined never to be appreciated by anyone other than his loving cousin, a fellow outcast from House Anzelm*

—*a politician who stood by his beliefs until his bloody and brutal end*

Tom knew what was happening. The lives he was experiencing belonged to Aitan's family! Azazel had seared the remnants of Aitan's loved ones into the angel. Branded his soul with them. Tom, in his efforts to burn away the corruption of the land, was destroying them, one at a time.

With Grin, it was different. Tom found himself experiencing all of the memories that had caused Grin to doubt the sanity and reason of the Vessels. Experiencing them— and burning them away. If he did not stop, he would find himself facing a zealot who knew his secrets and would not rest until his heresy was expunged from existence!

"*Everything comes at a price,*" Azazel said. "*This is mine.*"

"*And mine,*" Abaddon said from above.

Tom was about to pull away from the angels. Kayrlis sensed it and moved to stop him.

"No," she said, placing her hand over his and Grin's. "You have to keep going."

"Kayrlis—"

"I don't care whose side Mithra was on," she hissed. "He told you that it was all a matter of faith, and I don't have to own some divine Power to know that of all the things he was saying, that much was true. Believe in yourself, Tom. The way I believe in you."

Tom thought of all the people who would suffer if the lands of his home and those of the True Lands came to this place. He couldn't allow it. No matter the cost.

And the only way to stop it was to fulfill the charter

Komm Kayriel had set for him and bring Aitan Anzelm back to the mortal plane.

"I'm sorry," Tom said, and pressed on.

He watched the lives of the burning angels pass into nothingness. He experienced the knowledge that Grin had gained over years of service to a mad god.

Then it was over. Exhausted, he fell away from the angels, though Kayrlis never released her grip on his hand. He saw that Aitan and Grin had been restored. But there was a sadness in Aitan's eyes and a confusion within Grin that quickly turned to hatred.

"Whatever your problems are with me, we have to leave now," Tom said. "Right now."

The angels nodded and came toward him.

Then a voice called, "NO. NOT YET."

Everyone looked up. The chain of burning angels was once more in the sky. But they were no longer in torment.

Tom had not destroyed them at all. Instead, he had set them free!

"KNOWLEDGE," one whispered, as he gestured to Grin. "KEPT SAFE FOR YOU."

The former Emissary buckled as the angel worked a strange magic on him, and his memories were restored.

"No!" Abaddon said. *"I won't permit this."*

"YOU HAVE LITTLE CHOICE," another of the angels said.

At once they vanished.

Azazel stood. *"All of you will pay for this!"*

"No," Tom said. Malkiyyah's sword appeared in his hand. Tom knelt and buried it in the land. There was a roar as fingers of pure white flame rippled through the earth and raced toward Azazel. Fissures opened in the land and thousands of beings rose, freed from their torments, burning with the blazing white light of purity.

They flew to Azazel, who backed away from them, and quickly realized that he had nowhere to go.

Tom grasped Aitan's hand. Kayrlis took Grin's.

They were away mere seconds before lightning raced through the palace of Azazel and brought it down around the Lord of Darkness.

Epilogue

THE PEOPLE OF GENESIS HAD WATCHED AS THE PORtal of darkness had exploded into one of light, and a city of darkness fell before the will and goodness of a single man of faith. They saw the sky restored and watched as the man and his beloved helped a pair of weakened angels down the Spire of Truth's staircase.

"Lilith, Matthew," the man had whispered upon reaching the shadows at the base of the spire. He'd looked around, but seen no trace of those he sought. An expression came upon his strong face that said perhaps this was for the best.

The strangers were given food and a place to rest.

And it was in this place, the home of the newly devout Robert Maslin, that one of them, the woman, looked out the window, to the sky, and saw that it was far from over.

"Tom," Kayrlis cried. "You have to see this. Look!"

He came to her side. The angels crowded in around them.

In the sky, a ring of winged men flew over the city. They looked like the visions of angels from books long forbidden, yet somehow not forgotten.

Other beings appeared in the air. Horses with wings, others with the torsos of winged men.

And at their center, a single being who defied description. Who appeared different to each who gazed upon him.

Tom had seen this being's like before. The words of the renegade angel Mithra rang in his head. Tom had asked the angel to name his true adversary.

You have a journey to make, Young Master Keeper. When it is over, it will fall to you to name that enemy. I can't do it for you.

Now Tom knew who it was. "The Fourth Vessel," he whispered. The keeper of God's creativity.

A being who had gone irrevocably mad. And even at this distance, Tom sensed why this was so.

There was another within the Vessel. A being the Vessel had attempted to destroy before he spread his madness and pestilence across two words.

The Angel of Holocaust.

Haborym.

"Tom," Kayrlis whispered.

"I see it," Tom said.

Everyone in Genesis saw it. The Fourth Vessel had pointed in their direction. Then He and the creatures He had created as his heralds, slowly descended to the earth....

to be concluded in
The Elven Ways, Book 3: Night of Glory

AVONOVA PRESENTS
MASTERS OF FANTASY AND ADVENTURE

BLACK THORN, WHITE ROSE   77129-8/$5.99 US/$7.99 CAN
edited by Ellen Datlow and Terri Windling

SNOW WHITE, BLOOD RED   71875-8/$5.99 US/$7.99 CAN
edited by Ellen Datlow and Terri Windling

FLYING TO VALHALLA   71881-2/$4.99 US/$5.99 CAN
by Charles Pellegrino

THE IRON DRAGON'S DAUGHTER   72098-1/$5.99 US/$7.99 CAN
by Michael Swanwick

THE DRAGONS OF THE RHINE   76527-6/$5.99 US/$7.99 CAN
by Diana L. Paxson

TIGER BURNING BRIGHT   77512-3/$6.50 US/$8.50 CAN
by Marion Zimmer Bradley, Andre Norton and Mercedes Lackey

THE LORD OF HORSES   76528-4/$5.99 US/$7.99 CAN
by Diana Paxson

Buy these books at your local bookstore or use this coupon for ordering:

Mail to: Avon Books, Dept BP, Box 767, Rte 2, Dresden, TN 38225   E
Please send me the book(s) I have checked above.
❏ My check or money order—no cash or CODs please—for $_____ is enclosed (please add $1.50 per order to cover postage and handling—Canadian residents add 7% GST).
❏ Charge my VISA/MC Acct#_____ Exp Date_____
Minimum credit card order is two books or $7.50 (please add postage and handling charge of $1.50 per order—Canadian residents add 7% GST). For faster service, call 1-800-762-0779. Residents of Tennessee, please call 1-800-633-1607. Prices and numbers are subject to change without notice. Please allow six to eight weeks for delivery.

Name_____
Address_____
City_____ State/Zip_____
Telephone No._____   FAN 0197

RETURN TO AMBER...
THE ONE *REAL* WORLD, OF WHICH ALL OTHERS, INCLUDING EARTH, ARE BUT SHADOWS

ROGER ZELAZNY

NINE PRINCES IN AMBER	01430-0/	$5.99 US/$7.99 Can
THE GUNS OF AVALON	00083-0/	$5.99 US/$7.99 Can
SIGN OF THE UNICORN	00031-9/	$5.99 US/$7.99 Can
THE HAND OF OBERON	01664-8/	$5.99 US/$7.99 Can
THE COURTS OF CHAOS	47175-2/	$4.99 US/$6.99 Can
BLOOD OF AMBER	89636-2/	$4.99 US/$6.99 Can
TRUMPS OF DOOM	89635-4/	$5.99 US/$7.99 Can
SIGN OF CHAOS	89637-0/	$4.99 US/$5.99 Can
KNIGHT OF SHADOWS	75501-7/	$5.99 US/$7.99 Can
PRINCE OF CHAOS	75502-5/	$5.99 US/$7.99 Can

And Don't Miss

THE VISUAL GUIDE TO CASTLE AMBER
by Roger Zelazny with Neil Randall
75566-1/$15.00 US/$20.00 Can

Buy these books at your local bookstore or use this coupon for ordering:

Mail to: Avon Books, Dept BP, Box 767, Rte 2, Dresden, TN 38225   E
Please send me the book(s) I have checked above.
❏ My check or money order—no cash or CODs please—for $_____is enclosed (please add $1.50 per order to cover postage and handling—Canadian residents add 7% GST).
❏ Charge my VISA/MC Acct#_____Exp Date_____
Minimum credit card order is two books or $7.50 (please add postage and handling charge of $1.50 per order—Canadian residents add 7% GST). For faster service, call 1-800-762-0779. Residents of Tennessee, please call 1-800-633-1607. Prices and numbers are subject to change without notice. Please allow six to eight weeks for delivery.

Name_____
Address_____
City_____State/Zip_____
Telephone No._____   AMB 0197

Avon Books Presents
THE PENDRAGON CYCLE
by Award-Winning Author
Stephen R. Lawhead

TALIESIN
70613-X/$6.50 US/$8.50 Can

A remarkable epic tale of the twilight of Atlantis—and of the brilliant dawning of the Arthurian Era!

MERLIN
70889-2/$6.50 US/$8.50 Can

Seer, Bard, Sage, Warrior…His wisdom was legend, his courage spawned greatness!

ARTHUR
70890-6/$6.50 US/$8.50 Can

He was the glorious King of Summer—His legend—the stuff of dreams.

PENDRAGON
71757-3/$6.50 US/$8.50 Can

Buy these books at your local bookstore or use this coupon for ordering:

Mail to: Avon Books, Dept BP, Box 767, Rte 2, Dresden, TN 38225   E
Please send me the book(s) I have checked above.
❑ My check or money order—no cash or CODs please—for $_____ is enclosed (please add $1.50 per order to cover postage and handling—Canadian residents add 7% GST).
❑ Charge my VISA/MC Acct#_____Exp Date_____
Minimum credit card order is two books or $7.50 (please add postage and handling charge of $1.50 per order—Canadian residents add 7% GST). For faster service, call 1-800-762-0779. Residents of Tennessee, please call 1-800-633-1607. Prices and numbers are subject to change without notice. Please allow six to eight weeks for delivery.

Name_____
Address_____
City_____State/Zip_____
Telephone No._____   PEN 0996

The Chronicles of Fionn Mac Cumhal
Prophet, Poet, Warrior, Outlaw

by Diana L. Paxson & Adrienne Martine-Barnes

MASTER OF EARTH AND WATER
75801-6/$4.99 US/$5.99 Can

Safely hidden from the world of men, an ancient warrior will teach the child called Demne many things—but never speak about the boy's mysterious parentage.

THE SHIELD BETWEEN THE WORLDS
75802-4/$4.99 US/$6.99 Can

Now the time has come for Fionn to assume his tribe's mantle of leadership—to restore his fian to its former greatness.

SWORD OF FIRE AND SHADOW
75803-1/$5.99 US/$7.99 Can

It is the bitter twilight of a noble hero's life as enemies mass on all sides, waiting to strike the killing blow. But from the terrible wreckage, he will arise victorious once more.

Buy these books at your local bookstore or use this coupon for ordering:

Mail to: Avon Books, Dept BP, Box 767, Rte 2, Dresden, TN 38225   E
Please send me the book(s) I have checked above.
❑ My check or money order—no cash or CODs please—for $_____ is enclosed (please add $1.50 per order to cover postage and handling—Canadian residents add 7% GST).
❑ Charge my VISA/MC Acct#_____ Exp Date_____
Minimum credit card order is two books or $7.50 (please add postage and handling charge of $1.50 per order—Canadian residents add 7% GST). For faster service, call 1-800-762-0779. Residents of Tennessee, please call 1-800-633-1607. Prices and numbers are subject to change without notice. Please allow six to eight weeks for delivery.

Name_____
Address_____
City_____ State/Zip_____
Telephone No._____   PMB 0796